WELCOME TO THE WORLD OF

Shallow Cove™
DARKDIMENSIONS

HUNTED SWEET

EVEN THIS MONSTER DESERVES SOMETHING.

SWEET

THE MONSTER STALKER SERIES BOOK 1

JANUARY RAYNE

DEDICATION

To your pussy, with how she will weep for me when you read this.

AUTHOR'S NOTE

Heads up: Everything in this book is fiction. If you find it hard to believe that any of this would happen in real life, you're right. Nothing about this story is believable. My imagination went wild.

Content Warnings: This book contains stalking, dark themes, nonconsent, S/A, somnophilia, forced pregnancy, birth control tampering, blood sharing, a drugged FMC, and murder. Please refrain from reading if you are affected by these subjects. Mental Health matters. You matter.

PROLOGUE

CREED

Shallow Cove Institute

Time is relative. When you've been in the same exact place for so long, you can't seem to remember anything else.

That's how it is for me. I can't remember when I got here, and no one has told me why. All I know is that I ache in my fucking bones. My skin has been cut open. My blood has been drained and replaced. My organs have been removed and put back in me. My bones have been broken and shattered. I've been injected with unknown substances a hundred times.

And one thing always remains the same.
I never know why. No one has ever explained anything to me.

All I know is that I've forgotten what the sun feels like and how the breeze feels on my skin. I've forgotten what it's like to laugh. I actually don't remember the last time I found something funny. I can't remember much of anything. Everything is dark. My heart, my mind, my soul.

I've come to the conclusion that I'm going to die here. Whatever they are trying to do— or trying to make me be— isn't working.

Their attempts will kill me, and I welcome death.
I *want* it. I *crave* it. I *wish* for it.

The people that are doing this are sick and twisted. They call themselves scientists, but they give science a bad name. They are fucked up in the head.

They are trying to create a new form of life. That is what I've concluded in my time here.

Has it been days, months, years? I don't know. They keep me in the dark.

Literally.

I close my eyes and lean my head against the concrete wall while sitting on my cot. My body is shaking from how cold it is, yet at the same time, my skin is on fire. My teeth clink together and my head swims with sudden dizziness.

Cries from down the hall make my ears ring and a pain begins to throb in my head.

I squeeze my eyes shut, rolling my head over my shoulders to try to relax, but the cries get louder. Next, I hear laughter from a guard who is on his break. I know because he loves to tell me when he'll be back to watch me get tortured.

But *why* can I hear him? He isn't close to me at all.

The sounds blur until the cries return and they turn to sobs. I don't know who is crying. I'm the only one on this floor that I know of.

What the fuck is happening to me?

I hold my head in my hands, wanting the noises to go away. They are clashing together, becoming louder, blurring together until it's white static that has me falling to the floor. I can't catch my breath.

My fingers begin to hurt, and I hold my hands out in front of me, my vision blurring and sharpening as if it was a camera trying to focus. How can I see them in the dark? My nails are bleeding, and the sight of my own blood has my teeth hurting. The lights in the cell come on as the guard flips the switch in the hall, disorienting me even more.

"Well, look at you." The guard, Franklin, drawls in his southern accent. "All this time, I didn't think any of their poking and prodding was working. Something is." He leans against the bars of my prison cell, shelling a peanut before popping it into his mouth.

He tosses the shell on the floor, then steps on it, the crunch reverberating inside my mind and it makes me want to rip him limb from limb.

"The doctors will be happy to hear about this."

"Fuck you," I growl, my voice deeper and not sounding like my own.

He chuckles, tapping the metal bars with his baton, and speaks into the radio. "We're showing progress with subject 1-5-4-3," he says. "Nail bleeds, erratic behavior, voice differentials."

"Get him ready," they say from the other end of the radio, the static cutting off when they end the conversation.

"Gladly." He doesn't say it to them but to me.

I flip onto my back, all the noises fighting inside my head end, and the pain in my nails vanishes. All that's left is blood.

My prison door opens, and Franklin is standing there with a tranquilizer gun pointed at me. He grins, showing his yellow teeth, bits of peanuts stuck in between them. His partially bald head shines under the fluorescent lights. The thin strands of brown hair are combed over the greasy dome.

It's sad when he's the one I look forward to seeing the most because he isn't the one who inflicts the pain.

I used to fight him. I'm bigger and much stronger, but they do a great job at keeping me drugged enough so I can't truly fight for myself now. They liked watching me defend myself in the earlier days. They took notes on my words and movements.

Now that I look back on it, I'd say they were taking a pre-examination, compiling data for their study.

I just wish I understood what they were trying to accomplish and what they were injecting me with.

Franklin shoots, the puff of the dart leaving the barrel is louder than usual and the needle hits me in the side of the neck, pulling me under until I'm deadweight on the floor. My eyes struggle to remain open, so I lock my sights on the wall, thinking back to the one memory I do remember. The one that keeps me sane.

It isn't much, but I remember the smell of something sweet. It was honeysuckles. I remember plucking the flower and bringing it to my nose and inhaling so deeply, my lungs ran out of room to expand. Then I pinched off the end before popping the sweet treat into my mouth.

It's all I have of the outside world and every time they do their tests, I latch onto it. Out of all the ugly I've seen while being here, it's the only beauty I have to hold onto.

Multiple sets of footsteps echo in my cell and my ankles are grabbed as I'm dragged out of the room.

"It's good to see progress, Creed. I was worried you'd die before we saw any sign of promise. I think our attempts are finally working."

I try to move my body, but I can't. All I have is my mind, and like always, the memory fades to the time I was hit over the head while walking home from the bar. Nothing special. I wasn't celebrating anything. I only wanted to take the edge off of a stressful day. My parents had just died and left me with their fortune.

A fortune I never wanted because I hated them.

And then I woke up here.

The skin on my wrists is pulled when they restrain me on the table. Next are my ankles and the table lifts to a standing position, bringing into view the three men in front of me. I've been in this room so many times, I wonder if they have any other unwilling subjects.

"Let's see just how far you've progressed." The one with circular glasses and a thin mustache above his upper lip announces with a sardonic smile. He has a giant gap between his crooked front teeth and nothing but curiosity in his eyes.

One of the other scientists with a receding hairline, has his long thin hair pulled back into a greasy thin ponytail. He adjusts something above me.

I tilt my head back to see something that reminds me of one of those salon hair dryers. The release of metal sounds and something sharp threatens to pierce my temples.

"What the fuck are you doing? What are you doing to me? Get away from me!"

"Give him more sedation. He's moving too much." The third scientist has his arms crossed as he leans against the wall, the darkness of the room hiding his face, but not the rest of his body. He seems to be the one in charge, watching his project from afar, seeing what he likes and dislikes as his men work.

My breath hitches in my throat when the pressure on my temples becomes more intense, but right as I'm about to scream, the medicine works its way into my system, and I relax. I still try to struggle, but it's like moving my body through mud or quicksand. The more I try to fight, the more I sink into death.

"What are you doing?" I slur, still trying to move my arms. "Please," I beg pathetically. "Please no more." I squeeze my eyes shut when a knife pierces my skin, cutting so deep, I swear I feel the blade nick my bone.

I scream as much as I can while drugged. The pressure of the needles passing through the thin skin layer at my temple stops me from moving too much. Looking down, I notice my left arm filleted open like a fish.

And I can see my bones.

Blood pools under me, dripping freely like a waterfall.

"What the fuck?" The words are muted, but also an attempted yell. My tongue is thick and feels swollen. Tears gather in my eyes as I watch my skin stitch together, healing the horrible wound they inflicted on me. "What did you do? What did you do to me!" I scream again, trying to will myself to beat the drug in my system and fight like hell to get out of here.

But will isn't stronger than medication.

Nothing is.

"Oh my God. It worked! He's going to be the first of many," the man with the circular glasses says, pushing the frames up his nose.

"Not so fast." The one leaning against the wall comes into the light and I'm finally able to see his face. "He can heal, but I want to know what else he can do. We've injected him with so many different kinds of DNA. I want to know what stuck."

What are they talking about?

"Please, let me go," I mumble, a haze teasing my vision. "I won't tell anyone what you did. Please," I try one last time.

The man in charge grips my chin and forces me to look into his eyes. One is dark brown while the other is milky white. "You can beg all you want 1-5-4-3. You are no longer Creed Blackstone. This is where you're reborn. You're going to be so much more than you were that night walking all alone on the street. I saw you and I knew you'd be perfect for what I had planned. You seemed so lonely. We will be your new home."

I try to shake my head but the needles threatening my temples stop me.

"Insert the needles," he announces.

I don't have time to try to stop him, not that I could, I am useless. I'm their toy to play with and I have no choice but to let them.

The needles spear my temples and I scream again, this time the agony guttural. My pain echoes off the stainless-steel walls. My entire body tenses and sweat is a thick coat over my skin while a fever burns my insides.

I stop moving. I have no control over what I can do. My body is still. I can move my eyes and breathe, but that's it. My thoughts turn darker, more violent, and rage unlike anything I've ever felt before swims through my veins just like the blood pumping through my heart. My vision tunnels and everything heightens.

I can smell them.

Each of the three men has a different scent and they are all repulsive.

My eyes drift to the one with glasses and a gap between his teeth. The pulse in his neck jumps as I watch every rise and fall of his flesh. My mouth waters, wanting to rip his fucking throat out and guzzle his blood until I'm full.

"Look at his eyes." The leader points to my face. "They are shifted. A gorgeous golden color with thick black rings. Looks like the wolf shifter gene, perhaps." He writes something down, the pen scribbling across the paper makes me growl. It reminds me of nails on a chalkboard.

"The growl is definitely wolf, perhaps werewolf?" stringy ponytail suggests.

The leader grips my chin and lifts my upper lip, grinning when he sees something he likes. "Werewolf. Look at those fangs."

I don't know what the fuck he is talking about, but I manage to jerk my chin from his grasp, the needle sinking further into my head. I'm frozen.

"Good. Don't fucking growl at your creator, 1-5-4-3. Send the shock," he orders.

A jolt flames through my mind, zapping down my spine, and every inch of me quakes.

"Enough," he orders again.

When the electricity stops, I'm unable to sag in relief, the needles piercing my brain keep me upright. My teeth chatter and the metallic taste of blood drips over my tongue. I must have bitten it.

"Again."

The electricity works its way inside me once more.

"Stop."

I'm barely able to take a breath before he signals them to go again.

And again.

And again.

The rational part inside me who is understanding, that knows the difference between right and wrong fades into the back of my mind.

I cock my head when the electricity no longer bothers me. If anything, it feels like a low hum. I look through my new eyes at the man with a gap between his teeth.

"Amazing," Ponytail states with awe.

A torch is lit next, a burning bright orange flame that turns blue at the end dances through the air. The man with a milky eye takes it from the one wearing glasses, then without waiting a second, he hovers the torch over my shoulder, working its way down my arm.

"Holy shit." Glasses runs to my side, analyzing my arm. "Scales. They are faded but seem to be a blackish-purple color. They appeared when the flames hit his skin. Maybe they are protecting him? Like armor," he admires, his gaze drifting up and down my arm, then turns to Ponytail. "He has dragon DNA too."

"Could be a snake," Milky-Eye says, tapping his chin thoughtfully.

Every inch of me, every cell in my blood, tries to break free from the restraints. I want to rip his heart from his chest and drink the warm blood from the organ while it beats for the last time. I'm going to hunt them down when I'm free and I'm going to kill them. I'm going to crush every bone, inhale the dust, and salivate from the taste.

Fuck. That sounds good.

There's a voice in the back of my head saying I shouldn't want that, but it's too distant for me to care.

"Dragon definitely." Glasses peels one of my scales from my arm and I roar, not wanting him to fucking touch me. Fire shoots from my mouth and smoke billows from my nostrils. I manage to catch his coat on fire. He shouts, shrugs it off quickly, and steps on it to put out the blaze.

"I'd be angry if I wasn't so fucking proud of our success." Milky-Eye walks up to me, wraps his hand around my throat, and leans in so close, I can smell the cigarette on his breath and the pussy he somehow managed to get. By the lingering scent, I'd say last night.

Who the hell would fuck him? He probably paid for it.

"You better remember where the fuck you are and who you serve. I am your father, brother, priest, or whatever fucking god you pray to now. Do I make myself clear?"

Rage burns so deep, heat flares in my throat and smoke drifts from between my lips.

Whatever the fuck they did to me, I'm not the same man they took off the street.

If I'm a man at all.

I don't say anything, and he shoves my head back. The needles twist and a slashing pain echoes in my head.

"I want to know what else you can do. What other abilities do you possess? Fireproof his mouth. We don't need to get burned alive for what we are about to do."

I narrow my eyes at him, the sweat from my forehead stings my eyes, and track him as he opens what looks like a fridge.

Something similar to a muzzle forms over my mouth.

"You can try to burn this, but it's made out of flame-resistant fabric. The same kind firemen wear. It might not be able to withstand a lot, but it will be enough for what we want to do," Glasses informs, clipping the muzzle on me as if I'm a dog.

"He's coming off the sedation. Since he's transforming, he's burning through it quicker. Insert more and start an I.V. drip so the dose is constant." Milky-Eye struts forward, a cloth is in his hand and in the other he has a small brown bottle with a corked top. He pops the cork, and it falls onto the ground while he shakes a few drops of whatever is inside onto the cloth.

Holy fuck.

I inhale.

"What the *fuck* is that?" A growl lives within my throat as I breathe the words with a harsh sneer, tugging against the restraints to get to the cloth. I want to roll around in it. I want my skin to smell of the scent and I want the fragrance to seep into my skin.

"You like that?" he chuckles, smelling the cloth himself. "I don't smell anything. It's interesting you do. Make note of that," he demands, snapping his fingers at Ponytail.

The guy listens eagerly, scribbling on his notepad like a good bitch.

The first thing I'm going to do when I'm free is rip his scalp off and shove his ponytail into his mouth, suffocating him with the one thing he can't seem to let go of.

"Seems you have acquired the mating traits of a shifter or werewolf. Perhaps when our experiments are over, I can get a blood sample to see."

Smoke sways from my nostrils again like an eerie fog drifting through the night.

He chuffs, smothering the cloth over my nose so the only choice I have is to inhale, and when I do...

Jesus fucking Christ when I do, my eyes roll to the back of my head from how good it smells. My cock thickens in my flimsy sweatpants they make me wear and a painful sensation overcomes it. I rip my face away from the cloth and groan from the misery.

"Fuck! What did you do to me? It burns." I snap my teeth together and then a whine escapes me because I want that cloth back. "Smells so good."

"I bet you want to fuck something, don't you?" He jerks the sweatpants down and his brows raise.

He's right. I do want to fuck something. My entire body burns with need.

"I didn't expect that," he mumbles, the other two men come to stand by his side and Glasses takes a picture of my erection.

"Interesting."

"Unbelievable," Ponytail agrees, taking a step closer. He leans down, getting a better view of my cock.

I haven't been hard in ages because I've been here. I had no urge to until I smelled whatever he put over my mouth.

"Don't—" I cut him off when he reaches his hand to touch me "—fucking touch me," I mumble through the muzzle.

"I want to see what else he is capable of." Milky-Eye grabs a scalpel from the tray and stands in front of me. "You're exceeding all of our expectations."

Another debilitating wave of sedation hits me, and my muscles relax against the standing table. My torturer raises his hand and removes the needles from my temples. Then there's pressure behind my eyes, a ringing in my ears, and I feel like my head is about to explode.

"This will only hurt for a minute." He turns his head over his shoulder. "I'll be starting at the knot and working my way up the penis."

"What?" I ask, barely able to keep my eyes open. "What are you going to do?"

He stabs the tip of the scalpel into the base of my cock, the pain unlike anything I've ever felt, and a primal sound escapes me. My teeth ache for a moment and the scream turns into a roar, the kind that shakes my core.

Glasses and Ponytail cover their ears but Milky-Eye only cringes, continuing to drag the scalpel down my cock until it's nearly split in two. I can't tear my eyes away from the gruesome sight. My head sways and I can't help but wonder if I'm in a dream. If it isn't, I'm losing every bit of my humanity.

They are breaking me.

My cock bleeds, dripping red in heavy streams onto the floor. I turn away from the sick view to dry heave at the sight of my mutilated body.

It's the last of my humanity leaving my body because I will not let them take anymore from me.

I sag against the table until movement between my legs drags my eyes back down. The blood has stopped— I can't possibly be seeing what I'm seeing.

I shake my head, wanting my vision to stop playing tricks on me when my cock fuses itself back together, lengthens to become bigger, the width larger, and suckers appear along the shaft. The skin has a variation of color too. The shaft is a shade of purple while the suckers are red.

"What the fuck," I whisper in horror, wondering how the fuck that happened.

This can't be real.

"Just kill me," I say to them. "Kill me. I'm begging you. I have nothing to give you!" I yell, tugging at the restraints as hard as I can, but I'm still too weak. "I have nothing to give you." The admission is whispered.

"You've given us everything, 1-5-4-3. You're going to be the start of something... revolutionary." He turns away from me, excited, and begins to pace. "It seems the trauma inflicted on his penis caused it to morph into a better appendage to protect itself, but will also be of better service to him. And he knots like a wolf. Tell me all of our findings," he snaps at Glasses.

He pushes his glasses up his nose again. "Shifted eyes, fangs, scales, fire breathing, smoke, healing abilities, knot, reaction to a woman's heat pheromones, and tentacle traits," he rambles off the list. Then he lifts his finger, heads to the fridge, and pulls out a bag of blood. "Pull off the muzzle for a sec," he instructs ponytail. He tears the top off and comes closer, waving the blood in front of my face.

The smell of blood causes me to groan. Glasses swipes blood across my lips and my tongue flicks out, forking like a snake, my fangs aching to sink into a vein.

"And he has vampire qualities as well with his hunger for blood. Along with the snake DNA trait! His tongue has shifted." He yanks my mouth open. "But when his tongue is inside his mouth, it is normal, replicating a human tongue. So just when it is in use does it shift."

I hiss, yanking on my bindings.

"So all the DNA we have pushed into his system has genetically mutated his. He has the traits and attributes of all. Werewolf, dragon, vampire, snake, and cephalopod. Do you know what this means? This will change medical, science, and military history, and the future. We won't have to kidnap people or monsters to test our subjects anymore. We are going to be millionaires," he announces, and the other two men begin to celebrate.

"Stop it, you fools. We still have a long way to go. I want you to bring in the omega girl. She's in heat, yes? I want to know what their mating will be like. I want samples of his sperm."

"I'll go get her." Ponytail spins on his heels and marches away, disappearing down the corridor.

The table lowers until I'm lying horizontally and staring up at the ceiling. There's a jab into my arm and when I look down, I see the syringe Milky-Eye is holding.

"You'll love it. You'll never want to fuck another woman when she isn't in heat."

The drug hits me hard and I can't keep my eyes open. My head swims and I dig down deep for whatever lives inside me now, but it's quiet.

"Plus, you'll be doing her a favor. Poor thing is in pain. Don't you want to relieve it?"

I shake and nod my head in confusion, groaning. My heart races when I realize what's about to happen. I don't want this. I don't want this at all. I need to get out of here. I need to— my mind comes to a halt when I smell her.

Her whimpers of need cause my cock to harden, and the suckers along my shaft move of their own volition, an odd, but not unwelcome feeling.

I stare down at my cock, my eyes straining to focus, and I notice how much different it looks now. I tug on my restraints when she gets closer, knowing I need to do my best to get out of here, but it's too late for that.

This is my reality.

I don't want this. I don't want her. I mean— I do. She smells so fucking good and all I want is to bury my cock inside her.

"You're thinking too much." Milky-Eye stabs the needles back into my temple and sends a powerful jolt of electricity through my system, numbing me. "Release her," he says.

Squinting my watery eyes, I try to focus on the woman running to me as if I'm her savior.

"No," I mumble, tugging on the ties that hold me, but I'm too weak. "This isn't..." My thoughts trail off when her scent overwhelms me.

"Watch him for every sign or shift. We need to have detailed descriptions," Milky-Eye says.

The woman is young, early twenties maybe, and her hair is a mess from not being brushed or washed in who knows how long. She's naked and too lean, her tits barely bouncing as she hurries to me. I can't see any details of her face, I'm too drugged.

But I don't need to see her face.

Her scent is enough, and she needs me.

A low growl sounds in my throat as she straddles me. Her thighs are wet and when she grips my cock, I groan.

"I'm sorry," she whispers. "But I can't do this alone again."

I nod, not wanting to speak because I do want this and that makes me a bad person. If I wasn't restrained, I don't know what I'd do to her. I think I'd fuck her anyway.

Turning my head to look, long black talons have replaced my regular nails right as she slides herself down on me.

I sneer, lifting my head so hard, I break the contraption keeping the needles embedded in my temples.

"Oh finally," she sobs, rocking herself on me as if she's been waiting ages to seek relief. "You feel so good. I'm so sorry," she chants, tossing her head back while she uses me.

I inhale, her scent is still amazing and strong, but it isn't right. *Something* isn't right.

She isn't... she isn't...

I can't find the word. It's on the tip of my tongue.

No. No. I don't want this. I don't want her. It's too late though. She's already on top of me, taking what she needs, stealing the rest of my control.

She isn't *mine*.

The words are whispered in my mind, and I don't know exactly what they mean, but they make sense.

"Smoke, talons, but no knot," Glasses advises, doing a once-over of my body. "In fact, according to his vitals, he isn't interested in her."

The strange woman stares down at me, tears in her eyes as her hands land on my chest. "I'm not either, but I need this burning pain to go away. I need to be able to breathe."

Flames lick my teeth as they try to escape my throat. "Take what you need and get the fuck off me," I grumble, the new monster inside me revolting at the stranger riding my cock.

She nods, closing her eyes as tears fall down her cheeks and I look the other way as the woman fucks me. Any man would be pleased right now, but that isn't how I feel.

I feel guilty and a sense of mourning falls over me as I think about the one who is supposed to be mine. I've betrayed her.

"Hey! Fuck her, 1-5-4-3. Do what you're fucking told."

Flames leave my mouth again, but I remain quiet, small grunts leaving me here and there because she still— unfortunately— feels good.

"I said do what you're told!" Milky-Eye slaps me across the face and I don't know what happens, but something powerful emerges from me.

The drugs burn off and I break the restraints. Sitting forward, I wrap my arm around the woman and turn my head, letting the burn that's been trapped in my throat free. Fire weaponizes from me, hitting Milky-Eye in his face.

He screams at the top of his lungs, and it gives me enough time to slide the woman off me and place her on the floor.

She sits down, cradling her stomach, whimpering from the pain that I have no doubt these men inflicted. Glasses charges at me with another needle and I dive right, take his head in my hands, and snap his neck easily.

Too easily. The man I was yesterday couldn't do that.

I wait for the guilt, but I don't feel it.

I don't feel anything anymore.

Ponytail tries to run away but I grip him by his hair and sling him backwards. He hits the back wall, slamming into the counter, and bottles filled holding the substances they injected me with fall to the ground.

They shatter.

Pieces of glass slide across the floor. Ponytail tries to stand but slips on the liquid.

"Listen. Please. We had to. Do you know what this could mean for the world? The people it would save? The wars we would win."

I look down to see Milky-Eye's burned face and his skull showing through his scalp, still smoking from the fire.

"I don't give a fuck about your plans or your wars." I grab him by his throat and lift him to his feet. "What medicine can I give the girl? And I'll let you live." I won't. I'm going to free the prisoners and kill everyone who kept me trapped here. "The medicine," I grit because the thought of fucking her makes me sick.

"Fridge," he croaks.

I don't release him. My talons grow and threaten to rip out his throat. I drag him to the fridge, open it, and have no fucking clue what I'm looking for.

"Where the fuck is it?"

"It's that one." He points to the red bottle labeled 'Heat Reversal.'

That seems too simple, but I'm not in the position to argue.

"Thank you." The urge to rip his heart out overcomes me so I do just that. I plunge my fist into his chest and rip it out. His mouth falls open and his eyes are saucers as he watches me sink my talons into the beating heart before his dead body sags to the floor.

I drop his heart as I stare at my dripping hands. My mouth waters from the iron scent of the blood. My teeth ache and I reach into my mouth to feel the pointed tips.

Fangs.

They've turned me into a monster.

Whimpers from the left remind me of the poor girl and I snag the bottle from the fridge, heading over to her quickly.

She scurries closer to me, reaching for my cock, which is flaccid despite her delicious scent, but she isn't mine. I think when I first smelled her, my body never experienced something so intense before, so I reacted, but then the actual act happened, and whatever beast they've turned me into made itself known. I don't want her anymore.

I don't know why.

"No. We aren't doing that. I know. I know you're in pain." I wrap my arms around her to keep her still, twist the cap off with my teeth and shove the bottle between her lips, tilting her head back. "Swallow it down. Come on. Drink up. It's the only way you'll feel better."

She does what I say, grabbing the bottle as if it's water and she's been dying of thirst. While she drinks, she rocks her wet pussy up and down my leg, seeking relief.

I don't even want her to do that. I understand why, but I'm not hers. I don't belong to her, and I don't want to feel her. I lift her from my leg, fighting the urge to become violent.

None of this is her fault.

I have to remember that. Keeping myself together is becoming too difficult. I need to get out of here.

Her hips finally stop rocking in the air as she sags against the wall, the bottle falling from her hands and shattering on the ground. She cries, covering her breasts to hide herself. I walk over to one of the dead bodies, pull his coat off, then toss it to her.

"Get out of here. There won't be much left of this place when I'm done." My eyes shift, my vision tinted in amber. Everything sharpens, becoming crisper. My ears are sensitive and sounds from across the building seem like they are only a few steps away. Smoke swirls from my mouth, my throat heating from the fire burning below, and I'm reminded of what I've become.

I grab my file from the counter and vanish down the hall, my talons, and fangs at the ready.

And I get lost in the screams and the blood.

I don't know what I am, but I'm no longer a man, yet the memory of honeysuckles has me grasping onto what's left of my humanity.

CHAPTER ONE

CREED

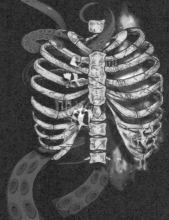

Beauty can be admired from afar, but it can also be ruined and damaged. It's interesting how fragile someone becomes when they are beautiful. All the ways their lives become easier are ways that can easily be destroyed.

Just like mine.

Now, I make sure I stay in the shadows where I hope no one can see me. Ever since I broke out of Shallow Cove Institute, the world isn't the same. I'm not the same. My mind is darker. My body has been modified in certain aspects within the few months I've been free. I'm not sure if it's because whatever DNA they pumped inside me needed time to grow and overcome the other cells in my body, but whatever they did, they succeeded.

I'm a monster.

I have permanent black and purple scales on each shoulder, spreading across my chest and down my biceps. My eyes are in a permanent state of amber. The irises are huge with a thick black ring around them. My fangs are always elongated. My cock is bigger, replicating a tentacle. It has red suckers up and down the length while the shaft is a deep purple now. I have two additional tentacles that have grown next to the base of my cock that stay wrapped around my shaft unless I want them to move.

My tongue is forked like a snake when I shift it and my ears are pointed with long hair. I'm assuming that's the werewolf inside me. My skin is gray, and my fingers and toes are webbed while my nails are long, black talons.

My nails and tongue are the only things I can willingly shift.

Everything else, I'm stuck with.

While my appearance has transformed, I can't lie and say I don't find the new powers I have fucking incredible. I'm powerful. I'm fast and strong. I can hear a heart pump from a few miles away. I've killed so many men since I've been free.

And I've loved every minute of their fear and screams. I loved the taste of their blood. I loved ripping into their hearts. Hunting them, feeling their flesh tear, their blood spilling over their sides while my tongue lapped up the red, succulent juice.

It sated the monsters inside me.

There's one last urge that has yet to be met and I'm not sure what it means. I don't know what it is but there's been a pull in my chest directing me across town. I've been ignoring it, but it's too strong now. It's a need. A compulsion. An obsession for me to figure out what it is.

There's a word that's whispered by one of the beasts that always confuses me.

Mate.

Just the thought has a few different growls of pleasure ringing through my head.

"I know, I know," I say to them in the middle of my cabin that's nestled in the woods. One of the men I killed lived here and his home was perfect for my needs.

I live away from everyone and everything. To protect myself. The last thing I want is to get captured and tortured again.

Zipping up my black jacket, I lift the hood over my head to hide my ears and the majority of my face.

"We're going. Tonight is the night we find out what the fuss is all about." I stare in the mirror, knowing I'm talking to myself, but the monsters are the only company I have.

Next, I tug on my pants, tie my boots, and make sure all the odd parts of me are covered for the most part. My hands are showing, but I can say they are tattooed gray, if anyone asks.

They won't.

People tend to stay away from me. It's as if they know I'm a predator looking to make them my prey.

Smoke billows from my nose and fire warms my chest as my dragon makes himself known. The vampire inside me is next, craving to feed, to drink, to have blood.

Beloved.

Another term that's whispered to me. When I didn't know what it meant, I researched and found it's a term used in myths about vampires. Beloved is the term vampires like to use for their soulmates. Thinking about my beloved's blood has my fangs aching and my cock hardening which is insane because I don't have a beloved.

Looking into the mirror of my reflection, my eyes glow, the fierceness of this pull has every instinct I now possess right under the surface.

I flip off the light and the thud of my steel-toe boots resonates throughout my empty living room as I head to my front door.

I don't regret taking this cabin from the man I killed. He was the first unfortunate soul I came across in the woods when I had escaped the institute. I was angry and hungry. I was a savage and he just so happened to be in my path.

Slamming the door behind me, I tuck my hands in my pocket and begin to walk toward town, letting the pull in my chest guide me to where I need to go.

Leaves and twigs snap under my heavy steps. Soft chewing sounds coming from the left have me turning my head. A deer stands with large antlers reaching toward the sky. The wolf inside me wants to hunt it and feel its bones break under my teeth, but the urge to follow this pull outweighs the need to kill.

I drag my claws across the tree trunks, sliding my eyes to the right where the road is. I can hear the hum of tires. The radio is on, and the driver is singing at the top of his lungs thinking no one can hear him.

He's terrible.

The urge to rip his throat out is nearly impossible to deny, but I refrain since I have other things I need to do tonight. The horrible singer will live another day.

A fog rolls in as twilight descends. I look up, the stars are nothing but faint small dots above the treetops. The wolf inside me wants to howl and the dragon wants to fly, but there are no wings to make that happen.

I feel the need though. It's like an itch I can't scratch on my back. It almost... hurts.

Not having wings makes the dragon roar in irritation. Warmth spreads through my veins causing me to stumble right as I get to the tree line at the edge of town.

The heat bubbles up my throat, giving me no choice but to open my mouth to allow the fire to be free. Orange and red flames pierce through the air, a whoosh sounding from the force. The lower branches of a nearby tree catch on fire.

Seeing it has me snapping my mouth closed to stop the spread of destruction. It's one of the many... gifts I haven't been able to control yet.

"Fuck." I wipe my hands on my jeans and stare at the leaves burning. Sighing, I leap into the air and dig my claws into the trunk. I climb, reaching for the branches that are on fire, and snap them away easily until they fall on the ground.

Pushing from the trunk, my talons scrape the bark leaving behind my mark. I land with a thud and pat away the small fire I've started. The branches are burnt and smoking, but at least the entire forest is safe.

I snort to myself. "You're a fucking monster, not smokey the goddamn bear."

I wouldn't be surprised if I had creatures inside me I didn't even know about though. The file I stole had notes of the DNA they tested on me, but what if they didn't list all of them?

There's no point in wondering or questioning. I am what I am now, and I've embraced it.

I'm a killer.

I'm a hunter.

I'm beyond anything a human could ever comprehend.

Wiping the soot from my palms onto my black jeans, I head out of the tree line. The small town is nestled between two mountains which gives it the appearance of being safe.

It used to be.

Until I arrived a few months ago.

Tilting my chin, I walk down the hill. A light mist of rain begins to fall, slicking the grass, and cooling the fire simmering under my skin. Thunder grumbles through the black clouds meshing across the night sky. Lightning crackles, sending bolts down to the ground a few miles away.

The rain blooms new scents as it falls. The musk of the ground permeates the air. Mud begins to form under my boots with every step that disturbs the ground. Tucking my hands back into my pockets, I keep my head down while following the sidewalk.

Fog swirls around my feet as I quicken my steps, the pull becoming stronger. I can't help but follow it, chasing it like a fucking high. I don't bother looking as I cross the street and a car honks its horn at me for a little too long.

I slam my hands on the hood, my talons screeching across the metal to leave five long marks. I see the person beyond the windshield. My vision sharpens until I can see every line on his face. His lips part and his eyes widen when he sees me.

He pushes his black frame glasses up his nose, staring at me in disbelief. Smoke ripples from my mouth, my dragon irritated from the interruption of following the pull in my chest. Instead of killing the driver, I dive to the left, dropping to all fours, and dash down the nearest alley to avoid the people on the sidewalks.

Snarls leave me and my talons dig into the pavement. My werewolf chuffs at the distinct smell of trash as I pass dumpsters behind the businesses that sit along the downtown strip. A rat scurries away and I dive to the right to play with its life before the pull tugs me back on track.

As quickly as it started, the rain stops when I get closer to the source, and a strong sweet scent reminding me again of the best memory I have hits me so hard, I stumble. I fall to my chest, my jacket scraping against the concrete. I sneer at the inconvenience and push myself up to stand. I crack my neck with a growl and watch as the wounds on my palms heal. All that's left is blood dripping down the sides. I wipe them on my jeans.

Taking a deep breath to calm the rage, to ease the fire swirling inside my chest, that fucking scent hits me again. I follow it, my cock hardening behind the zipper of my jeans. The sensation of the suckers moving feels so damn good as they search for the cause of their ecstasy.

Stuffing my hands in my hoodie pockets, I tilt my head down and start walking. A puddle reflects my face, forcing me to stop in my tracks to stare at the creature I've become.

I crouch, wanting to get a better look at myself. My brows pinch together when I notice my features are sharper than they have been before. My beasts are close to the surface. A hint of scales glistens on my neck, my cheekbones are sharp, and my fangs are longer than usual. My bottom and top cuspids settle over my lips. I take a deep breath, trying to gain control of them, but the more I try, the more the beasts slam against my chest wanting out.

"We can't see the source of the pull if we can't be in public," I whisper out loud, hoping these sharpened features will ease. On a good day, I still look like a monster, but people think I'm wearing contacts or tattooed my skin this odd gray color. They look at me like I'm something from their nightmares.

If they only knew the truth, I'm exactly what they fear.

The creatures inside me listen and fall back, the powerful hum of them simmers in my bones. The humanistic side of me returns to my features, my eyes still holding onto a savage nature.

I step into the puddle, rippling the water.

The pull tugs me right, so I move swiftly, the connection and scent getting stronger the closer I get to my destination.

The windows glow from the bright lights in the quaint stores I pass that consist of coffee shops, boutiques, hardware stores, and restaurants. People laugh and a little girl runs from the ice cream shop, nearly slamming into me. She stops, looking up at me with big brown eyes. Vanilla ice cream is smeared all over her mouth and the cone is almost gone from the delicious treat melting all over her hand.

"Sorry, Mister Eyes," she says in a high-pitched voice she hasn't grown into yet.

I grunt in response, debating on knocking the cone from her hand just to watch her cry, but I decide against it. "Be more careful," I growl in warning, letting my eyes flash. "You never know who you'll come across." I step around her, only to stop, staring down at the cone with fucking sprinkles on it. I haven't had ice cream in ages. With one quick swoop, quicker than she can recognize, I swipe it and take a bite, only to quickly spit it out.

It doesn't taste as good as I remember.

"Here. The sprinkles ruined it." I shove the ruined cone in her hand and walk away. I roll my eyes when I hear her cries from behind me.

I'm testy. I have someplace to be.

I'm getting closer. So close, I begin to run. The sensation in my chest is so intense, my heart is about to rip from my body. At least, it feels that way.

When I get to the corner of the street, I stop, noticing a diner just across the road.

Demi's Diner.

The name of the place is a bright pink neon sign. It has a classic feel. The kind of place that's been around forever, the kind of diner regulars come to because there is no other place that has better coffee.

I assume Demi's Diner has good coffee with "The Best Endless Coffee in Town" painted in white on the windows.

While I live on the outskirts of this town, I have never explored my new home. For... reasons.

Obviously.

I look both ways before crossing the street. When I get to the diner, the first thing I notice is all the plants outside. Vines crawl up the stucco building, winding around the windows delicately. There's a bench too, old, and wooden. It looks like it's about to fall apart. Stepping closer to the window, I'm able to see inside.

My breath catches. I stop breathing. My beasts roar, pounding so hard inside me, I nearly double over.

Mine.

Mate.

Beloved.

I don't know what that means but I can't take my eyes off her. She's beautiful. She's wearing a classic style uniform, something from an earlier time. A dark apron wrapped around and then tied at her waist. Her hair is short, cut just above her shoulders, and is a vibrant pink.

She places a few plates down for a group of rowdy men and one man slaps her ass.

Smoke pours from my nose and mouth. The urge to burn the man to a crisp is overwhelming but I realize I can't do that here.

All I know is I have to protect her, but I won't protect her from me.

CHAPTER TWO

DEMI

The door chimes and I'm unable to look up to see who has walked through the door. I'm too busy cleaning up another spilled drink from these drunken assholes.

"Welcome to Demi's! I'll be right with you," I shout as happily as I can, cleaning up the mess.

The new customer doesn't reply, but the air charges with electricity. The hair on my arms and on the back of my neck stand. Goosebumps travel all over my body. A sense of fear, danger, and curiosity has me lifting my eyes from the floor to see where the new person decided to sit.

I don't see him. I stand, tucking the dirty towel in my apron, and look around for the stranger when I catch sight of him in the furthest corner. It's darker over there, away from the main crowd that flocks to the well-lit dining area.

Pulling out my order pad to go talk to him, Daniel Dickhead grabs my ass again for the third time tonight and I slap his hand away.

"That's enough, Daniel. Do not touch me. I own this place and I'm one more spilled drink away from banning you and your friends from this diner."

"Aw, Demi baby, don't be like that. You know I'm just having fun. You know how I feel about you." His glazed eyes tell me he has had one too many beers as he checks me out.

I roll my eyes. "I know and I don't care," I mumble.

He snags my wrist when I try to move, and I swear I hear a growl in the building.

"Let me go." I tear myself from his grip. His fingers leave marks around my wrist.

"Don't go sassing me, Demi. You know damn well we are going to be together. Hell, all of us wanna a taste of the famous Demi pie. Isn't that right?"

I glance around the table at his friends. They have different expressions on their face, but they all say the same thing.

Want.

"Caden will be your server for the rest of the night," I say, my voice shaking as I try to remain calm and professional.

I've known Daniel since we were kids. He has been around for nearly my entire life. He's seen this diner get passed down from my grandmother to my mom, and then to me. This diner is all I've ever known. It's all I've ever wanted. I'm proud of myself for taking over after my mom retired and decided to travel the world. I knew I'd be able to take over Demi's without an issue. My mom had taught me everything I needed to know. Including how I'd never have to spend a ton of money rebranding since the diner is named after the women in the family.

The Demi name goes back seven generations and I happen to like it. I've yet to meet another with my name.

"Oh, come on, Demi. I'll be good. I promise."

"I don't care, Daniel. You're being a jerk. Caden will be your waiter." Blinking away tears, I push the kitchen doors open and sag against the nearest counter, catching my breath.

The bang of the back door opening makes me jump, pressing a hand to my chest. "Caden. You scared the crap out of me."

"Sorry, D. You know how I need my smoke break."

I muster up the saddest damn grin I have. It's the only one I have the energy to give.

He cocks his head and looks me over. His eyes stop at my wrist and the tears gather in my eyes. "Did that mother fucker put his hands on you, D?"

"Don't worry about it. Can you please take over their table?"

"We need to ban them from coming here. It isn't right."

"I know, and if they didn't spend nearly three hundred bucks every time they were here, I'd consider it. He and his friends are in here two, sometimes three, times a week. We need that."

"From now on when they come in, I'm their waiter, okay?" He gently grabs my shoulders. "Okay?" He gives them a firm squeeze.

I look up at him and sniffle, nodding. "Yeah. Thanks, Caden."

"Anything for my favorite boss," he teases.

I dry my eyes and straighten my spine. "I'm going to take care of the customer in the back. If you need me, that's where I'll be."

"You got it."

Caden's smile eases me. He's the kindest guy. Gorgeous too. He has wavy brown hair that falls naturally as he combs it back, striking green eyes, and a perfect smile except for the small gap between his front teeth.

I find the gap endearing. I hope he never gets it fixed.

Nothing romantic has ever been between us though. He's my best friend.

"You got this, Demi. Just another night. Daniel is just an asshole. Not all men are like that." Snagging a fresh pot of coffee, I plaster a smile on my face and head out of the kitchen, the doors nearly hitting me on the ass.

Taking a left, I hurry to the new customer.

The closer I get, the more intense the need is to be by his side. It's as if a rope is tied to me and he is the person tugging me closer.

When I stand by his side, I notice smoke. "I'm sorry, but there's no smoking in the restaurant."

"Sorry," he grumbles, keeping his head down.

The hood covers him for the most part. I can't get a good look at him, but I guess that doesn't matter.

"What can I get you?" I ask, filling his coffee cup even though he didn't ask.

"Does he bother you a lot?"

The rough gravel of his voice has my stomach clenching.

"It's fine," I say sweetly. "It isn't a big deal."

"Does. He. Bother. You?" he clips and if I'm not mistaken, I see a flash of pointed teeth as he turns his head just enough for the dim light to catch.

"He's just drunk, which is more often these days. Nothing I can't handle. Can I get you anything?" I try to change the subject. I'm nervous around this guy. With Daniel, I know what to expect, but with this guy? I don't. It scares me.

"Just the coffee."

"Sure." I take a step away and look over, noticing his eyes for the first time. I gasp in awe. They are glowing a bright golden color. "Your contacts are really beautiful. Striking, even. They look so real."

He hides his mouth with the coffee cup as he takes a sip, his attention never leaving me. His sights are set, and I don't move away. I'm caught in a trance, leaning in his direction, and I have this urge to crawl onto his lap. The longer our eyes are locked, the further away from reality I become.

A loud crash sounds from behind me and the connection is lost.

"What's your name? I've never seen you here before. Are you new to town?" I sit down on the other side of the booth, folding my arms across the table.

Every instinct inside me is telling me to run away but at the same time, if I run, I think I'd want him to chase me.

He keeps his head down, not allowing me to see his face.

"Creed Blackstone," he grumbles sounding irked.

I grin, his name sounding eerie and mysterious just like him. "I'm Demi Hawthorne," I say, holding out my hand to introduce myself. "It's nice to meet you, Creed."

He does it again. He lifts his head just enough for me to see the glow in his eyes. He stares at my outstretched hand and right as I'm about to drop it, his giant one slides across mine.

I lick my dry lips, staring at where his hand engulfs my own. Long, thick fingers swallow me. He tightens the hold, another growl surrounds me, something animalistic, and it's coming from him.

His skin is rough and immediately I think about him gliding those rough hands down my body.

"How old are you, Demi?" he asks, tightening his hold on mine as if the answer might cause him to break my bones.

"Twenty-four," I say on a near whimper when the pressure almost becomes too much, but not because he is hurting me. The longer his touch lingers, the more I yearn for more. The more my body aches with agony for something other than his touch.

He hums. "Good." The tight hold loosens. "That's real good, Demi."

I nibble my bottom lip, wondering if I've passed some test. "How old are you?"

"I think I'm thirty-two."

I frown. "You think?"

He lets go of me and picks up his coffee again, tilting his head so far down all I can see is the top of his black hood.

"I'm sorry. I shouldn't have asked. I need to go. I have to get back to work. I hope to see you again, Creed."

"Oh, you will."

I'm not sure if I like how that sounds. There's an obvious tone to it, one that says he doesn't have anywhere else he'd rather be.

I give him a tight smile, knowing I don't need to give Creed another look.

But I do.

And he's smoking again.

Only this time, I let it go because trauma comes off him in waves, and who am I to stop him from feeling better? He's different. That much I can see.

Different isn't always bad, but it isn't always good.

And something about him is telling me Creed isn't all *that* good.

He's a red flag.

Tall, dark, and mysterious with a brooding demeanor. He is the kind of man I lock my doors for but here I am, introducing myself as if he's my next-door neighbor.

I really need to get a grip.

"You guys have had enough. We close in five minutes. Get out before I call the cops."

I spin around to see Caden holding the front door open. Sweat begins to form on my forehead as Daniel's eyes find mine. I don't like the shift in his features. The muscles relax and his eyes narrow, then his lips tilt in a wicked smirk.

"No harm, no foul, Caden. We're going." Daniel doesn't leave. Not yet. He walks around the table and eats the distance away between us.

My fingernails dig into the table as I grip it.

Another deep rumble sounds from behind me and my racing heart calms knowing I have someone nearby.

"For you," Daniel says, holding up a one-hundred-dollar bill.

"That's Caden's. Give it to him."

"I don't think so. You did a lot of the work." He takes a step closer, sliding the cash across my lips.

I jerk my head to the side. "Daniel. Get out. You're drunk."

He rolls his lips together, the smell of beer wafting from his mouth, and it causes me to hold my breath. "Fine, but one of these days, Demi. You'll come around." He slips the money into my apron pocket before zigzagging away in his drunken stupor.

I release the breath and cup the back of my neck, stretching it to the right. I'm exhausted. I'm ready to go home and crawl under the covers where I'm safe.

"I'm sorry, Creed. We're closing—" I begin to say as I turn around, but he's already up and on the other side of the room. He's a huge man, well over six feet tall with broad shoulders, but he makes himself look small by hunching and keeping his hands in his pockets. His presence fills the room with that unknown and dangerous power he carries. He can't hide that kind of energy.

He dips out the door and Caden locks it. I frown, wishing Creed would have said goodbye. I blame it on wanting to know all the people who live in town, especially new people. I want them to feel welcome and loved. After so many horrible disappearances of residents in town lately, we need new blood.

"What a night, right? I fucking hate those guys," Caden spews.

I blink away my thoughts when I hear Caden's voice. "Right," I agree with a slight chuckle. "Let's split this hundred Daniel gave me. You did half the work."

"You better keep that. I wasn't the one who got my ass grabbed. God, I swear if I actually see him do it, he is a dead man," Caden threatens while cleaning off the tables.

"It's fine. I can handle it."

I think.

"You shouldn't have to handle it."

"Well," I set the black bin down and help him clear the table. "We shouldn't be doing this. This is a busboy's job. We need to hire someone. It can't just be you, me, and Holt." Holt is our cook. He's mute and doesn't make much noise. I bet he's already out the door and on his way home.

There are times when I forget he is here because he is so quiet.

"I'll put up a flyer tomorrow. Deal?"

I nod eagerly, my eyes beginning to hood from exhaustion. "Deal."

An hour later after cleaning, I pour myself a small coffee to sip on the way home, so I don't fall asleep at the wheel. When we step outside, Caden walks me to my car like he does every night to make sure I'm safe.

It hasn't always been like this. Safety was never an issue in town but ever since a few residents from the Shallow Cove Institute escaped, everyone has been on alert. Everyone has their guard up. They are even armed— not that it has mattered for those that disappeared. The joy from the town has been removed.

Even the weather seems dim. The nights have been damp, dark, and foggy.

The perfect environment for something bad to happen.

Creed flashes in my mind as I drive home. Is he good or bad?

Only time will tell.

CHAPTER THREE

CREED

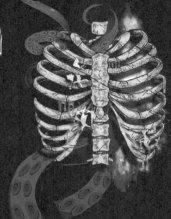

    I didn't know I had so much self-control. As I sat in the booth, surrounded by her scent, my beasts were clawing at my insides to be set free and to ravage her. I wanted nothing more than to lie her flat on her back, tear her clothes off, fuck, and bite to claim her as mine.

    Mmm, my beasts love that idea. I love that idea.

    I want to tie her to me. I want to bind her to me.

    Mine to have.

    Mine to own.

    Mine to fucking claim.

    And when I witnessed her being harassed by that guy in the diner, it took all I had not to tear him to pieces. I didn't want her to see me like that. She'd never want to see me again and I can't risk that.

    Which is why I left the diner so suddenly. I've followed the group of men who harassed Demi outside into the dark.

    Mate.

    Beloved.

    The words are whispered to me again, echoing back and forth between all my beasts and the small human part of me doesn't understand. All I know is that it feels important. She feels important.

    No one can hurt her. No one can take advantage of her. No one can have her.

    Except me.

I stick to the shadows outside, staying quiet as I follow the group through the parking lot. They parked behind the building.

They laugh and Daniel gets shoved, stumbling until he hits a car.

"Fuck," he bursts out laughing, the annoying sound has my ears ringing and my talons lengthening.

"You good, Daniel?" one of his friends asks.

"I'm good. I gotta piss. You guys go on. I'll see you later."

I crouch behind a truck, watching each person get into their own car. Daniel strolls to the dumpster, leans on the rusted bin, his head resting on his forearm as he unzips his pants and begins to piss.

My werewolf comes to the surface, wanting nothing more than to hunt and play with our food, but that would mean missing the moment when Demi gets off work. I can't have that happen, but another day? I'd take Daniel to my cabin, scare him so much he begs for his life, and then let him run to try to escape.

All the while, knowing I'll hunt him down and feast on his fucking bones.

I lick my lips, saliva gathering thickly in my mouth. A drop drips down my fangs and falls to the ground.

When he's done, he tucks himself back in and zips up his pants. He fumbles with his keys, the metal jingling together. The keys fall from his hand and with the new vampire speed I've acquired, I blur to him to take him by surprise.

"Allow me." The words are grumbled, laced with the hate and violence that I want to unleash on him.

"Shit, you scared me, man." He holds his hand to his chest. "You came out of nowhere."

I pick up his keys and stand. He holds out his palm and I cock my head, staring at the hand that touched my... mate.

I drop my hood and drive a key through his hand until blood is dripping down his wrist. Daniel tries to scream, but my vampire takes over, having me lock eyes with the creep in front of me.

"You will not scream," I say in a calm, soothing tone. "You are deathly afraid of me, but you will not make a noise." I yank him closer to me, tears swelling in his eyes and dripping down his cheeks. "Do you understand me?"

He nods, completely entranced. "Yes, I understand."

I keep my gaze on his and lift the hand that's bleeding before I flick my tongue across his wound. Alcohol riddles his blood, the taste bitter and unfulfilling. I hate it. I spit it out, confused as to why I couldn't manage to swallow it.

"Was it this hand you used to touch Demi?" I ask.

He nods again, grinning. "Her ass is perfect. You would too if you got the chance to be close enough."

I break his wrist. The loud crack of bone has my cock rising, the beasts in me wanting to hear it again.

He opens his mouth to scream, but it's silent.

"I've taken away your ability to call for help," I whisper, blurring us behind his car for better protection from prying eyes when I hear the back door to the diner open. He shakes in my hold, the smell of fear pours off him in waves and I inhale deeply, the scent nearly as good as Demi.

Nearly.

"What are you?" he stumbles over the words as his teeth clank together from shock.

I lean close, running a long talon down his cheek, applying just enough pressure to break the skin. Horrible or not, I lick the droplets of blood from his cheek and then spit it back in his face.

"I'm your worst fucking nightmare, Daniel," I whisper into his ear in a slight rumble I'm unable to contain in my chest. "You touched Demi. *My Demi.* Not yours." I break his other arm and his knees buckle, his cry of pain stuck in his throat.

I wish I could fucking swallow it. I bet it would taste so good.

Smoke drifts from my nose and fire boils in my veins. I lift his arm and blow fire across the skin, burning the flesh until it's ruined and charred. His eyes roll to the back of his head to pass out, but I catch his eyes again.

"You aren't allowed to pass out. You deserve the pain that's happening, isn't that right?"

His head bobs as spit drips from his lips and down his chin. "I deserve it."

"What else have you done to Demi?" I ask, bending his broken wrist back to inflict more pain.

His knees buckle and I allow him to fall to the gravel. The smell of his blood hangs heavy in the air and I look down to see a small puddle from the wound in his hand.

"I've grabbed her ass," he explains.

"What else?" I growl, knowing that isn't all that he has done. I drift a talon across his throat. Not deep enough to cause him to bleed out, but enough to get him to start talking. "What. Else?" I snap my fangs together.

"I've taken pictures. When she's wearing a skirt, I slide my phone so I can look under it."

I roll my shoulders, my muscles tensing as I fight the instinct to rip him to shreds. "Keep going. I know you've done more."

"I have an album of her at home. Even a few pictures of her naked. I've jacked off to those photos so many times."

"You've seen her naked?" I wrap a hand around his throat and squeeze. "How?"

"It was at night. I was outside her house. Her blinds were open."

"Have you fucked her?" The thought of her with him or any man has me seeing red. She's only ever allowed to be with me.

"No. She acts like she's too good for anyone. I don't think she's ever had sex. She's a prude."

With a savage growl, I punch through his chest and wrap my hand around his beating heart.

He struggles to breathe, his mouth gaping like the pointless hole it is and wraps his hands around my wrist to try to pull me away.

"You'll never see her again, Daniel. You'll never talk about her again. Your time with my mate is over." I rip his heart from his chest, my werewolf wanting to howl in victory, but I keep him quiet.

Blood trickles down my arm as I hold the heart up, watching it struggle to beat.

Daniel's hands fly to his chest and his eyes widen with the realization that he's dying. I squeeze his heart, his blood pouring from the useless organ, and he finally succumbs to his fatal wound. His body falls to the ground right at my feet and I sigh, annoyed that I have to dispose of the body.

I unlock the trunk of his car with his keys and toss him in there along with his heart before slamming it shut. Blowing a perfect stream of fire, the flames lick the metal together, allowing it to melt so it's difficult to open the trunk.

Then I do the same to the keys. I burn them until I can crunch what used to be metal in my palms and watch it blow away in the wind as ash.

I wipe the blood on my jeans, then grin when I remember I have three more men I have to kill at some point for Demi.

What would she think if she knew someone felt so deeply for her that they killed just so she had peace?

I'm doing this for her. She'll understand. Nothing can get in the way of us.

Her fate is inevitably bound to my unfortunate soul. If my mate is afraid of the dark, she'll have to learn to love nightmares. I was born in darkness and the only light I'll ever see again is the one I feel when I'm near her.

The door to the diner opens and I leap from the ground until I'm on top of the roof, swaying from the surprise jump I didn't know I could do. Crouching, I crawl to the edge, watching my mate walk to her car.

"Are you going to be okay?" The man from the diner walks her to her car, asks.

I growl again, my talons digging into the roof. He doesn't seem like a threat, but I'll have to keep an eye on him. He didn't hurt my mate, so I won't hurt him.

"I'll be fine. I promise. I'll see you tomorrow, Caden. Thank you," she says.

"Anything for my bestie." His head turns, and he sniffs the air, turning around to try to figure something out.

"What is it?"

"Nothing. I thought I smelled... you know what? It doesn't matter. It's probably me," he chuckles. "Tell me when you're home."

My vision tunnels to her and I'm able to see every line of her face. She smiles, but it's forced while she gives a slight tilt of her chin.

"I will." She climbs into her car and the headlights beam into the night.

My back begins to itch. The pain blinding for a moment before massive wings burst from me, spreading out on either side of me like black leather curtains.

And then I groan from how good it feels. It's as if they were trapped, waiting for the moment that they were truly needed. I test them out, gently flapping them, stretching them, then folding them down my back to make sure I know how.

One more thing to add to the list of reasons why Demi would want nothing to do with me. She backs out of her parking spot and begins to drive away from me. Desperately needing to be close to her, I push every ounce of strength I have into jumping into the air.

I spread my wings and move them up and down, bringing me higher into the sky until her car is nothing but a speck on the ground. The dragon inside me is at peace. The constant warmth I've felt in my chest from the fire is gone.

The air is cool as I fly with the stars and pierce the clouds. The scales are more prominent now since my wings are out. They travel down my gray arms, reflecting the light of the crescent moon.

There's a beauty up here, a realm of peace I haven't known in a very long time. I don't understand so many things that are happening and I don't understand why I feel this way. Perhaps, I never will.

All I can do is follow my instincts, even if they are violent, unpredictable, and promise blood.

Soaring through the air, I cut right, then left, spinning just to have fun and see what I can do. I'm tempted to smile, but I don't. I want to save my happiness for when I'm inside Demi.

Flying won't be able to compare to that.

From up here, I can see the red blink of her taillight as she signals her right turn into a small subdivision. She parks in the third driveway, and I focus on her, wanting to hear what she's doing before she climbs out of the car.

A song is playing over the radio, but it doesn't hide the sigh escaping her after a long day.

She opens the door and climbs out; her hot pink hair is a beacon and easy to spot from up here. When she's inside the house, I nose-dive, breaking my way through the clouds. Her house comes at me fast and when I'm close enough, I instinctively correct the angle of my wings which lifts me upright and I slowly land on her roof with a soft thump.

I tuck my wings behind my back, growling when they get caught in my ripped hoodie. Grabbing a hold of the sweatshirt, I rip it from my body which leaves me in my tattered black t-shirt. A tingle spreads throughout my back as the long, leather wings mend to my back, out of sight, out of mind. I grip my shoulder, trying to look to see where they could go, when I see what looks like a tattoo. I spin in the other direction, checking my other shoulder to see the same thing.

Large tattoos of my wings have been forever stained into my skin.

Jumping down from the roof, I land in her sizeable fenced-in backyard, then press my back against the side of her house before peeking my head around and peering through her sliding glass doors.

She's still in her work uniform and while she's walking to the kitchen, she begins to take off her apron. Demi tosses it on the counter before snagging a bottle of wine from the fridge, then she heads to another room while unbuttoning her shirt.

The suckers along my cock ripple as I harden, lust hitting me so hard, I nearly come on the spot. It isn't going to be as easy as walking in there and claiming her.

All I know is that I have to be near her. I have to know what she's doing at all times. Her life from this moment on will never be the same. She'll never walk alone again. I'll be her shadow, and in the night, I'll be her dark. I'll consume her so she never knows loneliness again.

When she's gone for a few minutes, I listen carefully, placing my ear to the glass and focus.

She's humming under her breath and the splash of water sounds, but it isn't a shower. It's a bath.

I groan, pressing my head against the glass at the thought of her naked. God, I bet she's fucking beautiful. I bet her skin is soft to the touch and her lips will give like pillows once I press mine to them.

Then the memory of Daniel saying he took pictures of her sends my primal instincts into overdrive. Everyone needs to know she's off-limits.

I walk over to one corner of her fence, growling at the fact that she isn't with me in my cabin. I'll have to make do for now.

Unzipping my pants, I free my semi-hard cock, and piss a steady stream around her yard. My werewolf huffs in approval, wanting to thump its tail— if I had one.

Inhaling, I grin when all I smell is my scent.

It will warn away predators. No one will come near her.

I zip up, feeling so smug, a purr builds in my chest. With a new pep in my step, I try the sliding glass door again.

It's locked.

"Oh, my smart mate protecting herself from the out-side world," I whisper against the glass, my breath fogging it. With my finger, I draw a heart into the condensation. "But it won't save you from me." I lick the glass, wishing it was her skin.

The hairs tipping my ears stand when the splashes become louder.

She's gotten in the tub.

I growl again, wanting to get closer— no— needing to get closer. My talons lengthen unwillingly as I wrap my hand around the handle and give it a tug. The lock snaps making the door slide open easily. The burst of her scent wraps around me as I step inside. My entire body is overwhelmed by it.

My cock becomes hard while my wings twitch to break free from my body and my fangs ache. All my new urges rush to the surface. My sense of smell intensifies enabling me to scent the cookies covered on the counter, the oil from something she fried a couple of days ago, the orange-scented candle lit in her bathroom, and then the rush of her blood.

Her heart pounds hard, slow, and steady as she relaxes. Even through the scent of the candle, the smell of her blood is what makes me ache the most. My mouth wa-ters and my cock has never throbbed so intensely. I can feel the suckers moving again, the tentacles wanting to unravel.

Gripping onto the back of the couch, my talons nearly slice through the material covering the cushions. Bend-ing down, I run my nose across the sofa, a moan catch-ing in my throat when one pillow is drenched in Demi's scent.

Smoke rolls from my mouth in fogged sheets, meshing with her scent, and my dragon's fire begins to swirl inside me.

"Can't," I whisper, rolling my hips into the couch to find some type of friction. "Can't yet. This is her home." The smoke turns from gray to black as the fire burns hotter inside me. Before the entire house smells, I'm able to cage that part of me. I regain my footing, taking in the living room, surveying all the little knickknacks on her entertainment center.

Taking a peek towards her room, I pay attention to the movement of water in the tub. I don't want to get caught.

Not *yet* anyway.

I'm grappling with so many emotions right now, so many insidious feelings, that I know I would have never felt before I became *this*.

The more I try to reason with my new instincts, with the little humanity I have left, the stronger those instincts become.

It isn't so bad anymore. Not since I'm used to the power, the enhanced senses, but I am on the outside looking in. It's lonely, but now I have my mate, whatever that means, and I'll do anything to be by her side.

Even if it means living in her shadows, in the darkened corners of her life, and I'll haunt her. I'll be the ghost that possesses her mind, body, and soul.

Until she has no other choice but to be mine— to want to be mine.

My finger glides over the wood of the entertainment center. It's very clean. No dust. She cares for her home. I like that. Maybe she'll make my cabin a good home too. I'll build whatever she likes. We can't stay here. I need space. I need the woods now.

The town is no place for a monster like me.

I come to a picture of her and two older people that must be her parents. Both have gray hair, but everyone seems happy. Demi's smile is bright and wide, wrinkling the side of her eyes. She's in a cap and gown.

Obviously graduation day.

I grab the picture and rub my finger across her beautiful face, smearing the clean glass. She's perfect. I wish I could remember aspects like this of my life, but I can't.

Whatever the scientists did to my mind when they electrocuted me, damaged that part of my brain. Certain things are murky, but one thing always rings clear.

Honeysuckles.

I place the picture down where it was and slowly walk the length of the entertainment center, noticing books on the shelves. Curiosity wins and I reach for one, noticing a woman on the cover in basically a sheet but she's in the arms of a sea monster.

The kraken inside me rises and the tentacles push at the crotch of my pants, wanting free, wanting my mate.

If she likes books likes this... maybe...

I shake my head and put the book back. Fantasy is often better than reality and the reality of me is far worse than how monsters are portrayed in books.

Taking a step away, I look up, studying the ceiling, wondering which place would be the best for a security camera so I can keep an eye on my mate.

I grin and head to the kitchen, inhaling the scent of fresh cookies but all I want is her blood. My stomach grumbles for it, but I can't feed from her yet. I want to. My tongue is dry, and I crave to drink from her while I'm fucking her sweet cunt.

More smoke escapes me and my wings try to burst free as they ripple across my back, but I grip the edge of the counter to control myself.

I'm only here to learn about her.

For now.

My eyes catch another good spot for a camera. My mate has done well by herself. Her home is nice. Small. Too small for us and the kids we will have.

Fuck.

I need to get out of here. The urge to go into her room and breed her is so strong, I can't think straight.

Yet I find myself walking to her room and pushing open the door. The carpeted floors cushion the heavy clunk of my footsteps as I enter. Her scent is the strongest here. It hits me so hard; I have to catch myself on the wall.

My head becomes dizzy as I follow to where her smell is heaviest.

Her laundry hamper.

On top are a simple pair of black panties and I reach for them, bringing them to my face.

I inhale until my lungs can't expand anymore then let out a shaky breath. Looking over my shoulder to her bathroom to make sure she can't see me, I tuck her panties in my pocket, then dig through the dirty laundry like a fucking dog burying a bone.

I find two more, tucking one in the other pocket, then keep the other one in my hand. Nothing has ever smelt better to me. It's so good, the knot at the base of my cock begins to swell, filling with come, and I want nothing more than to lock it inside her.

Placing my back against the wall next to her open bathroom door, I take a chance, peeking inside to see what she's doing. The lights are off and the candle glows brightly as it sits on top of the counter.

Demi has a mask over her eyes while her body is covered in bubbles. Her tits tease me, barely breaking the surface of the water, but I can still see the curve of them. I bet they'd feel so good in my palms.

Unable to stop myself, I step into the bathroom, needing to be closer to her. The music blares, hiding the soft scuff of my boots as I cross the tile floor. The bubbles in the tub jiggle from the speaker sitting on the edge of the tub, the song playing on full blast. It's so loud, I can barely hear myself think, but that's probably the point. Demi works so hard and wants to forget the day.

My eyes travel the length of her, from her head to her toes, and I'm fucking enamored.

I press the crotch of her underwear under my nose to smell her pussy's juices, then drag the panties to my lips. I suck them into my mouth, and her flavor bursts across my tongue.

Unbuttoning my pants, I freeze when she moves, the water splashing over the edge of the tub. She settles, sighing again as if she has no worries in the world when the biggest one is standing right in front of her.

Carefully, I unzip my pants, and my tentacles stretch out to Demi immediately, twisting and turning in the air. Wrapping her panties around me, I begin to stroke my cock. My eyes roll to the back of my head when I apply added pressure on the suckers. My knot fills more, the round base growing so much, I'm afraid it's about to burst. I hold in a growl to keep quiet, but I can't stop the smoke drifting from my nose.

I feel like I'm about to catch fire. My bones ache and my body burns, my skin is hot. My scales become more visible. Blue and orange flames lick my skin as I hold in my dragon wanting to burst free.

My mouth drops when my orgasm bursts from my cock. My knot pulsates, sending streams of come into her bath. My talons dig into the vanity of her sink so I can hold myself up as my legs give out from the intensity.

The white ropes disappear into the bubbles, the evidence gone, and the come wasted.

I sneer with discontent. Every drop deserves to be inside her.

Demi swirls the water with her hands, splashing it on her chest, and every part of me purrs with satisfaction.

She's bathing in my come. She's marked.

Unwrapping my hand and her drenched underwear from my cock, I notice my entire palm is coated in come. My brows rise when I realize the suckers must secrete it as well. Even better, so when I fuck my mate, and lock deep inside her, my suckers sticking to her and my knot locking us together, she'll be full of me.

She'll be bred.

Backing away from the bathroom, I step aside so I'm officially out of sight. Propping my elbows onto her long oak dresser. The top of it has an array of perfumes, jewelry, and makeup laid on top of it. I grab a perfume bottle and untwist the top, then pull the pump out.

Wiping my hand on my pants, I hold my cock again, placing the opening right at my slit. I only need a few drops of my piss. I don't want it to be overwhelming, but enough to make her smell of me.

Everyone will know she's mine.

I don't need to go after marking her entire backyard, but a few drops dribble free just like I wanted. My toothy smug smirk catches my attention in the mirror. The animal stares back at me with glowing eyes and long fangs.

Placing the pump back where it belongs, I twist the top on, give it a good shake, and leave before I risk getting caught.

But not before I give her pillow and blanket a few sprays of her perfume. When she sleeps, she'll be covered in me. That soothes the primal instincts roaring inside my sardonic heart.

Safety is no longer her concern because nothing can save her from me.

Her life is mine.

I exit how I entered her home and my wings rip free from my back just as I need them—when I need them to—and fly into the sky.

I'll show her the stars even if it means dragging her through the darkness of hell.

CHAPTER
FOUR

DEMI

DEMI'S DINER

I'm about to open the car door when the hairs on the back of my neck stand up. The reflection from the driver's side window shows my surroundings. The trees behind me sway from the morning breeze and the clouds move slowly in the bright blue sky.

It's the figure at the edge of the tree line that has me gasping, spinning around so fast, I drop my keys. They clatter to the ground, the metal scraping against the driveway.

Only to be met with nothing.

I place my hand over my heart and chuckle at myself for being so paranoid.

"Oh my God, you're losing it, Demi."

"You okay, Dem?" Mr. Pete, my neighbor, asks me while he waters his precious plants that he babies more than his own kids.

"I'm fine. I just startled myself." I bend down and pick up my keys to notice they are scratched from dropping them.

"You shouldn't be living by yourself. A girl like you needs to settle down. If you had someone here, maybe you wouldn't be so scared."

It's a sincere statement, but he sounds grumpy as usual.

"Thanks, Mr. Pete. I'll keep that in mind." I finally get into my car and slam the door, pausing a moment to take a few deep breaths.

I know what I saw.

Someone was there.

I'm about to start the car when my phone rings and I jump, dropping the keys on the floorboard.

"Jesus, Demi. Get it together. You're a damn mess today." I rummage through my mess of a purse that contains a hundred receipts, emergency makeup, tampons and pads, a travel-size sewing kit because no one knows when it might be needed, and my pepper spray until I finally find my phone at the very bottom.

Of course.

Caden's name is flashing across the screen, and I swipe it across to answer.

"Hey, what's up?" I ask while fumbling for the keys.

"You need to get to the diner now."

The urgency in his voice has me straightening in my seat, keys in hand. "What's wrong?"

"I don't know. The cops are here. They won't tell me why until you get here since you're the owner."

"Oh my God. Okay. I'll be there in ten minutes. Tell them that for me."

"Sure thing. Drive safe."

"I will." I hang up and toss my phone in the passenger seat, wondering why the hell the police are at my diner.

Damn it, I hope I don't have to close for the day. The morning surge is my favorite. I always earn a lot of tips from the men who work at the local logging factory when they come in before work. The diner usually gets a rush of them after they get off work too. They come in filthy, covered in dust, and sometimes blood, depending on if they got injured or not. I always give them a discount on their food. The men are always appreciative and leave me a nice big tip, but I feel so bad for them. Those guys always look so tired. The job is kicking their ass, but that factory is where most of the town works. It's where all the money is made. Without it, the town would be nothing.

Even with the amazing tips, one day of being shut down will be a nightmare for me and Caden. The diner does well, but one day without it is a massive loss because we are one of the only restaurants in town. If the cops need me to close, I'm not sure what I'll do. If I had a food truck, I could park it in the factory parking lot. It would help with the loss.

It's an idea for another day.

I arrive at the diner in record time, the car dipping as I pull into the parking lot. My heart begins to pound harder when I see the red and blue lights flashing. My stomach sours when I see Daniel's car in the very back, a few officers walking around his vehicle.

Something is *very* wrong.

The brakes squeak as I park the Chevy Bel Air, reminding me I really need to get to the mechanic to get this car pampered. The sound gains the attention of the police officers, and they all stare me down. All four of them walk toward me in a synchronized stride. It's intimidating. My mind whirls, wondering if I've done anything illegal that will warrant arrest.

I did run that stop sign the other day, but that was an accident. I didn't even see it. How is it my fault that it wasn't closer to the road and hidden behind bushes? I know I got lucky not getting into a car accident, but running stop signs doesn't equivalate to jail time, does it? Or what if Daniel told them something horrible I didn't do? I wouldn't put it past him since I've rejected him more than a hundred times.

Oh my God, what if I go to prison?

My hands begin to shake with anxiety and before I can open the door, Caden is there. A burst of the cool morning air hits my heated face and immediately, calmness washes over me, enabling me to breathe again. A quick shadow passes over me, blocking out the sun as Caden helps me get out of the car.

Covering my eyes, I search for the shadow, but the blue skies stare back at me. There's nothing to be seen.

"Are you okay?" Caden waves his hands in front of my face. "I need you here with me, Dem."

I blink away my trance and my eyes meet Caden's. His are full of concern. "Sorry, I thought I saw something. What's going on, do you know?" I slam the car door, trying to get inside the diner before the police get to me. If I'm inside, I'll be more comfortable than being out in the open.

"No. All I know is when I came to the diner, I noticed Daniel's car. I didn't think anything of it. I figured he drank too much and went home with his friends, but I overheard the cops talking and they said Daniel never made it home."

I bump the front door open with my hip, the jingling of the bell louder than usual because of the circumstances.

"Oh my God, that's terrible. Do you think he's okay?" I hurry to the employee closet I keep locked and set my purse inside.

"The part of me that hates him hopes he isn't, but the decent man inside me hopes he is," he answers genuinely with his arms crossed.

Tying my apron behind my back, I nod in agreement. "I know how you feel. I only wanted him to stop grabbing my ass. I didn't want anything bad to happen to him."

"Karma is a bitch." Caden shrugs his shoulder. "I'm going to go put on a fresh pot of coffee. I'm sure the officers would appreciate it."

"Good idea."

The bell jingles as the cops enter. Because it's such a small town, everyone knows everyone.

"Demi." Jake Holland tips his hat to me before taking it off.

"Jake," I greet, wiping my hand on the apron. "I mean, Officer Holland," I correct myself.

"You know you can call me Jake. We've known each other too long for you to call me officer." He walks over to give me a hug and I take it, but something feels different. I don't feel like I should be hugging him.

I pull away quickly and wave to the three other men. "Waylon. Jenkins. Zig."

"Hey, Demi," Waylon answers for all of them. "We hate to come to you like this, but we have a few questions for you."

I swallow, knowing they won't interrogate me, but they are still the law. Naturally, I'm anxious.

"Sure. Caden is putting on some coffee. Do you want some?"

"That would be lovely, Demi," Jake reports, adjusting his utility belt carrying his gun. "We might need to close the diner for an hour. Is that okay?"

"I'd prefer if we didn't. I have the factory men coming in soon and they really need their breakfast, but maybe between Caden and I, we can manage?"

Jake sighs, gripping my shoulders. "I'm sorry to use my authority, Demi, but the diner is closed for now. Why don't we take a seat, and we can discuss why."

"Okay. Let me tell Caden to make enough coffee to put outside with some muffins for the factory workers then? Please?"

"Always so thoughtful, Demi. Sure, that will be fine. We will take the booth in the corner since it can fit all of us."

"Okay," I whisper, trying not to show the tears swimming in my eyes. I'm so afraid I'm in trouble. I start walking away and stop. "Jake?"

He turns, flashing a concerned expression at me with his dark eyebrows furrowing together. The other men get settled while Jake's large strides eat up the distance between us. "What's wrong?"

"Am I in trouble? Are you here to arrest me?" My voice comes out as a tremble. I've never done well with authority.

He rears back. "God no, Demi. We are only here to ask questions." More sirens sound in the distance and they get closer to the diner with every passing second. "The fire department is on their way too."

"Okay." I'm able to function now that I know I'm not being hauled off to jail. Jake goes to his booth while I disappear into the kitchen to see Holt making muffin mix.

"Before you ask, I already told Holt to make enough muffins for an army. I have all the coffee pots full." Caden places a pitcher in the middle of the tray surrounded by clean coffee mugs that say Demi's Diner across them in bright pink.

"You're too good at reading my mind. I'd question it if I cared enough."

He snorts in laughter, handing me the tray. "Just be thankful I know you so well. Let's not keep the nice cops waiting." He spins me around and pushes me out the kitchen door. "The muffins will be done soon. Let's leave Holt to his mastery."

"Thanks, Holt!" I shout over my shoulder and hear a grunt in return.

It's typically the most we ever hear from him anyways.

When I enter the dining room, Caden and I head over to the booth. I set the mugs down and fill them with coffee.

All of them take it black.

I sit down and Caden slides in next to me. He falls into a coughing fit, and I pat his back.

"Are you okay?"

"Are you wearing your typical perfume today?" His eyes water as he chokes out the question.

"That's not important right now," Jake interrupts, giving Caden an annoyed glare. "Demi, when was the last time you saw Daniel?"

"He was here last night with his friends. They left drunk as usual, and I didn't see him after that. Caden and I stayed until closing, cleaning up."

"Was anything out of the ordinary? Do you know if Daniel had any enemies?"

"Enemies? What is this about? I'm sure he's drunk in a ditch somewhere," Caden says.

"There was a lot of blood found outside of his vehicle and the trunk is welded shut. With that amount of blood, it's unlikely anyone would survive that."

"Fuck." Caden rubs his fingers through his hair and leans against the booth, scooting away from me before coughing again.

"Oh my God. You think he is dead?" My head spins from the news, and memories from childhood with Daniel flicker through my mind like an old movie.

"We can't say for certain. Did you know anyone who wanted to hurt Daniel? Did he have an argument? Have you noticed anything out of the ordinary?" Jake asks, tiny notepad and pen in hand to write down my replies.

Caden snorts. "The guy was a fucking asshole who assaulted Demi left and right." He leans forward and crosses his arms on the table. "And I can bet he did it to a hundred other women. He made an enemy of everyone the moment he opened his mouth."

"Did you ever file a report, Demi?"

The laugh that leaves me is sad and sarcastic. "Come on, Jake. You and I both know nothing would have happened."

"I would have tried," he explains with a frown.

"I know that," I say to him, gently touching his arm from across the table. "He grabbed my butt when he got drunk. He didn't take no for an answer, but he never went further than that. He was an asshole, but I never wanted him dead, Jake. And nothing has happened that has been out of the ordinary. I get new people in here every day that are just passing through."

"Anyone unique? Did anyone stick out to you?"

Creed flashes through my mind, but he'd have no reason to hurt Daniel. The thought of him warms my insides, and I relax again. My gut tells me to protect him even if I don't know him well enough to truly care.

"No," I lie, nibbling my lip, then shake my head as I pretend to think. "I'm sorry. No one. Daniel wasn't a nice guy. I didn't want him dead, but I also can't say I'm surprised." I hate that I wipe a tear away because even though he wasn't a good man, I had still known him for most of my life.

"And can you account for where you were last night with a witness?" Jake asks, his face softening as he does. "It's procedure. I have to ask."

"I understand. Caden and I, along with Holt, my cook, were here until closing. It had to have been another hour or so before we all went home."

"Did anyone see you go home?" Waylon chimes in.

"No." I raise my voice, offended. "I live alone. Caden and Holt live alone. Caden walked me to my car and we both left. We have nothing else left to say."

"I'm sorry, Demi. We have to ask these questions."

"I know. I'm sorry. I didn't mean to snap." I rub my temples and think about how poorly I slept because of the dreams I had.

All night I tossed and turned, waking up in a fever from lust. My entire body was drenched in sweat and no matter how many times I made myself come, it wasn't enough.

Creed took over my dreams and I barely know the man, but my orgasms have never been so intense. My want for him is unlike anything I've ever felt before. Even now, I feel like I need him by me, touching me, inside me, his lips on mine, him owning my body.

My cheeks heat and I have to look away from the men staring at me. It's as if they know what I'm thinking.

The bell jingles above the door, saving me from embarrassing myself further.

"We're ready when you are," the fireman says, poking his head in.

"We'll be right out." One by one Jake and his colleagues stand.

"I'll keep you updated, okay?" Jake informs.

"I'm coming out there with you."

"Demi, I don't think that's a good idea." Caden and Jake say in unison, but I am already walking across the main floor and out the door before they can catch me.

The firetruck's engine grumbles, the vibrations tickling under my feet. An officer is blocking off the entire border of the property I own with yellow crime scene tape, and seeing that makes this all too real.

The hair on the back of my neck stands up again. Goosebumps travel down my arms. That feeling is back.

Someone is watching me.

I study the parking lot, narrowing my eyes to block the sun. Firemen are barking orders and pointing at one another. A metal saw grinds through the air and sparks fly as they try to cut the trunk of Daniel's car.

Something shifts out of my peripheral vision, and I turn my head, only to find nothing there.

"What the fuck?" I whisper, wondering if I'm losing my mind between what happened this morning and now.

"Let's get closer to see what's going on." Caden grabs my arm, yanking me across the parking lot.

We get so close to the car, I can smell the harsh scent of metal from the saw cutting into it. The sparks from metal grinding against metal almost land at our feet.

"I can't let you come any closer." Jake steps in front of us, his lips stern and tone full of that power only a police officer can possess.

He does it well.

"Got it!" the fireman handling the saw proclaims, lifting the mask from his head. The sun hits his sweaty face just as he backs away and for some reason, I take that moment to look down.

Next to the tire is a dried puddle of blood and my hand latches onto Caden's arm. My nails dig into his skin. My entire body begins to tremble when the severity of the situation hits me.

Caden wraps his arm around me as we watch the firemen pop the trunk open.

"Oh shit," one of them says, but all three of them turn their heads.

"We have a body," Waylon announces, sighing as he looks away. "It's Daniel."

"What?" I shout, pushing by Jake to see what Waylon is talking about.

I'm about to round the car when Waylon wraps his hand around my eyes, spinning me around so I don't see Daniel's body.

"Let me go! Waylon! Let me go!" I fight to get out of his hold, but he's so much bigger than I am.

"You can't see that, Demi. I won't let you see that. He was a rat bastard, but he didn't deserve to die like that."

"Let. Me. See."

He spins me around, forcing me to look him in the eyes. "There won't be going back if you see this. You'll change."

"Then I'll change, but I need to see it."

"Let her go, Waylon. Maybe she needs to learn the hard way," a fireman I don't know says with a cocky smirk. "Sometimes pretty things love horrible nightmares," he chuckles, blowing me a kiss.

"Shut the hell up, Ricky. Now isn't the time for your bullshit. We have a murder." Jake points his finger at Ricky. "I'm going to talk to your chief about this."

"Demi," Caden's whisper of my name freezes me mid-step. "Don't."

Not even my best friend's pleas are enough for me to stay away. I can't say why I want to see Daniel's body. Maybe I need to know it is him, but I know that isn't it.

Deep down inside my soul, past my heart, mind, and the difference between right and wrong, I know what it is.

Seeing Daniel dead would be a gift.

A fucked up, sinister gift.

And I think someone left him for me.

Creed comes to mind, but I have only seen the man once and my obsession with him is becoming questionable.

Why would he kill for someone he doesn't know?

I break eye contact with Caden, slowly glancing down in the trunk. Time slows to a standstill. The wind blows my perfume around me and while it reminds me of a beautiful childhood memory, it isn't powerful enough to wipe away the stain of what I'm seeing.

Daniel is dead.

His face is contorted. His mouth is wide open as if he died on a scream and there's a giant hole in his chest where his heart used to be.

The organ is lying next to him, so the person went out of their way to kill him but did not take the heart they ripped from his chest.

Dried blood is under him. I have an image of him lying there, fresh and dead, blood dripping from his chest cavity to the carpet.

Lifeless.

It should scare me. It should haunt me and cause me nightmares like the fireman said, but it doesn't terrify me like it should.

Maybe I'm a little more broken than I thought since all I feel is relief.

The feeling of someone watching me hits me again and I back away from the dead body and look around one more time to see if I can spot the person who is giving me this feeling.

I can't see him, but I know he's there.

And I think...

He killed for me.

CHAPTER FIVE

CREED

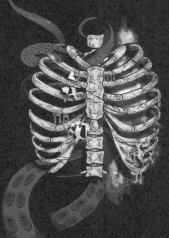

As much as I wanted to stay and watch Demi all day, I couldn't, but damn it, I wanted to. I loved her face when she saw Daniel's body. She didn't seem upset like I'd thought she'd be.

She was impressed.

And I want to keep impressing her.

It's why I'm taking advantage of her house being empty today. I have cameras I need to install.

I can't wait to be able to watch her. I'll probably break into her house and watch her sleep, but on the off chance I can't do that, I need to be able to see her.

My feet hit the ground of her backyard and I tuck my wings against my back, rolling my shoulders as they mesh into my skin. I inhale to make sure my scent hasn't faded.

It hasn't.

Growling in delight, I open the sliding glass door again, frowning when it glides open too easily.

Anyone could get in. I should have thought of that before I broke in.

"Fuck." I snap my fangs at the damn door, wanting to burn it down for pissing me off. I'll have to fix it and find another way into her house.

The only man allowed in her home is me.

I wait for guilt to eat at me for what I'm doing, but it doesn't exist. I'm meant to be here, to watch over her, to protect her, and to love her.

What I'm doing saves her.

I drop my bag on the table, unzip it, and dump all the supplies. I place a camera in the living room, dining room, kitchen, laundry room, and spare bedroom.

Her room is last. I'm standing just outside her doorway, cocking my head as I stare at her bed. The comforter is still messy from her sleeping last night. I inhale as much as I can until my body aches for oxygen. Her scent drowns me, fusing with my blood, working its way into the marrow of my bones, and the chambers of my heart.

The tentacles around my cock tighten, then move up and down to stroke me.

I want my mate. All the beasts inside me are clawing at my chest to claim her. The thought of anyone else makes me sick which is a problem because I'm hungry. I'm starving.

And any blood I taste, I find disgusting. I want my mate's blood.

Beloved.

My vampire side corrects me.

Mmm, yes. My beloved. I want to sink my fangs into her neck and drink long swallows until I'm full.

I step into her room and debate where to put the camera and decide on the small crack in her vanity. It's the part that connects to the mirror and I slip the tiny camera in there, then do the same with the bathroom. I settle it in the middle of the shower head. The thought of being able to watch her slide her hands down her own body has more desire building the fire in my chest.

One day, my hands will be caressing her curves. One day, my talons will be scraping her skin until pale pink lines appear and she's gasping for breath due to pain and pleasure.

One day, she'll be screaming my name as I pound her tight pussy with my cock.

I groan, my cock so hard it fucking hurts. I grip the trim of the doorway in the bathroom, my claws digging into the wood. The warmth in my chest spreads, fire threatening to burst from my mouth. My wings twitch, wanting to spread out and stretch.

My entire body feels hot.

I get undressed, stripping down until I'm naked.

A rumble is constant in my chest as I inhale her scent. It's so potent, I feel it seeping into my skin, in my lungs, making itself at home in the abyss of my soul. My cock is hard and heavy, weighed down by the size of it. My tentacles sway, dancing to reach the bed, and I listen.

Gripping the edge of the mattress, I lean down, burying my face in the sheets, and moan. Lowering myself, I slide against the soft sheets bathed in the smell of my mate. I fist the blankets, my wings lash out, and wishing they could wrap around Demi to hold her close. I want to block the world out, darkening our surroundings until all there is, is us.

"Demi," I whisper on a whine into the bed, biting the sheet as I rock my hips into her mattress.

The soft friction of the sheets coasts across the suckers lining my shaft causing me to gasp.

"Fuck," I groan, stretching my arms out to clutch the other side of the bed while I rut into the mattress.

Her scent drugs me. My body is lightweight, and my mind is dizzy. She's the slow buzz of alcohol while I'm the lethal injection that kills. She's the graceful sleep and I'm her paralysis demon freezing her body so I can possess her.

"Goddamn it, Demi," I moan for her. "I need you. Fuck, you're going to feel so good." I bury my nose into the blankets, then roll, cocooning myself in the same sheets she's wrapped her body in. The thought is nearly too much. My orgasm threatens and I have to reach down, squeezing the shaft so hard it hurts.

Snagging the pillow, I place it over my face, smothering my nose and mouth so I'm suffocating in her.

I stroke myself hard and fast. I bite the pillowcase and the scent of her bursts across my tongue. I can taste her.

I lick the pillow, sucking on the material before moving to a dry spot so I can do it again.

My Sweet Honeysuckles.

She even tastes of the beautiful flower.

"You're mine," I moan. "You're mine forever, Demi. No one will take you from me." I bite my bottom lip, my fangs aching to sink into her neck to drink her blood.

Rolling onto my stomach, I grip the headboard, and imagine she's beneath me, legs wrapped around my hips while I own her tight cunt.

"That's it. Take my cock, Good Girl. Feel it stretch you beyond your limits," I bark to the ghost of her under me, the one begging for more, the one begging me to fuck her harder.

The headboard slams into the wall, my cock viciously rubbing against the crumpled blankets.

My orgasm hits me, and I toss my head back, groaning at the same time fire escapes my throat. My wings flap with every spasm that leaves me. A pathetic whimper escapes my throat because that orgasm only took the edge off.

I need her.

I'm burning for her.

Lifting from the bed, I stare down at the mess I made. I don't want my come to go to waste. Bending down, I suck my seed into my mouth, cleaning the sheets before it's too late and it dries.

I want Demi to have it.

There's so much and it belongs inside her, but since she's not here, I have to figure out another possibility.

My eyes land on the bottle of lotion by her bed. I untwist the top and spit my come inside, place the cap back on, and shake it.

She'll never know.

Every time she puts on lotion, she'll be marked in another way.

My cock stirs again. Looking down, the suckers are still secreting come, but my tentacles are at rest. I lean back, studying the empty room, and begin to wonder if this is all I'll ever have with Demi.

The chances of her loving a monster like me are slim to none. I have to take what I can get even if it means watching her from the shadows.

Her bed squeaks as I stand, trying to gather the energy to get dressed and leave. My dragon likes it here. It's warm and safe compared to the cold cabin I killed for.

Begrudgingly, I tug my shirt on, then my pants, and head out to the living room where my bag is.

"Let's see if these cameras work." Snagging the tablet from the table, I turn it on, punch in my code, and bring up the security program I've coded so no one can track me down if they discover the cameras.

Feed from all the cameras appears in squares. I click camera one and the entire screen fills with the image of me behind the couch. Next, I pinch my fingers and zoom in.

I do that for every screen, so I know it works. Grinning, I tuck the trash from the cameras in my bag, the tablet, and do one last sweep to double-check that I didn't leave any evidence behind.

Her bed is messy, but it was like that when I arrived, so hopefully she won't think much about it.

But.

I hope she does.

I hope she lies there tonight, feeling that something is different. She'll be able to smell me and not know why. She won't be able to put her finger on what seems so out of order. She'll toss and turn all night, casting her eyes into the darkness of her room. She'll imagine something there and get scared, that's when she'll think of me.

That's when she'd wish I was there, to hold her to scare away all the bad and frightful things.

Not knowing that I'm who she needs to be afraid of.

I don't know what I'm capable of, but I know I'll find out soon enough when it comes to Demi.

Forcing someone to love me won't be easy but it's better than being alone.

Taking one last look around, I slide my arms through the backpack straps and walk out the back door.

I want to go see Demi.

"Who the hell are you?" an old voice says from the other side of the fence.

With a growl, I turn my head, annoyed when I see an older man staring at me with wide eyes.

Fuck.

By the smell of it, he's watering his plants.

"I knew I heard something going on over here. Demi is at work. I know she isn't dating anyone. Who the hell—"

He shuts the hell up when I use my vampire speed to be directly in front of him. I wrap a hand around his fragile throat, debating if I want to snap his neck.

My amber eyes glow in the reflection of his aged blues. Fear is potent and it causes my mouth to water.

I show my fangs, snarling at the stranger.

When he stares at me long enough, he falls limp, his eyes glazed over from being held in my trance.

"I'm no one," I bite out, lifting him into the air. "You did not see me. Everything is fine at Demi's house. Nothing is out of the ordinary."

"Nothing," he repeats, letting out a dreamy exhale.

I still want to snap his neck, but Demi might like this old man, so I think better of it. Carefully, I lower his fragile, delicate body until his feet touch the step stool he was using to pry.

One by one, I release my fingers, scratching my talons along the wrinkled folds of his neck.

"And you never see me when I'm here," I add to be safe, glowering.

"Never."

"Good." I step away and launch myself into the air, high enough that no one can see me.

The sun is hot and warm on my wings the more I ascend. I shut my eyes, relishing the freedom of flying. I try to think of my human days before I was kidnapped and tested on. I do my best to remember anything, my friends, my family, but again, all I smell are honeysuckles.

Snarling in frustration, I nosedive to the ground. The man I used to be is gone, replaced by a savage selfish beast.

I land in the tree line behind Demi's diner, about a third of a mile away. It's further than I'd like to be, but I can't risk her seeing me.

The *full* me.

The cops are still there.

I focus on their conversation, slowing my heart rate and breathing until all I hear is them.

"Poor bastard," one cop says as the ambulance drives away with what I assume is Daniel's body. "Heart ripped out? Who has the strength to do that?"

"I don't know," another states. "I hope this town doesn't have a serial killer on its hands. We aren't prepared for something like that."

Demi's voice from inside the restaurant cuts through the chaos and the sound of her has me sinking into the side of the tree, suddenly sleepy.

"I'm fine, Caden. Daniel was a childhood friend, but he was an ass. I won't miss him."

Then, I did the right thing.

"If we find the guy who did this, we don't ask questions, we shoot. My son is dead. I want the person held accountable."

"Yes, Mayor. We'll keep you updated as the investigation progresses."

I tilt my chin down, thunder vibrating my chest.

I'll kill the mayor too if they try to sweep this under the rug. Daniel deserved to die the way he did.

Anyone who gets in my way. Anyone who threatens Demi. Anyone who dares to challenge me.

I'll rip their hearts out too.

Slinking into the forest to head to the cabin, I take one last look at Demi's Diner.

When the night finally swallows the sun and the moon takes its place, I'll be back.

Maybe with the cover of the shadows and corners, I can somehow have Demi want me.

Love can't happen in the daylight because once she sees all of me, she'll understand why light can never shine on me.

CHAPTER SIX

DEMI

It's been a long day. My feet hurt. My head hurts. My back aches. I'm ready to go home but there's still two hours before the diner is due to close. I think everyone thought today would be the day to come get their free coffee to get an up close and personal look at the dead body.

Not thinking that they wouldn't actually be able to see the body.

"Have a good night," I wave to the last customer, plac-ing my hand on my lower back, groaning when it pops. "That's the stuff," I sigh.

"If you want to go, I can handle the rest of the evening." "No, Caden. I appreciate the offer, but really, I'm fine." "Your friend died. I doubt you're fine."

I snort in disbelief while scrubbing a table with a clean rag. "He wasn't my friend, Caden. For the hundredth time. He was... someone I knew. Nothing more. I'm fine. I promise."

"Still. Today was insane, right? I mean, you saw his body, Demi. That can't sit well. If you need to talk about it—"

I stop scrubbing the table when the image of Daniel's lifeless face flashes in my mind. The hole in his chest was unlike anything I've ever seen. I could see right through it to the bottom of the trunk he was stuffed in. His heart lying next to him, useless.

And the only thing I can think is, what a waste of a perfectly good organ. It's terrible to think that. A man lost his life. A man I've known since I was a little girl. But Daniel didn't deserve kindness after all the disrespect he liked to spew.

Hate breeds hate and he died by the hands of it. I'm not surprised and honestly, I'm relieved I never have to deal with his wandering hands again.

"I don't need to talk about it. I appreciate what you're doing, Caden, but if you were assaulted every day by that man by having some part of your body squeezed, the last thing you'd feel is remorse. It's harsh, but it's true."

He picks up the tub of dirty dishes to take them to the kitchen. "I can't say you're wrong there. Just know I'm here for you, okay?"

I smile at my friend. "I know."

The doorbell jingles, signaling someone coming into the diner. I lift my head to greet them when I notice a man standing in the entryway, blocking the door from shutting. Rain pours behind him, the static of it whispering its way into the dining room. His clothes are soaked, water dripping off him in rivulets to create a small puddle on the tile floor.

His clothes stick to his massive frame, revealing how wide his chest is. The definition of his muscles peek through the fabric, leaving nothing to the imagination. The hood is up and water drips down from the edge of it, his face safely hidden in the shadows the hoodie and nighttime create.

The man's eyes lift, and the glowing ambers steal my breath. His attention is only on me.

Eyes like that only exist in one man that I've met.

"Creed," his name falls from my lips in breathless relief. I don't understand why, but him being here makes me feel protected; like I have nothing to worry about.

I'm safe.

"I'm glad to see you again. I thought you were only a passerby. Take a seat. I'll get you some coffee."

"Demi." Lightning strikes right behind him outside, the loud crack causing me to jump.

My name is seductive drum rumbling his throat causing my pulse to race.

"You're soaked. I don't have any dry clothes."

"It's okay. I don't mind being wet." His attentive gaze doesn't move away from me as he keeps to the side of the room, hiding himself in the shadows.

His boots squeak on the floor from being drowned, leaving a trail of water in his wake until he's at the same booth he sat in yesterday.

Tucked away in the darkest corner, trying to hide in plain sight, but a man like him could never hide.

He's... different.

I don't understand why or how, but being near him is all I want right now.

If he is a storm, I want to be caught in the middle of it and risk destruction.

"I'll be right out with a fresh pot of coffee for you, Creed."

"I'll be looking forward to your presence, Demi."

Such an odd thing to say, but regardless, I blush, watching as his eyes close as he inhales. When he opens those smoldering amber gems, they are burning brighter than I've ever seen and smoke drifts into the air again.

But he isn't smoking.

I dip into the kitchen and lean against the wall, my heart hammering in my chest from the unexpected connection. I close my eyes and my hand presses into the middle of my chest, feeling the strong slam against my breastbone. I couldn't have seen what I thought I did.

Smoke coming from his nostrils? Without a cigarette? Impossible.

A grunt has me opening my eyes and Holt is standing there with his huge arms crossed, staring at me. He points at me then gives me a thumbs up, asking silently like he always does if I'm okay.

"I'm fine. There's just... there's someone here who just makes me flustered. In a good way," I add on quickly, so he isn't worried.

Holt is the type to show how he feels with every action since he's mute. He'd beat someone to death with a ladle for me if he had to.

He grins, shooing me to go back out there.

"I'm not ready. I need the coffee pot. I'm not—" I yelp when he thrusts the coffee pot in my hand and shoves me out of the kitchen.

I'm left standing outside the swaying doors all by myself. Embarrassed about being kicked out of my own kitchen, I turn toward Creed, smiling when I see his mysterious figure sitting in the booth like a statue.

I pour him a cup of coffee and he immediately wraps his giant hands around the mug, bringing it to his lips.

I wish I knew what was so different about him. His hands are larger than normal and gray with dark veins along the top. I'm not able to see the rest of his arms since they are covered by the jacket, but I am curious.

A voice in the back of my head is whispering that his black nails aren't fake, his skin isn't tattooed, and the color of his eyes isn't due to contact lenses.

"Sit with me," he states, hiding his face with the mug as he sips.

I figure if he wants me to see him, he'll show me. I won't pressure him about it.

Scanning the room, I'm pleased to see we are the only ones in it. I think the rush of the day is over and everyone finally got bored of all the commotion about a dead body.

"Don't mind if I do." I slide across the cushion until I'm directly across from him.

Nothing is said for a minute. It isn't awkward. I'm trying to hide my smile and this emotion of excitement building inside me that I get to see him again.

"I heard about the body found in your parking lot," he says at last, setting the cup down. He tilts his chin, hiding from me again. "Did it bother you?"

"Did it bother me?" I echo his question, thinking about how odd he sounds asking that.

"Does it bother you that man died after what he did to you?"

I lean forward, my fingers sliding across the slick red and silver tabletop of the booth to get as close to him as possible. "And what did he do to me, Creed?"

He growls and his fingers flex, the long nails digging into the table. "He... touched you," he snarls, sounding more animal than human.

"Does that bother you?"

"Yes," he bites out and I swear, I see a flash of fangs.

That can't be right.

"Why? We don't know each other. You shouldn't care what happens to me."

A crack of lightning sounds again, followed by the harsh rhythm of rain beating on the roof.

"I care," he grinds out, drifting his nails down my forearm. "Only I can happen to you." He applies more pressure to my skin, and I wince in pain when he breaks skin.

Lightning flashes once more and the electricity goes out, leaving me submerged in darkness.

Something wet, rough, and long rubs up my forearms.

Instead of being afraid like I should be, lust pools in my belly, and warmth spreads between my legs.

The array of emotions I feel when Creed is near, vanishes. The lights come back on, and I find I'm alone, wondering if I imagined him.

His mug is there, steam still drifting from the fresh coffee, but that isn't the only thing he left.

Written in blood, it says.

"Only I can happen to you."

A sliver of fear runs down my spine and a quick terror-filled fever heats my body. Sweat builds on the back of my neck while I stare at the threat. Yet, I find myself loving how it makes me feel.

Taking out my phone, I snap a picture, wanting it so I can look at his words whenever I want.

I must be fucked in the head if I like this.

"What in the world?" I check my arms when I notice no cuts, only smears of blood, and that's when I remember something wet gliding along my skin.

He licked me.

He tasted my blood.

And somehow, I have no evidence I was scratched at all.

Hearing a noise coming from the kitchen, I panic. Caden can't see this. He will become overly protective and hunt down Creed. Rushing to the register, I snag the cleaning spray and a rag.

"Fuck," I curse when I remember all my rags are white. I won't be able to hide the evidence.

I almost trip over my own two feet running back to the table. There's a part of me that feels guilty as I wipe away Creed's declaration.

That's what it has to be, right? Or maybe I'm delusional and he means only he can harm me.

"Hey, Demi?"

When I hear Caden's voice I tuck the rag in my apron and act as though I'm cleaning the table Creed just left.

"What's up?" My voice cracks a little.

I was never a good liar, but Caden doesn't catch on.

"Let's close early. This storm is bad and before it gets worse, we should try to get home."

I nod in agreement. "That's fine. Go ahead. I'll wrap up here."

"I'm not leaving you alone."

"Caden, I'll be fine just like I am every other time you worry. I promise. Go. I want to do a few things around here anyway."

"Okay," he says reluctantly. He sniffs the air, turns his head, and surveys the room as if he is looking for something.

"What is it?"

"Nothing. I just thought I smelled— you know what? It doesn't matter." He gives me a kiss on the cheek. "You really need a new perfume. Yours reeks, Demi."

"It's the same one I always wear," I argue, plucking my shirt to bring it to my nose. "It smells the same to me."

"Maybe it's a bad batch? Or maybe it's just me."

"Maybe. We have had a busy day."

"Tell me when you're home," he shouts as he opens the front door causing that bell to jingle.

"I always do!" I sing song.

"I just saw Holt leave out the back, so please, be careful. Maybe I should stay. I can wait." He tries to come back into the diner and I bodycheck him, slamming my hip into him.

We slip on the wet floor, then wrap our arms around one another to stop us from falling, but it's useless. We hit the ground on our sides, knocking the breath out of our lungs, then laugh until we can't breathe.

"Look what you did," I tease, wincing when I roll to my back.

"Me? You are the one who went crazed wrestler on me." He stands, groaning as he stretches his neck. Caden lends out his hand and helps me up.

"Sorry." I rub my hands down my apron. "But I promise, I'll be fine. Go home, okay? I'll see you tomorrow."

He tightens his jaw, and his eyes trail the dining room, checking for any inconsistencies. "Fine, but you'll text me."

I groan as I shove him in the chest and out the door. "Yes, for the love of all that's savory. Go!" I push him into the rain and immediately he's soaked.

I lock the door and wave at him, a smirk gracing my lips.

With a roll of his eyes, he takes his time getting to his car, tilting his head back to enjoy the rain. He'd stand out in a storm all day and night if he didn't have responsibilities.

The electricity goes out again and another crack of lightning strikes, giving a flash of light. In the distance, there's a figure, and I squint my eyes to try and get a clearer vision. Another bolt crashes down, so loud the diner shakes, but the person is gone. Then the lights flicker on again.

"I'm losing my mind. You're crazy. That's what this is," I tell myself.

I quickly mop up the water trail from Creed, close out the register, and tuck the bloody towel into my purse, before taking one last look around and shutting off the lights.

Locking up, I stand outside to watch the rain crash against the wall angrily. Lightning flashes. Thunder rolls, vibrating the ground. The wind howls like a wolf calling for its pack. My shoes are wet the moment I step into the parking lot, the water infiltrating my socks.

Ugh, I hate wet socks.

Right when I get to my car door, soft whispering words filter through the rush of rain.

"Only I can happen to you."

I spin around, the ends of my wet pink hair slapping my chin from the force. "Hello? Who's there?" I turn around again, wanting to see in every direction so I don't miss anything. "This isn't funny. Creed? Is it you?" I search for him through the weather, the rain making it impossible to see further than a few inches.

The feeling of someone watching me is there again, slithering over my skin. Swallowing, I fiddle with my keys, my hands shaking from the unknown entity surrounding me. The keys drop to the ground, and I bend down to search for them when my foot hits them, causing them to slide under the car.

"Come on," I half cry, hating to be in the dark all alone.

Any person is afraid of the dark after a certain amount of time being submerged in it. I don't care what anyone says.

The grinding of metal against concrete has me looking down and my keys slide from under the car, stopping right at my feet.

My breathing comes out in harsh pants as I stay still. My eyes dart back and forth to see if anyone is there. My body trembles from the cold and my teeth begin to chatter.

Not wanting to waste any more time, I bend down and snatch the keys as fast as I can, open the door, and slide inside. My fingers find the lock button, breathing a sigh of relief when I'm safely in the car.

"I'm losing my mind," I whisper, knowing I've lost my sanity. There's no other way to explain it.

I wipe my face with my hand, my cheeks burning from the harsh sting of the cold rain, and start on the journey home, wanting nothing more than to change into dry clothes and have a hot cup of tea like I usually do before bed.

The night is almost over, but for some reason, I have a feeling these hauntings have just begun.

Going home takes longer than usual. The windshield wipers can't swipe fast enough with how hard the rain is falling. I can't see anything. I lean forward, gripping the steering wheel tight, I squint my eyes hoping that will help me see.

"I hate driving in the rain," I whine into the empty car. I get so much anxiety and go way below the speed limit which only infuriates other drivers. I don't know how they zip right by me as if it's a clear sunny day.

If I went that fast while it was pouring, I'd lose control of the car and wreck. I should have stayed at the diner. Sometimes, I do that when the weather is too bad or if I'm too tired, but with Daniel's body being found in the parking lot, I didn't want to be at the diner alone all night.

Bright lights shine in my rearview mirror. I flinch from how blinding they are and the car behind me honks their horn, swerving to the left so they don't hit me.

As they pass, I don't bother looking at them because I won't be made to feel bad about being afraid to drive in this treacherous storm.

Finally, I take a right into my subdivision and press a button so I can pull the car into the garage. When I'm safe and dry, I put the car in park, and lean back in my seat to take a breath. My heart slows hearing the rain pummel the house around me.

I hurry inside, shutting the garage door, and the first thing I do, like I do every night, is heat the kettle for my tea. While the water is warming, I change into the huge, oversized shirt that falls to my knees that I sleep in.

Next, I brush, and towel dry my hair, noticing it's almost time for me to touch up the bright pink color. My bed catches my eye in the mirror, and I turn, leaning against my dresser as I try to figure out what's different.

"Nothing has moved, Demi. You're paranoid," I try to make myself feel better, knowing nothing is out of place in my room. I think the sheets look different, but what do I know? I've had a long day.

Yawning, my feet patter across the floor as I walk to the kitchen when the kettle whistles.

Stuffing the tea infuser with my new favorite white tea, I drop it in the mug along with some honey, then douse it in hot water. The smell hits my nose, and my entire body stops tensing, the familiar routine settling my anxiety from driving in the storm.

Exhaustion hits me hard, so while sipping on my tea, I head to my room, straighten the covers, and climb into bed.

I sniff, smelling something new. At least, I think I do.

"What the hell is that?" I grab my pillow and blanket, smelling something faint that I can't put my finger on.

It smells... really good. I've never smelt it before. I don't recognize it.

I bury my face in the pillow and inhale, a picture of Creed entering my mind. I bet this is what he would smell like.

"You have lost it," I grumble, tossing the pillow back on the bed. I don't even know the man, but he is intense, slightly terrifying with his looks, and the way he licked my arm and grumbled those six words still sends shivers down my spine.

"*Only I can happen to you.*"

I swear that's what I heard, but I have to be wrong. It has to be the exhaustion. None of that could have happened today.

Not him licking me.

Not him smearing my blood on the table.

Not him whispering those words.

That's insane. I should be afraid.

So why aren't I? Why do I want to see him again?

Knowing I won't have answers tonight, I type out a text to Caden.

Me: "*I'm home safe. I'm going to bed. Love you. See you tomorrow.*"

Him: "*Perfect. Love you too. Also, found more people to hire. No, you won't interview them. They are hired. We need help. End of story. Goodnight.*"

Me: "*So bossy.*"

Him: "*Someone needs to be ;)*"

I should have hired people ages ago, but I'm so picky with whom I trust at the diner, but now we are drowning, and it isn't fair to Caden or Holt. Poor Holt. He kills himself in that kitchen. He needs extra hands too.

Finishing off my tea, I turn off my light, and roll to my side, listening to the banshee of a storm. My eyes begin to hood, sleep finally calling to me.

A scream of lightning cracks, shaking the entire house and illuminating my room.

Someone is standing in the doorway.

Panicked, I hold my breath and sit up, flipping on my lamp.

But no one is there.

I rub my eyes and look at the doorway again. It's empty. My mind is playing tricks on me.

Flopping onto my bed, I decide to keep the light on. The fear of the dark creeps in just like it did when I was a little girl. I know the same thing happens in the light as it does in the dark, but I hate how evil things can hide by taking advantage of what we can't see.

Darkness is a nightmare within itself, holding all the horrors we never want to see.

Hugging the other pillow close, I bury my face in it and inhale, wishing Creed were here.

I bet he'd protect me from the dark.

CHAPTER SEVEN

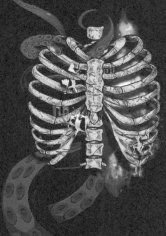

CREED

When she finally falls asleep, I step into her room and watch her. She's so fucking beautiful. I love her pink hair, how unique it is compared to other women. Demi hugs the pillow I buried my face in earlier and she's cradling it to her chest, her nose pressed against the section I bit and sucked.

She senses me too.

"I wish I knew what this all meant," I whisper, sitting on the edge of her bed. "I know I can't stay away from you." I lie down next to her, careful not to disturb her so she doesn't wake up.

It's imparative she never wakes up when I'm with her. Leaning forward, I smell her hair, my cock hardening as the familiar scent of home has me scooting just a little closer.

"You remind me of the only memory I can remember," I whisper into her ear, slightly dragging my nails down her arm.

"Mmm," she mumbles in her sleep, rolling away from me until she's lying on her stomach.

I wait a moment, so she remains asleep. "The only good I'll ever feel," I admit to a quiet room. "You deserve more than me, but I refuse to let you have it." Moving closer, I drag my finger down her arm, needing to know what her skin feels like again. "Just as soft as it was earlier." When I licked and tasted her forearm, I shot a stream of come in my jeans. My orgasm was too intense to deny the moment her blood burst across my tongue.

"I wanted death for so long. Nightmares are the only thing that live in my mind— at least they were. Every time I see you, those nightmares ease. I can't be without you. No matter how close you are, no matter what you give me, I know it will never be enough. I will never be sated of you. I will always want more." My voice remains a whisper and she continues to lie still.

My deep sleeper.

That will come in handy for everything I have planned for us. Grabbing the blanket, I ease it down, wanting to see more of her wearing nothing but that shirt. As I peel it back, her long, silky legs become exposed. Saliva pools in my mouth, my fangs lengthening to sink into her thigh and feed.

Her shirt is bunched around her waist, and she isn't wearing any underwear. Smoke leaves my nostrils when I see the perfect curve of her ass. I want to touch. I want to slip my finger inside her pretty cunt to see how wet she'll get for me. I scoot down, closing my eyes as I inhale, scenting her pussy.

"I bet you're so sweet." I gently kiss her right ass cheek, my breath shaking as it leaves my lungs as I fight every instinct all my beasts have.

She shivers, reaching for the blanket again. Wishing I was the one to keep her warm, I growl, sparks of discontent flying out of my mouth as I cover her body that I can't wait to defile.

Standing, I take one last glance of my mate, my beloved, my everything, and do the hardest thing I've ever had to do besides survive the experiments forced upon me.

I walk away.

My dragon has different ideas. I've done research on all the beasts that consume me and it seems my dragon loves gold. He wants to hoard. He wants to make Demi's house his den. I snag something small and irrelevant from her dresser, a bobby-pin, and replace it with a gold ring with an emerald stone in the middle I hope she likes.

Ever so slowly, I'll be making this place my home.

Until then, she'll be questioning everything, and I'll be answering nothing.

I sniff, turning my chin to my shoulder when a whiff of her tea ignites an idea. Following the source to the kitchen, the scent becomes stronger as I get closer to the container.

Opening the lid, I notice loose-leaf tea and grin.

I officially have a way to be with her at night. Now, I just need to find a pharmacy to give me the medication.

"Creed," I hear my name whispered and I freeze.

She can't know I'm here. It's impossible. I don't move. I don't breathe. I listen to her closely, paying attention to the rhythm of her heartbeat. It's calm and steady.

She's still asleep.

"Creed," my name falls from her lips again, the cloak of sleep suppressing my name as she calls for me.

I call upon my vampire, quickly blurring into her room until I'm by her side. I kneel by her bed, one arm caging her head in where it lies on the pillow while I tilt my chin to look at her face.

Her beauty is life-altering. The kind that fills a room with light when she walks into it, the kind that has you wondering why a woman like her would ever fall to such a low level to be with a monster like me.

"Creed."

Only this time my name is a moan.

I watch her intently. Her face pinches and her brows furrow together. Her plump pink lips part.

"I'm here," I growl, petting her head to push her hair back. "I'm here, my mate." With every word I speak, my dragon's smoke leaves my mouth and the threat of fire builds in my chest.

I want to set her on fire after I mark her, searing my claim into her skin, her soul, her body, and claiming it as mine.

Her arm begins to move under the blanket, her breaths come out in harsh pants, and my tentacles unravel around my cock when I realize what's she doing.

My sweet mate is having a dirty dream.

And she's dreaming of me.

I can't take her yet. Not with her knowing. She'll run away screaming. If she's touching herself to the thought of me, what does she think I look like? Am I everything she's ever wanted or am I what she's damned herself with?

Tugging the covers to her knees, I watch as she finger fucks herself lazily while she sleeps. She's deep into her dream. I can't help myself, I switch positions, crouching at the bottom of the bed. I'm perched like my dragon would be on a cliff. On their own, my wings open and spread out. The scales across my arms shimmer and the hair from my werewolf grows over my body as lust courses through me.

A constant thunder shakes the room, but it isn't from the storm outside. It's from me.

"Creed. Yes," she says so sleepily, mumbling the words, but I know in her dream, she's probably screaming my name.

I blow out a stream of fire, then suck it back in. It doesn't give me the relief I need. My fangs grow until they surpass my lip, my vampire dying of thirst, dying to bond. I can't drink anyone's blood. It has to be hers.

Just a drop.

Just a little.

I tear the zipper of my jeans with my claw, freeing my cock. The suckers move fervently, the tentacles reaching for her wanting nothing more than to fulfill their purpose.

Pleasure.

That's all they are for, and they are made for Demi.

I wrap my hand around my cock, watching as her hand moves quicker. The entire room smells of smoke and sex. Leaning forward, I drop a hand between her legs, pressing my palm against the mattress, my gaze locked onto her bare cunt. Her fingers shine from her slick and it takes all I have not to hold her down, force my cock into her, and take what's rightfully mine.

"Creed," she calls for me again.

I grunt as I stroke myself faster. "I'm here, Demi." Flames lick from between my teeth. "Fuck," I curse in a hushed tone, tossing my head back as I tighten my fist.

Her scent becomes sweeter as it thickens the air. My tongue flicks out and I groan when the flavor hits my taste buds.

"You're mine, Demi. You just wait. Soon, you won't have to dream of me. I'll give you everything you want."

Her mouth parts as her back arches. Her hand works quickly, rubbing her clit in fast circles as she comes. I aim my cock between her legs as my own orgasm rushes through me. Come leaks from my suckers, soaking my palm, and ropes of my seed hit her pussy while she still fingers herself. Unknowingly shoving my seed into her body.

A primal growl escapes me knowing I'm a part of her now. Unable to think straight, I lunge forward, sinking my fangs into her thigh and pull in a deep, long draft of her blood.

She cries out again, her hand still moving while another orgasm crashes over her.

"Creed," she moans, her hand finally slowing.

I ease my fangs free, licking the pinpricks so she heals. Her blood strengthens me. My mind clears. Exhaustion flees as energy takes its place.

I stare down at her, eyes slowly opening. Demi struggles to wake up, the grip of sleep still holding tight.

Tired slits land on me, a drunken smirk tilting her lips. "Creed?"

She's still caught on the edge of fantasy and reality. Not wanting to scare her when she realizes she isn't alone, I blur out of the room, out of the house, and soar into the air.

As I zip through the star-filled night, the blues and blacks painted in the sky form around me. I smile, thinking about what I just shared with Demi. I spin, twirl, and flip, having fun for the first time since becoming... this.

Maybe there is hope for us.

I nosedive, pinning my wings back. The air is colder from this height and right as I begin to feel the crispness of it, heat melts it away, my dragon keeping me warm.

When I land, I'm across the street from a pharmacy. The roads are empty downtown, and the quaint shops are dark. The only lights are the ones from the streetlamps.

This is where I belong, in pitch black, becoming a myth, the boogeyman, the ones people tell others about when they are around a campfire.

Walking across the street, my boots pound against the pavement.

A memory of something I read from a medical book in the cabin tickles my mind. The man I killed was a doctor, so inside his cabin were shelves of medical books. I read all of them thinking there was something in there that could fix me.

But there's no cure, I've concluded.

This is who I am now.

That fact becomes easier to accept with every day that passes.

As I stand outside the doors of the neighborhood pharmacy, a cute red-brick family-owned business, I remember reading about a drug that induces deep sleep. It's more like a sedative.

And I plan to put that in Demi's tea.

Clutching the door handle and using my supernatural strength, I yank it down, and the metal crumbles in my palm. I wipe my hands and open the door, the alarm blaring to signal the police.

I grumble when I think about the cop who was too friendly with Demi. She seems to like him, so I won't kill him, but it doesn't mean I won't imagine it.

Blurring across the pharmacy, I jump behind the counter and break the metal doors blocking the medications. While I move fast, I can still read every medication they have.

I need the aisle starting with A.

Finding it, I grab all the Ambien they have, then flee. My shoulder smacks one of the shelves and it falls, causing a domino effect.

Thump. Thump. Thump.

The shelves hit one another causing medications to flood the floor. Pills clink and clank in bottles, and spill across the carpet as the lids are knocked loose.

My shoulder slams against the back door, leaving a massive dent behind as it swings open. Wings spread, I jump into the air, flying away from the sirens getting closer.

My heart thumps with nerves and excitement.

Instead of going home like I should, I make a quick turn to go back to Demi's house. She should still be asleep. It's only around two in the morning. I just can't wait another day. The sooner I get these pills in her tea, the more I can advance our relationship.

It doesn't take me long. I land in the backyard and open her sliding glass door within ten minutes. Her house is quiet, and I listen to her heartbeat. I know the rate of it when she's asleep.

Ba-dum. Ba-dum. Ba-dum.

I'm in the clear.

My cock hardens again when I smell the combinations of our come still. This house reeks of me and what's mine. No other creature would dare to get near her.

My wing hits a jar on the counter, flinging it to the floor, and I use my vampiric speed to catch it just in time before it shatters on the ground.

Sliding it back on the counter, I empty all of my pockets, depositing pockets full of Ambien. Opening her tea leaf jar, I smash the pills with my palm until they are nothing but dust.

The fleck of humanity inside me urges me not to do this, but as quick as the guilt comes, it's gone, eaten within my beasts.

I tuck the jar between me and the counter, sweeping the drug into the container. The tea is coated in white and then I wonder if I crushed too many pills or if there wasn't enough.

Twisting the lid on, I shake it up, wanting every leaf coated in the only way I know she'll have me.

I'll finally get to experience her.

Having her while she's unconscious is better than not having her at all.

CHAPTER
EIGHT

DEMI

"You sure were loud last night. Don't you know people are trying to sleep?" My neighbor gripes.

My cheeks heat when I open the driver's side door. "Sorry, Mr. Pete. Won't happen again." God, I hope he isn't referring to what I think he is.

I had the hottest, most realistic dream. Creed was fucking me in every way possible and I orgasmed twice. I woke up sticky between my legs and had to really scrub to get the come off. It's unlike me to make such a mess, but that dream was almost real.

In the hot fantasy, Creed came too. He wanted to stuff me with his seed, going on and on about how he wanted to breed me.

Never in my entire life would I think that would be what I wanted, but it's all I can think about with him.

Not that it's even possible since I'm on birth control and don't plan to be off it for a while. Even though I'm a virgin and don't plan on having sex, there's nothing wrong with being safe. Maybe I'll meet a man tonight who will sweep me off my feet and I'll fall into bed with him.

Somehow, even the thought of another man besides Creed makes me feel guilty as if I cheated on him.

When I get in the car, something in the passenger seat captures my attention.

A flower sits on the cushion. One I haven't seen since I was a child.

A honeysuckle.

Creed's dark, rumbling voice echoes in the back of my mind. In my dream, I think he called me Honeysuckles. That wouldn't make sense.

I bring the flower to my nose, closing my eyes to inhale. It smells sweet and citrusy. Tugging the stem at the base, a bead of nectar begins to form, and I suck it into my mouth.

Delicious.

It's the folded-up piece of white paper that has me nervous because I know I didn't put it there. Tucking the flower behind my ear, I pinch the paper together between my fingers, debating if I want to open it.

"Just do it, Demi." I open it fast as if the message won't be there if I don't. I glance down, that well-known fear I've been experiencing slithers down my spine.

There's nothing out of the ordinary. Mr. Pete is watering his plants as always. The neighbor across the street is washing his car. The kids a few doors down are playing in the sprinkler.

But that sense of someone watching me gets stronger.

I read the note again, my throat suddenly dry, when I start to wonder if I have a stalker.

"*You are mine, Demi. You are beautiful. I can't wait to experience you falling apart.*"

What does that mean?

I flip the paper over but there's no signature. I have no idea who could have left this. Crumbling the paper in my fist, I toss it on the floor and put the car in reverse. The tires skid on the pavement, the smell of burnt rubber drifting through the vents.

I crinkle my nose, my eyes falling to the floorboard to stare at the note as if it's going to bite me.

"Oh God!" I swipe the flower from my ear in chaos like it's a bee buzzing around my head.

I'm not paying attention as I reverse, too busy swiping at my head and freaking out in general when I hit something. The car jerks and my head smacks the seat.

"Ow." I rub the side of my head.

"What the fuck, Demi!" Keith shouts from outside of my window, holding a soaking-wet sponge in his hand.

"Oh, no, no." I hide my face in my hands, tears burning my eyes when I think about the coming confrontation.

I hate confrontation.

Keith isn't the nicest guy. Out of all the cars I had to hit, why did I have to hit his?

The universe hates me today. Between the note, the flower, the dream, and now this.

I open the door to the teal 1957 Chevy Bel-Air that belonged to my grandmother, dreading to see the damage. This car was in pristine condition. The paint was redone, and the interior had just been reupholstered to a beautiful cream with teal stitching. Everything about this car is practically new. I drained my savings into it.

"Keith, I'm so sorry. I... there was a bee in my car. I freaked out and I wasn't paying attention to what I was doing." I swallow my fear and brace for the horrible damage.

The side of his truck is dented. The driver's side door will need to be replaced. My car on the other hand only has a broken taillight. Not even a scratch on the new paint.

"Oh, thank God," I say out loud.

"What the fuck do you mean, thank God?" He points to his truck. "Look at my truck. I just got it waxed. You've ruined it. Are you fucking stupid, Demi? I always believed a woman shouldn't be allowed behind the wheel. All of you can't pay attention to shit."

I cross my arms, the conflict is making me very uncomfortable. The feeling of being watched returns and I don't bother to search for who it is because I feel relieved to know someone is witnessing Keith's behavior.

"Keith, I'll pay for the damage done to your truck. I'll give you my insurance. Take pictures. There's no reason to be so upset about this."

He shoves me against the car, the sponge in his hand squeezes above my head, and filthy water drips down my face.

"I'm pissed, Demi. How about you go inside, bend over, and I'll think about forgiving you."

"Fuck off, Keith. You're an asshole. I'd never do such a thing." I shove him away and he grabs me by my arm, only to be interrupted by police sirens.

"I guess today is your lucky day, Demi," he whispers so no one can hear.

Officer Jake Holland steps out of his vehicle, fingers hooking into his belt. "Everything alright here, Demi?" Jake narrows his eyes at Keith. "Take your hand off her." Jake grips his gun, readying himself to remove it from his holster.

Keith does as he is told and raises his hands in the air. "Everything is fine. She was just getting her insurance card. Isn't that right, Demi?"

"Officer Holland," I remember to use his title since we are in front of someone he doesn't know. "It was my fault. There was a bee in my car, and I freaked out. I batted my hands at my head. I wasn't paying attention. He's right. It is my fault." I hate to lie to my friend since there wasn't a bee, but I'm not sure if I should tell him. What can he do? There's no proof. No harm has been done. The only thing this stalker has successfully done is rattle me a bit.

"A bee? Are you okay? Did it sting you?"

"Do you hear yourself, Officer? Look at my truck." Keith points to the massive dent in his driver's side door. "Who gives a damn about a bee. File a report."

Jake pushes me behind him, protecting me, and I glance over his shoulder to watch the scene unfold.

"I know it might be hard for your inferior brain to compute, but she could be allergic to bees. I might have to call an ambulance. There are other things in this world bigger than you. Your truck can be fixed. And if you keep on, I'll write up this report in a way that makes it your fault. So keep your damn mouth shut or I'll arrest you for assaulting a woman. I saw you put your hands on her."

If it were possible, smoke would be coming out of Keith's ears. His face is red, his jaw is tight, and a muscle flexes in his cheek.

"Good choice," Jake tells him with a shake of his head before pinning me with his authoritative gaze. "You okay? Hey, why are you wet?" He spins to Keith. "What the fuck did you do?"

"It's fine, I promise," I tell him. "I have a busted taillight. Think I can drive it without one of your men giving me a ticket?"

"I'll follow you to work and fix it myself, okay? Let's write this report up and get on with our day so this asshole can go back to thinking he is God's gift to the world." Jake writes the report and takes our information. "You sure he didn't do anything else to you? You can tell me. I'll believe you."

"You're sweet, Jake. I'm fine. I promise."

"I look at you like my little sister. I can't have anything happen to you. You're family to me."

"That means a lot," I whisper, not realizing how much I've missed my mom as she travels the world. I'm an only child. I don't have anyone. I have Caden, but I don't have any other friends. Not really. I'm always working. I don't have time for anything else. "Thank you, Jake."

"No problem. Come on. Let's get you to work." He opens my car door for me. "And I'll be keeping an eye on you, Keith," he shouts from the bottom of the driveway to my rude neighbor.

Jake flips on his sirens and that cuts the time it takes to get to the diner in half. When we pull into the lot, it's packed, and guilt swarms in my belly just like that fake bee did around my head.

Dark gray clouds roll in and when I step out of the car, the temperature has dropped. The wind is cooler with the promise of rain.

"What is going on with this weather? It's crazy lately. It's rained every day."

"Just that time of year, I suppose." Jake's window is rolled down, his arm perched on the edge, and his aviators are on. He fits the cop persona perfectly. "If you need anything, call me. I'm going to go get the part for your car."

"You don't need to do that. I can do it later and order it online." Jake's dad is the only one within a five-hundred-mile radius who will have the part for my car, and they do not get along.

In fact, they hate one another.

"I don't want you to go through that. I know how he makes you feel." I tie the apron around my waist.

"I'll live." He smiles, tapping the side of his car. "I'll catch you later, Demi."

I sigh, shaking my head. "Bye, Jake. Catch you later. Oh, Jake!"

The breaks squeak when he stops and turns his head out the window.

"I am allergic to bees."

"Good to know!" he shouts, waving his hand out the window as he leaves again.

Opening the door to the diner, a brisk draft of air conditioning rushes over me and a cold chill drifts down my back.

"Demi! Hey." Caden waves at me from the register. "Are you okay?"

"I'm fine. A little fender bender." I step closer and I swear, Caden's eyes take on an odd hue. "Are you okay?"

He inhales, then coughs. "I'm fine. Your perfume is getting to me for some reason."

"That's so odd. I'm so sorry, Caden. I'll try not to wear it to work anymore."

"It just smells like..." he shakes his head, clearing his throat. "Doesn't matter."

I lift my arms to double-check I put on deodorant. I did. I'm in the clear. "If you're sure. I mean, you'd tell me if I…" I lean in to whisper "If I smell, right? I showered and everything this morning."

"Of course, I'd tell you. I think it's just me because there's just… I know you… so there's just no way."

"No way, what? You're confusing me, Caden."

"Sorry. It's been a busy morning. Ignore me." He points to a few extra people wearing the diner uniforms. "That's Mickey, the one with the black hair. She's a new waitress. That's Minnie. Her sister. They arrived in town yesterday and I met them at the Upsie-Daisy, you know the bar downtown," Caden goes on to explain. "They were look-ing for work, but he wasn't hiring so I jumped in and said they could start immediately. They have experience too."

"Mickey and Minnie?" I know he can hear the curiosity in my question.

"Their parents must have really loved Disney. I don't know. We have Milo… their brother," he mumbles when I roll my lips together to hide a smile. "Anyway, he is the one cleaning the tables. Holt has two new chefs to help him, so food will be coming out faster. Their names are August and Jude."

"How did you meet them?"

"They were outside the diner this morning, asking for work. I gave it to them."

"We got very lucky, didn't we?" I say. "I'll meet them later. I can actually get caught up on administrative work. I don't even want to know what it looks like in that room." I wince thinking about it. I can't remember the last time I actually sat in the chair and did payroll.

I pay Holt and Caden under the table. They get cash, but I suppose that's come to an end now with the extra help.

"I need them to bring—"

"—Already done. It's on your desk. It isn't that bad in there. I opened the window to air it out though. It was musty."

"I'm promoting you to manager."

He rolls his eyes. "I've been manager, but I'll be happy with that pay increase."

"You know when you start getting a check, it will be lower because it will actually take taxes out."

"I set aside for those anyway." The doorbell rings, signaling more customers. "Welcome to Demi's Diner. How many today?" Caden responds automatically.

Taking the chance, I slither through the tables to head to the backroom, passing the bar. The red stools are actually full and one of the sisters is behind the counter, taking orders and making milkshakes.

My mom and grandma would be so happy seeing the diner flourish. I kept the classic aesthetic to it. Neon lights on the inside, the red booths, the silver and crimson cushions on the barstools, the uniforms, and even the jukebox in the corner. It only costs a quarter to play a song.

Before I disappear into the office for who knows how long, my eyes dart along the dining room floor, taking it all in. I remember growing up here and watching my mom take orders on her pad, smiling at all of the customers. There would be times when I'd pretend I was helping her. I'd run up to the tables to ask them what they wanted to drink, scribble down what they wanted, and would run to my mom.

Everyone was always kind about letting a little kid pretend she was an adult.

Now here I am, an adult, and not one person warned me how lonely adulthood would be.

With a heavy heart full of nostalgia and longing, I enter my office, shutting out the clinking and clanking of dishes behind me.

I blow out a breath when I see my work environment for the rest of the day. Boxes of old files dated from when my mom still worked here are stacked in the back. She always kept everything for tax purposes, but I think I might find the time to scan it so I can have more room.

Grabbing a rag and cleaner, I dust the desk off, plug in the laptop since I'm sure it's dead, and sit down, noticing something gold and shiny where a picture used to be. At least, I think a picture used to be there. It's been too long since I've stepped foot in the office to know.

"What in the world," I whisper, squinting my eyes as I lean forward.

It's a gold pair of earrings. I know they aren't mine. Maybe they belong to one of the new employees. They are beautiful though, enough for me to wonder if I want to ask them or keep these earrings for myself.

I tuck them in my apron pocket, saving the question for later, and begin catching up on all administrative tasks. I legally hire all the employees, enter their payroll information, catch up on a few invoices I haven't paid from the IRS, and print out new inventory sheets.

My eyes begin to burn, and my neck begins to ache from staring down at the computer screen for too long. I check the time as I rub the back of my neck, kneading the tight muscle. I'm not used to being so stagnant while I work.

My dream from last night creeps into my mind since I'm alone and my eyes shoot to the door to check to see if anyone is standing outside of it. I don't want to get caught.

And as I place my hand on my cheeks, I know Caden would catch on quickly because my skin is warm.

There were so many parts of that dream that felt real. I swear, I could feel him. I could hear him whispering to me.

When he came, the warmth of his orgasm coated me, and when I woke up, he was there at the foot of my bed, but that's impossible. I must have dreamed him into reality— a ghost of him.

I fan myself at the thought.

Even the ghost of him was fucking sexy.

A knock at the door startles me and I lean back in my chair too far, I try to balance myself but it's too late. I fall back, the ceiling is all I can see now as I slam against the floor.

"Demi?" Caden knocks on the door. "Are you okay?" The creak of the door fills the room while my head rings.

I groan deciding to just... lie there for a minute. I lift my hand. "I'm fine," I grumble, crinkling my nose when I notice how dirty the corners of the wall are. "We really need to clean in here."

It's actually kind of nice down here as long as I don't think about how I need to vacuum the floor.

"Where are you?" He peeks his head around the desk, staring down at me before holding out his hand. "What happened?"

"It's been so long since I've sat in a rollie-chair that I forgot how to sit, apparently." I slam my palm in his and with a hard tug, he helps me to my feet.

"You've been in here for hours. The sun is down, but we have a problem."

I pick up the chair, sliding it back in its place under the desk. "What's wrong?"

"Cops are here again."

I tuck a piece of wayward hair behind my ear, shaking my head with a smile. "Oh. No, don't worry about that. Jake said he was going to replace my taillight."

"Is that a euphemism?"

"What?"

"Nothing. Bad joke. Jake and his partner are here, and they aren't here about your taillight."

I rub my hands down my uniform. "I've told them everything about Daniel. I wonder what this is about." I smile at the customers, trying to seem calm so they don't get stressed out.

They are curious, whispering amongst themselves in hushed tones.

"Officers, is there a problem? I really hope you're here for the taillight." I lick my lips, trying to remain hopeful, but when Jake firms his lips into a straight line, the wind is blown from my sails. "Or coffee?"

"Let's step outside, Demi. We have a few questions for you."

I follow them, confused. "If this is about Daniel, I don't know anything. I've told you everything."

"This isn't about Daniel. This is about Keith."

"Jake— I mean, Officer Holland— I told you everything I know." I try to sound as sincere as possible.

A gust of wind blows sending a chill over my arms, the clouds are gray and building into large thunderheads. My instincts tell me to turn around and when I do, nothing is there.

But I feel it again— someone watching me.

"Demi? Is something wrong?"

I give Jake my undivided attention. He glances over my shoulder to see what I'm staring at.

"I'm fine. So, what's this about?"

"Keith Higgins is dead, Demi."

My eyes round in shock. "What? That's... that's impossible, Jake. I saw him earlier. You were there."

"And I know you weren't too happy with him," he implies.

I scoff in shock, taking a step back, appalled at his accusation. "You think I killed him? Jake, I've been here. I've been in my office all damn day catching up on paperwork. Caden can tell you. The computer with timestamps can tell you everything," I spew angrily.

"I'm just doing my job, Demi. I don't think you're a killer, but I think anyone is capable of anything. I had to ask. Do you know anyone that would kill him? Any enemies?"

"I'm sorry. I don't know. I didn't know him well. You're better off talking to his family. If he acted that way with everyone, I'm sure he has plenty of enemies."

"I think it's interesting," Waylon, Jake's partner says after writing something down on his notepad.

"What?"

"There are two dead people and both of them are connected to you, Miss. Demi Hawthorne."

I think about the sensation of being watched over the last few days, wondering if my mysterious person is protecting me somehow. I like how it feels and that frightens me a little.

"Well, that's a coincidence. I had nothing to do with it. Their deaths aren't my fault."

"You know what I think of coincidences?"

"I'm sure you're going to tell me anyway, Waylon." I suck my tongue across my teeth, doing my best to remain calm. The last thing I need is to get arrested for assaulting a cop. I wouldn't hit him, but I'm thinking about stomping on his toes.

Just a quick little slam to his foot.

"If it happens once, fine, twice, it's questionable, three times? It's a pattern and enough for a warrant. If I were you, I wouldn't leave town."

"Jake, you can't be serious. You can't be listening to him! I had nothing to do with their deaths."

"I know, but I'm sorry, Demi. He's right. You can't leave town. You're a suspect."

I throw my hands in the air, pushing between them, needing some air that isn't around those two.

Tucking my hands in my apron, the metal of the earrings hit my fingertips. I pinch them together, rolling the jewelry back and forth, stirring my thoughts.

What if the person watching me is saving me for last?

My phone buzzes, yanking me from my twisted thoughts for a split second.

An unknown number.

I click on the message and as I read, my heart drops to my stomach. Frantically, I spin and turn, searching for any sign that someone is watching me. I know they are. I feel them.

But all I see are the cops. Jake gives me a reassuring wave, then tips his hat to me. My vision blurs with panic. Dizziness grabs hold.

"You're pretty when you look for me."

I hold my hand over my mouth, holding back a scream.

Not wanting to back down, my fingers fly over the screen, tears prickling my eyes.

"Who are you? What do you want?" I reply, bringing my fingers to my mouth. I begin to chew on my nails as I wait for their response, debating if I should go to Jake. I know he'd believe me, but there would be nothing he could do. There's no proof the person stalking me is the person who is killing people.

"*Isn't it obvious, Honeysuckles?*"

A second later, the phone buzzes again.

"I *want you.*"

CHAPTER NINE

CREED

A *few hours earlier*

I land on the roof of the house that belongs to the man who dared touch my mate earlier. Demi had done nothing wrong. She accidentally ran into the man's truck after being so stunned after seeing my note.

She must have been very happy to lose focus.

I'll have to leave more special letters for her to find. More jewelry too. I want her to always feel appreciated.

So when this fucking asshole touched my mate, I knew I had to do something about it. No one touches my mate but me.

Growling as I crawl along his rooftop, my sharp talons scraping the shingles. I leave gouges in my wake, making as much noise as I can to get him to come outside to see what the fuss is about.

He has no idea he is trapped in his own home. I've sliced his tires, cut his brake line, and stabbed the gas tank of his motorcycle sitting next to his dented truck.

One. Little. Breath.

That's all it would take for me to burn this fucking house to the ground.

Lowering myself to the roof, I spread my arms and legs out, nearly slithering around the chimney. I dig my claws into the brick, perching myself up as I hear him open his back door and step outside.

Titling my chin, flames lick the corners of my mouth. I'm desperate to breathe fire, to burn him alive, to hear him scream, to smell his skin shriveling from dehydration.

"What the fuck is going on?" He marches outside, hands on his hips as he tilts his head up to see what is causing all the commotion.

I dip behind the chimney, my tongue flicking out so I can I taste his confusion.

It's delicious.

The door closes again, telling me he has made his way back inside.

But I want to have a little fun.

Dropping to my hands again, I scurry along the roof until I get to the very top edge where it slants down. I rip into the material, straightening my body, and gravity takes hold.

The shingles and wood tear in five long grooves as I slide down. I'm enjoying myself a little too much. I should stop playing with my food even if I can't eat it, but new habits die hard.

When I reach the edge, I stop, prowling to the other side as I wait for him. I crouch, my mouth salivating as I think about ripping his heart out. I'm biting at the bit to feel the insides of his chest.

The sliding of the door sounds and he comes marching out in his khaki shorts and teal polo shirt.

"My roof!" he shouts, the damage impossible to miss. "I'm sick of this day. First my truck, then my roof. Stupid fucking neighbor. I bet she's behind this. That bitch," he seethes, kicking one of the chairs tucked under his patio table.

He spins around, hands on his hips again, and looks back and forth across his property to see if the person responsible is still here.

Using my new enhanced abilities, I blur until I'm behind him. I tower over this pathetic excuse of a man. I look down on him, smoke clouding the space in front of me.

"What is that smell?" He sniffs the air, turning around, and his eyes widen in fear when he sees me.

He only reaches the middle of my chest.

Trepidation trembles his body. He tilts his head back, swallowing when he sees the monster standing before him.

He tries to run, sidestepping me, but a sardonic chuckle escapes me at his efforts. My arm shoots out quicker than he can take another step and I wrap my palm around his throat.

I'm so much bigger that my fingertips touch around the back of his neck.

"I'm that smell." I blow a large, hot breath of smoke in his face, sending him into a coughing fit.

With a tight grip around his windpipe, he gasps for air, struggling to take his next weak breath. I drag him inside, closing the door behind me and shutting the blinds so no one can see.

I throw him on the floor and his ribs hit the side of the dining room table on the way down. A crack sounds, tempting me to finish the job off quickly.

Biting the air, I cock my head, watching him squirm.

"Please." He shakes his head. "Please, don't. I don't know what you want, but I can get it for you. I can do anything you want."

Stabbing my claw into his ankle, I tug him under me, placing my other hand on his windpipe so he struggles to breathe. His eyes and cheeks turn a dying shade of red as he gulps and gasps to try to breathe.

Such pathetic and annoying sounds.

He thinks he's so much better than Demi and I was brought here to become this monster to prove to him, or anyone, that they are not.

I lift my top lip, showing the dangerous row of teeth, growling while I cock my head and lean forward. My tongue flicks out, tickling his cheek, and a delightful rumble fills my chest when I taste his fear.

So potent.

If I could, I would drink him dry and be drunk on his cowardice.

"What... are... you?" he rasps, trying to free himself from my grip.

He'll never be able to.

I'm so much more than he will ever be.

"I'm Demi's," I answer, snapping my teeth together in an audible bite. "And you dared touch her. You dared to get angry at her." I blow smoke in his face again, sending him into another coughing fit. "You dared to threaten her."

"She hit my truck!" He tries to defend himself as if that is a reasonable explanation for how he treated her. "She needs to be held responsible."

I rip the claw from his ankle, take his foot in my hand, and with a little pressure, I break it. The bones snapping reminds me of a crack of lightning. It slithers down my spine, seducing me, edging me, begging me to take more from this man.

My cock hardens from this bastard's pain as he screams.

I want him to beg for his life.

And I want him to die begging me to take it.

If I can wait that long.

Picking him up by his throat, I toss him across the room. He shouts, slamming into the wall. A giant dent is left from the force. He lands with a hard thump, groaning in agony. He begins to crawl away from me, dragging his useless body across the floor.

My wings stretch, then I tuck them where they belong while I walk over to our new friend.

I step onto the middle of his back, holding him in place, thinking about all the ways I could have fun with his body. I can't be here for too much longer though. Demi needs me and the cops will be here soon if anyone cares enough about the noise coming from this house.

"I swear, I'm sorry." His fingernails dig into his hardwood floor. "I won't bother her again. I won't. I'll move. I'll do whatever you want. Please," he begs just like I knew he would.

Grabbing his side, my claws puncture his skin, slipping into his insides. I flip him over, pulling my nails from his body one by one.

Wanting to make a show of it, I lick each claw clean even if his blood is the vilest thing I've ever tasted. Before I tried the sweet nectar of Demi's blood, I noticed that everyone's blood tasted different depending on the type of person they were.

If they treated their body like a temple, then they tasted of wine made from the gods, but if they hated themselves, then their blood was tainted.

The man below me seems to treat his body well, but his hate is what really curdles his blood.

"Oh my God." The words are a shaken breath followed by the smell of piss.

I glance down, watching his khakis turn to a darker shade of brown as he relieves himself. Crinkling my nose in disgust, I lean forward until our noses touch.

"You think I give a fuck about your promises? You're a self-righteous asshole who thinks women need to praise you. I'll tell you one thing—" I shove my hand into his chest, his beating heart thumping against my palm. "—The only man Demi will kneel for, is me." I rip the organ from his chest just like I did to Daniel.

It beats erratically, trying to pump the remainder of the blood. It drops down my hand in thick, delicious rivers. While they look appetizing, I know they aren't. I'll need Demi's blood to nourish me. I don't understand why that's the case, but she is the answer to my survival.

Like Daniel, he watches helplessly, the last few moments of his life slipping away.

"You can no longer make promises in a world where you always break them," I say, squeezing the blood out of his heart.

He exhales the last of the air in his lungs, dying with his eyes open and his lips parted. I drop his heart back into his chest cavity, appreciating my skills.

Unlike him, I kill to keep my promises.

Present time

I still smell the blood on my hands even after I showered. I think it might take a while for the rancid scent to wash away completely.

Sighing, I sit on the couch, watching the seventy-inch flat screen flicker between the rooms at Demi's house. She should be home any minute now.

I'm nervous.

Tonight will be the first time we will be together. Just the thought has my cock aching. People on the outside will think it's wrong for what I'm going to do, but they don't understand my need. They don't know what it's like to have these strong, animalistic urges for one person.

It's more than an obsession.

If I can't have her, I'll die. My life is tethered to her. This is survival. And why would I choose to die when it means I could experience the best part of life?

Demi.

"There you are, my beloved," I say to the screen, falling to my knees. "Welcome home. Did you have a long day?" Sliding closer to the TV, I raise my fingers, tracing the outline of her body.

She hangs her purse on the rack, stretching her neck to the side.

"It's so good to see you. I've missed you." My eyes lock onto her figure, watching as she heads to the kitchen to flip on the kettle. I've learned it's the first thing she does when she comes home.

Which works out perfectly for me.

In the day, she's nothing but a wish, but at night, she'll always be mine.

She begins to undress as she walks to her bedroom, untying her apron. It drops on the floor, then she begins to unbutton her shirt.

Smoke fogs the screen while I watch her undress, her beautiful body on display.

Unable to stop myself, I flatten my tongue on the screen and lick, dragging my tongue up her body, wishing I could feel her under me.

The screen switches when she steps into her bedroom. I zoom in, wanting a closer look at her body. The uniform slips off, her round ass on display. Demi steps out of her clothes and turns, tugging the hairband out of the ponytail. The camera doesn't catch the pink color of her hair tumbling down, but I imagine it.

I love her hair. She's so different. I could pick her out of a crowd. She's easy to find and hunt.

The sides of her breasts are revealed when she turns, stretching her arms over her head. Her nipples are hard, pointed, tempting me to go over there before my plan goes into effect.

"You're so fucking beautiful." I flatten my hand on the TV, freeing my cock from my pants when it begins to throb with desire. I give myself a tight stroke, but I won't come.

I'll edge myself. I'll push myself to the brink, bring my come so close to the surface, I'll have to control myself not to give in to the urge.

But I'll wait.

Because when I'm inside Demi, I want her to have every fucking drop that exists inside my body. I want to fill her, breed her, and possess her.

I want to claim.

I want to own.

Demi steps into the bathroom and flips on the shower, so I switch camera angles again.

The water slips down her body causing it to shine. She tilts her head back, her chest on full display. The hot liquid sprays across her chest, her perfect tits begging to be grabbed. I bet they would fit in the palm of my hand.

"Fuck. Oh, fuck. Demi. Demi. Demi." I gasp, mouth parting to inhale and exhale while I stroke myself faster.

She turns around, soaking her hair, then begins to wash it. Every move she makes I'm obsessed with. The way her fingers curl into her scalp, I want them to curl into my skin while she holds onto me. My forehead thuds against the TV as I watch myself fuck my fist.

The suckers are secreting precome, drizzling it all over my hand, the wet sounds erotic and not leaving anything to the imagination if someone saw me.

"The things I'm going to do to you," I growl, blowing smoke from my nose and mouth from the intensity of how much truth there is to that statement.

I lift my head, suds all drifting down her body now, hiding the parts I want to explore.

The shower is quicker than I like, simply because I'm not in there with her. "If I were with you, I'd fuck you until the water turned cold, and you were screaming with my knot stretching you." My orgasm heats my shaft and I squeeze it hard to stop myself from coming. I have to save it.

She wraps a towel around her body, brushes her hair, and stares at herself in the mirror for far too long. Her gorgeous, soft hand grabs the edge of the vanity and when I zoom in, her lips purse as if she's letting out a breath.

"What's on your mind, Honeysuckles? What do you need?" I turn my head again, brushing her face with my fingers.

She pushes away, strolls through the bedroom, and out the door.

My fingers become needy, pressing the button to the next camera.

My humanity, the sliver I have left, whispering in the darkness of my mind, past all my beasts roaring in my head.

Something flicks in my chest, something about right and wrong, but the brutality of the monsters silences it.

Demi pours the hot water in a mug. I zoom in, grinning when I notice the coffee cup is from the diner.

The Demi's Diner logo is on it, pink to match her hair.

I hold my breath while she stuffs the tea leaves in the steeper. This is it. This is where everything changes.

Change in life is inevitable. I'll be the reason for her to adapt. I'll better her life. She'll see.

Demi sips the tea, closing her eyes as if it's the best thing she's ever tasted.

"You're just waiting for me, aren't you? You know I'll be there for you tonight. Drink, Demi. Drink, so I can come and haunt your dreams. Let me be your nightmare," I whisper, tracing the outline of her body with my finger.

If there's one thing I know I can never be, it's her daydream.

She travels back into her bedroom, puckering her pouty lips to blow into the hot liquid before taking a sip. She slings her towel off and tosses it in the hamper, then slides one of her dresser drawers open. She tugs on an oversized shirt, similar to the one from the night before.

Only this shirt is white.

Her nipples are peeking through the material, tenting it, daring me to rip it to shreds so I can see them.

She stumbles, squeezing her eyes shut.

"Oh, it's working," I grumble in delight, tucking my cock in my jeans to prepare myself to leave. "Drink it dry. Make me proud." It's as if she can hear me, downing the last of it. "Oh, Good Girl," I praise, biting my lip when she tries to place the mug on the dresser, but stumbles. "Oh, no. Do you need help?" She sways, reaching for the dresser.

Missing again.

The mug drops from her hand, clattering to the floor. The handle breaks off, her foot almost steps on it as she struggles to stand.

The back of her knees hit the bed, her body falling until her back hits the mattress. She manages to flip to her stomach, fists the sheets I've made such a mess on, and pull herself to her pillow.

"Sleep tight, Honeysuckles."

I'll be there soon.

CHAPTER TEN

CREED

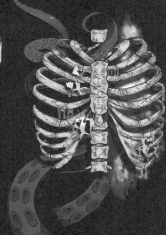

She's beautiful when she's asleep.

"That tea hit you hard, didn't it?" I tuck a piece of hair behind her ear, wanting to touch her, and also wanting to see if she wakes up from the simple gesture.

She doesn't move.

"I'm sorry." I trail my talons down her chest, her shirt ripping from the sharp points. "I'm sorry it has to be like this. You don't understand my need. You don't understand the constant battle inside me between all my beasts. You don't understand how much I crave you. It's... all consuming." I spread her shirt apart, my tongue sliding across my fangs when I see her tits.

I wait for her to move, to awaken, to scream when she sees me, but she's out cold.

"You are fucking stunning." I slide my hands up her body, her tits fitting perfectly in my palms. My mouth parts and an unsteady breath escapes in broken pants. I shut my eyes, groaning as I slide my thumbs across her nipples. They are hard, reacting to my touch. "You like that, don't you? You're asleep, but I bet you can feel me. God, you feel so good. So soft and perfect. Have you been using your lotion?" I ask, bending down to inhale.

"Mmm," she hums.

I freeze, tilting my chin up to stare at her, my entire body paused. Her eyes are shut.

"Your body is the light I never dreamed I'd touch." My tongue shifts, forking at the tips and flicks out, dragging it across her stomach.

My scent spreads across my tongue. "Mmm, Demi. You have been using the lotion. Good Girl. You taste just like me." I straighten, staring down at her flawless figure, her arms spread out as if she's presenting herself to me to be devoured.

"Don't mind if I do, Sweet Mate." I strip off my shirt, groaning as my wings stretch from being confined in the tatters of my shirt. I am going to have to buy some more before too long. I don't know how my wings keep going away, but they always burst out when I need them, or I lose control of my emotions. I've torn a lot of shirts apart. Rolling my head over my shoulders, my neck pops.

I hear her blood pumping through her veins, saliva pooling in my mouth saturating my tongue.

I undo my belt, the leather cool to the touch as I slip it through my belt loops. "You're probably wondering why I call you Honeysuckles." I toss the belt on the floor and the buckle clinks on the floor. It's loud and it would wake a normal person.

Demi doesn't move.

Unbuttoning my pants, I slide them down my hips, then kick them off as well.

"There are two reasons, Demi." I slide my body over hers. "Oh, fuck." I gasp, the air broken as it leaves me. I kiss the middle of her chest, sliding my hand behind her head to lift her just enough so I can take the remnants of the shirt from her body.

I bury my nose in her hair, inhaling her scent while she grumbles in her sleep. "You remind me of the only memory I have from when I was only a human. A field of honeysuckles. Every time I think about it, it's happiness. You are happiness. You are the field." I kiss down her neck, stopping at the strong pulse in her jugular vein. A low hiss escapes me, my now forked tongue flicking out to taste her skin. "But do you know how to taste the nectar from a honeysuckle? You pull the stem and suck the end of the flower to taste how sweet it is. To taste the honey." I wrap my mouth around her nipple, wondering if this will be the moment she wakes up to try to push me off her.

"That's what I want to do to you, Demi." I lick across her chest to the other breast while kneading the left in my hand. "I want to suck the honey from you." I lightly blow on her nipple so I can watch it become tighter. "I want to taste how sweet you are on my tongue."

Her brows pinch together, her lips part, and her body begins to move under me. Demi's back arches for a moment before she lies back down.

"I don't know how much time I have before you wake up. I hate to be quick. I want to take my time with you but if you see me... I can't imagine what you'd do." I take her hand, pressing it to my chest. "You would never want me. Not when I look like this." My gray skin in stark contrast to hers. "I want to imagine what it's like for you to want me, which is why I'm here." I kiss her lips and while hers are unmoving, feeling those soft clouds give under me suffocates me with desire.

I kiss down her body, my fangs scraping her skin, and she whimpers in her sleep.

"I'm going to make you feel good, Demi. I promise. You'll feel me in your dreams." I settle between her legs, spreading them wide to put her beautiful pink cunt on display.

She's already glistening and wet.

She knows I'm here.

"You're so pretty." I slide my clawed finger through her lips, watching for her reaction.

Another high-pitched whimper escapes her, but she remains in a deep sleep. I probably put too much Ambien in her tea, but I couldn't risk her waking up. I have to be able to drink from her, to claim her, even if it's only at night.

I circle her clit, wishing she was awake so I could hear her true screams of pleasure. The sounds she is making right now are muffled, almost slurred, as if she's trying to shout but can't.

I've taken her voice so I can take her body.

And none of my beasts care.

"Cree—" is murmured from Demi and I lift my eyes from her pussy.

Her eyes are still shut but they are pinched, brows drawn, and I grin knowing she's thinking of me.

I pinch her clit, rubbing it faster. Her thighs shake and those little whimpers become more frequent.

"That's it, beloved. That's it. Come for me. Are you close already? Are you needy for me?" I ask her, even if I know she can't answer.

"Of course you need me. I'm yours. How could you not need what is yours?" I rub her clit harder, faster, the tentacles around my cock stretching for her cunt, wanting nothing more than to lock onto her.

Her back arches again, followed by more whimpers and fast breathing. Her orgasm slams through her, her pussy becoming wetter, slicker, and more divine. I slip my fingers through her lips again, the sweet petals hiding what I need to claim.

Lifting my finger in the air, my claw shines from her juices. My tongue flicks out and wraps around it before I suck it into my mouth, groaning from her taste.

"So goddamn sweet." I wrap my other hand around my cock. "Fuck, Demi. Oh, fuck." I squeeze, but it doesn't stop a stream of come that leaves or what my suckers secrete. I apply so much pressure around my cock, it's about to burst with pain when finally the urge to orgasm stops. I let out a breath. "Look what you do to me," I chuckle, bending down to suck my come from her thigh so she is clean.

Lying down on the soft mattress, I spread her pussy, mindful of my claws.

And then I spit my come onto her tight hole. It drips down her crease, and I plunge my tongue inside to stop it from leaking out.

"Mmm," I groan into her, watching for any sign of her waking.

Her body is nearly limp, showing me the drug is still working.

"Demi. You are the best thing I've ever tasted. Oh God." I dive in, desperate and unhinged, my forked tongue plunging into her.

Sliding my tongue as far as possible, her legs spread further in her sleep without her knowing, allowing me to get more comfortable.

My beasts sound all at once, roaring in my head. My fangs nip at her sensitive entrance and fire slowly dances along my tongue, marking her with my fire and smoke as mine. I know it's safe. I feel it in my bones. My dragon would never do anything to hurt her.

"Mmm," she mumbles once more, her orgasm drowning my tongue.

I drink her down, bathing my insides in her honey. Slipping my tongue free, I sink my fangs into her thigh as my control snaps. I feed, taking long swallows of her blood that stitch the weakened parts of me back together.

When I'm full, I lick the pinpricks, and the evidence disappears.

My eyes roll to the back of my head. This time, I sway. I feel drugged. I look over my shoulder in the mirror, blood smeared across my lips and chin, a stream of it trickling down my neck.

I swipe my finger up the red trail, not wanting to waste a drop, and rub her blood across my gums.

Now. I have to claim her now.

I wrap one leg around my hips, guiding my cock to her entrance. One tentacle stretches to the back while the other circles her clit. It suctions, pulling and tugging on the sensitive nerve.

I feel her pleasure as if it's my own. I inch into her, a constant purr vibrating my chest.

And then I hit a barrier.

My werewolf howls victoriously. I tilt my head back, fire spouting from my throat and licking the ceiling.

She will only ever have me.

"You saved yourself for me. What a good girl. I'll take care of you now." I drive in, crying out as I sink all the way in.

Her wet, velvet walls wrap around me tight.

She cries out the best she can in her drug-induced stupor, pain etched across her face.

The suckers along my cock massage her insides, locking and releasing in place to give her more pleasure.

Cupping one of her tits, I slide out, watching my purple and red cock disappear inside her.

I snarl, my control snapping, my beasts taking over, and I begin to quicken the pace. The headboard bangs against the wall, my talons dig into the sheets, her pussy grips me so tight, I nearly spill, and something shifts.

We become closer.

Not only do I feel her pleasure, but her confusion too. It's dampened by how good she feels. Demi thinks she's caught in another wet dream.

"I'm going to breed you." My voice isn't my own. It's deep, dark, the baritone rougher than it has ever been before. "You're mine, Demi. You're mine. You're fucking mine. No one will take you from me. I own you. You belong to me. I won't stop until you're pregnant. Until you are trapped with me. Until you have no choice but to love me. You're. Fucking. Mine!" I roar, my wings freeing from my back, and they wrap around us.

We're in a safe cocoon. Her breath tickles the flesh of my wings and I moan from how good that feels.

"Look at you, taking my cock like a good girl. Your cunt was made for me, wasn't it? Your body was made for me." I bend down, sucking a nipple into my mouth while pounding into her cunt.

Her virgin scent fills the air, the blood coating my cock, and I'm dying for a taste again.

"Creed?"

My name slips from her mouth with a sleepy groan. I look into her baby blue eyes, half-hooded, pupils blown from the drug.

And then they close again as she falls back into her slumber.

My talons dig into her hips, my cock driving into her over and over with force. My heavy sack slaps her ass while my tentacle plays with her entrance.

"Ah! Ohhh," she groans a bit louder, her palm landing on my chest.

Her touch is welcomed. "Oh, my fffuck. You don't know what you do to me. Your pussy feels so good. I'm going to take you every night, Demi. Every single night. You're going to be so sore and not know why. I'll know when I see you. I'll know what we do." My wings release us, tucking back into their position along my back.

Gliding my hands up her torso, her body dead weight in my arms, I lift her from the bed. Her neck is bared to me, daring me to mark her.

To claim her.

My werewolf is at the surface, snarling to knot her, to lock our come inside so she carries my child.

I can't leave my mark where it can be seen. Not yet.

The knot at the base of my cock grows. It becomes harder to slide out with every thrust.

Before I seal myself inside her, I slide out, flip her over so she's on her stomach, and stare down at her ass. Her cheeks are perfect. I squeeze them, dragging my claws down the flesh.

With a snarl, I bite just below her ass— more on her upper thigh so it remains hidden by the crease and curve of her cheeks. When my fangs meet inside her flesh, I release her with a growl before slamming myself back inside her with my knot. My mark is on her. Mine.

My knot inflates, swelling to the point I can't slide free.

We're locked together.

Demi's pain echoes through the bond as my knot continues to fill with come and stretch.

"Nothing has ever compared to this moment." I shiver as pure lust drifts down my spine. "I've claimed my beloved." I'm still confused on what that means, but all I know is I feel right, like I belong.

I slow my unforgiving thrusts until they are shallow, rocking inside her so she feels pleasure and not pain. The suckers latch onto her walls and something else slithers from my tip, pushing into her womb.

A savage roar shakes the room while my come pours from my knot into her belly. Flames bathe us as I lose control. My skin erupts in fire, dousing hers in my own signature heat no one else will possess. My mark on her thigh is seared into her skin.

Scarred for life.

Scarred to be mine.

"Creed." Her words a ghost across my lips.

"Oh. Oh. I can't stop. You are taking so much. Look at you. You're swelling." I press my hand against her stomach, noticing the large bulge made of my come.

I finally stop filling her, but I'm trapped inside her for I'm not sure how long. I kiss her neck, then her shoulder, situating us on our sides while we wait for my knot to release.

"If you only knew how much you love what I do to you in your sleep."

And to my surprise, her pussy clamps around me, another orgasm taking over her body.

"That's it," I urge her. "Drink in my come. Take it all. Take every fucking drop. Make it stay. Give me a baby. Give me our baby."

Another burst of come leaves my knot and another orgasm possesses her body.

"Pull me in, Demi."

I'm learning that she's in a constant state of orgasm because of whatever is latched into her. I wish I knew more, but I know my beasts feel sated. This is right. This is what I'm meant to do.

When my cock softens, a gush of our come spills from her, dripping down her thighs.

I drop between her thighs, licking, sucking, and swallowing our mess until she's clean.

"I taste your virgin blood, Demi." I kiss her inner thigh. "I'm so glad you're only mine. I would have had to kill anyone else who ever had you." I roll off the bed, bring the covers to her chin, and then head to the bathroom.

My cock is semi-hard, come is still pooled in the suckers, but they aren't secreting more.

Doing my business, I wipe my cock clean, and flush.

"What do you have in here?" I become nosey, wanting to learn anything I can about my mate.

Her medicine cabinet is older, the mirror rusting on the sides, and when I open it, I help myself to everything.

"Headache, itch spray, flu medicine," I rattle off.

Then I grab a pharmacy bag. "What are you hiding in here, mate?" I chuckle, a giddiness washing over me as I get to know her. Tearing it open, I pull the medicine from the bag and stare at it.

I click the case, then spread it, showing little pills.

Around thirty of them.

"What is this?" I sneer, stomping through the bedroom so hard the house shakes. I wave them at Demi's sleeping face. "What is this!" My heart is a jackhammer in my chest, chiseling away at the bone.

Grabbing my pants, I fish out my phone and type in the name on the sticker made out to Demi Hawthorne.

When the search pulls up, I growl so viciously, if anyone had been standing in front of me, I'd kill them.

Birth control.

"Not anymore." Everything we just did could be for nothing. I can't have this happen again. One by one, I break the pills from the package into the toilet.

Then flush them.

"Who gave you these, Demi? Who made you take these? Who is trying to keep you from me?" I rush to her side, sliding my knuckle down her cheek. "No one can keep us apart." I kiss her forehead and her entire body moves under the sheets.

Her eyes open again, a small smile tilting her lips as she stares right at me.

And then, she's gone, falling into the hell I want to keep her in.

I get dressed, knowing I need to leave soon before she truly wakes up. I'd morph her dream into reality. She would no longer be confused and it's the confusion I need to live in.

"Doctor Allen Douglas," I read the doctor's name who prescribed her these pills.

I tuck the pharmacy bag in my pocket along with the case, then grab her torn shirt to leave no evidence behind.

The only evidence I want left is my come in her belly.

"I'll be back, Demi. And I'll deal with this doctor. Don't worry." I kiss her forehead, then her lips, and take a picture of her for myself to have.

I tug the covers down, taking a few more photos of her body, then spread her legs to get a view of her swollen cunt leaking with my come. I want to be able to see what I've done anytime I want.

And then I tuck Demi in. "Dream of me in the same way I live for you."

Not even a doctor could tell me my heart doesn't beat for Demi. If they did, I'd kill them.

My heart bleeds for Demi.

And I'll bleed them for her too.

CHAPTER ELEVEN

DEMI

I'm sore everywhere. My head is groggy and I'm dizzy. I even ache between my legs. I don't know why.

Looking in the mirror, I see nothing wrong with my body minus a few bruises here and there along my hips.

I remember dreaming about Creed. He was fucking me hard, whispering words of absolute filth. He didn't look normal though. Everything about him screamed animal. His features were defined and sharp. His skin was gray all over. He had fangs that pointed over his lips.

That's impossible. A person like that doesn't exist. My mind is playing tricks on me. I know Creed is different, but he isn't that different.

Maybe I've been reading too many paranormal romance books.

I scoff at that ludicrous thought.

My dreams are getting more intense the more I see Creed. Maybe I need to bite the bullet and ask him out. We could end up not liking one another at all.

Just the thought makes an ache spread through my chest. I rub it with my hand, willing the pain to go away. My eyes begin to burn, tears threatening to spill over at the thought of not being near him. Even now, I miss him.

I miss him so much. If I don't see him soon, the aches in my body will grow more painful. I know it.

"What the hell is wrong with me?" I ask myself, taking a deep breath.

In and out.

Calm. Down.

Everything is fine. I'll see him, talk to him, and get this need out of my system.

Giving myself one last look in the mirror, I head into my bedroom, gripping the door trim when I stare at the bed. Closing my eyes, I do my best to remember what happened last night or if I drank more alcohol than I should have.

I know I didn't drink. Even when I do, I never drink too much. I had my tea and everything after that is black or a blur. I swear, I put on a shirt before bed, but maybe I just thought I did. I don't like to sleep naked. I get too cold.

I had to have been exhausted last night.

Slipping on my panties, I groan because of the ache between my legs. Dreaming of Creed last night must have made me lose control with myself. I bet I fucked my fingers hard last night and that is what the pain is from.

I finish getting dressed, throwing on my uniform, then finish it off with my apron as usual.

My phone dings at the end of the dresser.

I stare at it, remembering the messages from yesterday.

Tying my pink shoes, I decide to ignore it. Maybe I'll leave my phone today. If I take it with me, I'll look at it every few seconds, checking to make sure that unknown number hasn't texted me.

"Shit!" I curse when the cell begins to ring.

It's my mom's ringtone.

I don't hear from her often anymore since she's living her best life traveling the world.

A part of me wishes she would have taken me with her.

"Mom. Hey." I lean against the dresser, pinching the bridge of my nose. "I'm so happy to hear from you." Tears fall like the rain did the other night, cascading in a rush as if a damn has broken.

"Hey," she says softly, realizing something is wrong. Her signal is weak. The line is cutting in and out. Wind rushes across the connection and I have to tilt the phone away from my ear. "What's wrong, Demi?"

I shake my head, and the tears drop free, landing on the tips of my pink shoes. The color darkens. How do I tell my mom my body hurts? That I feel like I've had sex but I know I haven't? How do I tell her about Daniel and my neighbor? How do I tell her I think I might be losing my mind?

I sniffle, wiping my nose. "Nothing. No, nothing like that. I just didn't realize how much I missed you until you called. Where are you this time? It's been a while since I've gotten a postcard." I love to get her postcards. The messages are always short and sweet. She usually tells me something like, "Demi, this ocean reminds me of your eyes. I miss you." But I love those postcards. It lets me get a glimpse of where she's at.

"I'm sorry, baby. I miss you too. I'm sorry about the postcards. I've been away at sea with Fabian."

I grin, pushing off the dresser. A piece of jewelry drops to the floor. I bend down to pick it up, lifting the gold ring into the air.

This isn't mine.

It's different from the ring I found the other day. This one has a ruby center. The gem is cut in an oval, hugged by two diamonds. It could be mine, I guess. I have jewelry I don't wear.

Shrugging, I slip it on, a rightness settling over me like a cloak. I hold out my hand in front of me, the ruby glittering in the sunlight peeking through the curtains.

"Demi? Are you there? Are you listening? I think he's the one," she giggles.

So were the last four guys she mentioned on her post-cards. Dad died after I graduated college and mom has been searching for her purpose again. I don't fault her for it. I'm so happy she's happy, but I'm worried she's alone and filling it with people who lack the substance it takes to fill a void, to be permanent instead of temporary.

Everyone is temporary in a way, but there are the few that refuse to leave, they plant roots in your soul, and weather every storm life throws at you. They are built of concrete, even if they crumble, they find a way to remain. Those people are few and far between, but they do exist.

I'm worried she's on an adventure to find those people.

"Really? Fabian? Sounds like a Greek God with long black hair and striking blue eyes."

"How did you know?" She dreamily sighs. "Oh, Demi. He is beautiful."

"I'm sure he is as he takes you sailing across the Mediterranean."

"It's been an experience. It's wonderful. Enough about me. How are you? How is the diner? Do you need help?"

I grab my purse from the hook next to the front door and leave, locking the bolt behind me.

"I'm fine. The diner is great. It's busier than ever. I made all coffee free. It was a test at first, but people actually end up buying more food now so I might keep it going."

"That is such a great idea. I knew you'd do great."

I stop just outside the driver's side door of the Bel Air, staring at my neighbor's house across the street. There's yellow crime scene tape blocking it off from the road.

No one is allowed to enter.

But I want to.

I want to cut the yellow tape and walk inside. I want to know what happened.

"Demi? Honey, are you sure you're okay? You seem... distant."

"I'm fine. I promise. I didn't sleep well."

"If you're sure. Oh, we have to go. We are docking and Fabian promised to take me dancing."

"Mmmhmm. Dancing. Is that what they are calling it? Wear protection."

"Demi!"

I snicker. "Love you. Bye." I hang up before she can lecture me about condoms. She's been wondering why I haven't had sex, being a grown woman and all, running my own business, but I don't know, I've never found a man worth that kind of time.

I'm busy. I have things to do. Playing games isn't one of them.

And most of the men I meet love to play games.

"You won't be missed, asshole," I mutter under my breath towards Keith's house. It's cold-hearted, I know.

I'm a kind person, but sometimes kindness gets you nowhere, or people will walk all over you. Being *me* only goes so far until I have to dig deep to snatch those angry feelings I keep bottled up inside. I always tell myself the anger isn't worth being remembered by.

Today is not that day.

I lift my middle finger to his house and climb into my car.

Huh.

I actually feel better.

Turning the radio on until I can't hear myself think, I sing at the top of my lungs "Shivers," by Ed Sheeran. I can always count on this song to put me in the best mood.

I roll down the windows, moving my hand through the air like a wave. The wind rustles the pink strands of my hair while a rare peek of the sun hits my cheeks, melting my anxiety.

I'm lost in the song, and in the gorgeous day when I pull into the parking lot of the diner.

In swift, long strides, I hurry to the door when a rush of ice slides down my spine. There it is again.

The feeling of someone watching me.

My hand is on the handle, but I don't open the door. I wait for the eeriness to pass because this can't be happening.

I gasp when I feel a breath ghost over the back of my neck. It's warm and welcoming, something about it soothes the panic rising. I tighten my grip on the handle and lean back, the breath of air still whispering over my skin as if I'm being seduced by a feather.

The bell jingling as the door opens has me stumbling backward.

"Demi. How ya' doing?" One of the factory workers greets as he puts on his hard hat.

"Hi guys. Have a good day," I manage to say somehow, lifting my hand in a wave.

"Bye, Demi!

"Bye!"

"See you later for more coffee!" They shout their good-byes one by one, leaving me on the sidewalk wondering what just happened.

There's no one around. It's just me.

My phone dings again, helping me come back to reality. I have to get it together for work.

Fingers trembling, I swipe the screen and notice a text message from an unknown number.

"Oh God," I whisper, looking around to see if anyone is watching me.

I only see the window of the diner. In pink and white paint, it says The Best Endless Free Coffee in Town. To my right, there are a few cars parked. Nothing and no one else is around.

I click the message.

Unknown number: "You look beautiful today."

Unknown number: "I did it for you."

"Did what? Did what for me?" I ask with a hint of venom in my question.

Running my fingers through my hair, I turn around, searching the distance of the field between the woods and the parking lot. Police tape still ropes it off. The grass has gotten long but not long enough for someone to hide. No one could watch me from the woods either, it's too far.

Like an idiot, I reply.

Me: "Who are you? What do you want? What did you do for me?"

I wait for my phone to alert me, biting my thumbnail in anticipation.

Unknown number: "*You shouldn't bite your nails. Bad girl, Demi.*"

My entire world spins from his declaration.

He can see me.

Unknown Number: "*And I want you.*"

Turning off my phone, I tuck it in my back pocket. I don't look back. I don't look around to see who it could be.

The welcoming entrance of the diner has the anxiety vanishing. The eerie blanket of someone watching me is gone. I'm safe here. The diner is my safe haven.

The black and white checkered floors shine from being polished. The red barstools are half-full. There's a child drinking a strawberry milkshake, whipped cream spread all over his chin.

I hope one day I can have kids.

Creed pops into my mind and the thought of him doesn't scare me. He's intense, mysterious, and questionable, in all of the best ways that grab my attention. It's way too soon to say I'd have his babies, but the thought feels right.

"Hey, Demi!" Mickey greets, waving at me as she cleans a booth.

"Hey, Mickey. How have things been?"

"They have been great. It's been a hell of a morning though. Didn't you hear?"

I shake my head, not knowing what she's talking about. "Hear what?"

"That poor old man. Some type of doctor. He was killed late last night."

"What? That's terrible. Who is the person doing these things? It's awful."

"I know," she agrees. "I'm afraid to walk to my car anymore. I don't know what will happen."

"New rule, we always go outside in pairs. Okay?"

Visible relief has her entire body sagging. "Yes. That would be amazing. Thank you, Demi. I appreciate that."

"Us girls have to stick together, right?"

"Right." She smiles.

The bell sounds, announcing another customer. A big customer service smile plastered on my face, I spin around on my tiptoes, pad, and pen in hand.

And just like that, my smile falls when I see who is there.

Dark brown button-up shirt with khaki slacks, Jake stands there with the badge shining above his left breast pocket. His last name is stitched on the other side. He takes off his sunglasses while Waylon stands next to him, removing his stiff department-issued hat.

"Jake." I try to sound happy to see him, but the dread seeps through instead. "Waylon." I unclick the pen. "I'll get coffee. Take a seat anywhere. I'll find you." I know they are here to talk to me by the looks on their faces. Their lips are pursed, but Jake gives everything he feels away in his eyes. He's the kind of person that never needs to say a word.

One look and you'll know anything you want to know from him.

"Sure, Demi. We'll wait. Are you sure you don't want to speak in private?"

"Why bother? Everyone is going to know anyway." I don't mean to sass or be rude. It isn't like me. "I'm sorry, Jake. This isn't your fault."

He gives my arm a squeeze as he walks by me. "I don't blame you at all for what you're feeling. It's okay. We'll talk in a minute."

He lets go and I slink into the kitchen, only to be met with a mess. Pancake batter is everywhere. It's dripping from the ceiling, coating Holt and Caden both. Pancakes are burning by the smell of it too.

And they are arguing, but I can't understand what Caden is saying over Holt's grunts and wild hand gestures.

"Hey!" I throw my hands on my hips, but they don't turn my way. I've never been able to truly shout. It hurts my throat. I also don't think there is any need to raise your voice. What has raised voices ever solved? The action usually just makes people feel bad and I don't want anyone feeling bad because of me.

Taking a large silver spoon, a pot, and a good dollop of frustration, I bang the spoon in the pot, ringing it as if it's a triangle and I'm on stage with a band.

They stop, turning to me in unison. It would be funny any other day with them drenched in pancake batter, but I'm not in the mood to laugh.

"What the hell happened?" I ask, setting down my weapons, then check all six of my coffee makers to see if there is a fresh pot. "I do not need this today. I have Jake in here again to talk to me. I'm starting to feel like a damn criminal and you two are in here, arguing, when we have a room full of customers out there?"

"Jake is here? Do you need me with you?" Caden swipes his face with his hand, the batter landing on the floor with a splat.

"Don't change the subject," I scold, snagging three mugs to put on my tray.

I wish it wasn't so early or I'd spike my coffee with whiskey with the kind of day I'm having already.

"Holt and I ran into one another. He was holding the batter, and lost his footing, I tried to grab the bowl, but he tried to pull it from me. One thing led to another, then the bowl is flying in the air above us, dumping pancake all over us," Caden explains for the both of them.

"Is this the truth, Holt?"

Caden scoffs. "I can't believe you don't trust me."

"I do, but you two are acting like one tried to steal your second-grade girlfriend, fighting on the playground. There is no playground fighting in my diner. Clear?"

"Yes, Demi," Caden grumbles.

Holt grunts, nodding while casting his eyes to the floor.

"I expect this mess to be cleaned up. I'll send Mickey and Minnie in here to help. Caden, you'll have to work all the tables since you're the most experienced."

"I'll get cleaned up."

"Nope. You are going to go out there just like that. It's only fair since you aren't the one cleaning up."

Holt chuckles.

"Don't make me take away all your kitchen gadgets, Holt. I am not in the mood today, no Sir, I am not."

His eyes grow round, his nodding turning frantic.

"Thank you," I sigh, already feeling exhausted and my good mood has faded into wishful thinking at this point.

Grabbing the tray, I nudge the swinging door open and find Jake in the back corner where Creed sits. It takes me by surprise, but I don't like Jake sitting in Creed's booth.

That's our spot.

I don't want Jake and Waylon to ruin it.

"Hey Jake. Waylon." I slide into the booth across from them, pouring each of them a cup of fresh coffee, then my own. I load it with cream and sugar, hoping I'll get a sugar rush to get through the day. "What's this about?"

"I'm sorry, Demi, but Doctor Allen Douglas was found dead at his practice early this morning."

I swallow the hot coffee slowly, the burn igniting in my throat. "That's the doctor who died? That's terrible. He was a good gynecologist."

The silence falls between them. The two officers give one another the side-eye, waiting for me to catch on.

I set my mug down, keeping my hand wrapped around it to feel the heat. "You think it has something to do with me? I didn't kill him. I didn't kill anyone."

"We know you didn't, but whoever did, I think you're connected somehow. As small as this town is, you're still the only one with a connection to all the victims. We think the killer believes he is doing you *and* him a favor. If he feels anyone is a threat, he's going to get rid of them, so no one stands in his way to get to you. I don't think it's a good idea for you to be alone. You should stay with someone."

"I'm not being forced out of my house. I've been fine. And how was my gynecologist a threat? He is an old man, nearly forty years older than me?"

"We don't know," Waylon inserts, taking a drink of his coffee. "We haven't figured that part out yet, but trust us, okay? We only want you to be safe."

This is the part where I tell them about the text messages, but I know what would happen. They wouldn't be able to do anything since nothing physical has happened, but since it's Jake maybe he can help. I need to stop denying that these killings have nothing to do with me.

As I toy with the outline of my phone in my apron pocket, I'm hesitant to give over my evidence, my truth, the proof they need to pin this on my stalker.

I don't want to give anything to them.

"If I think of something, I'll let you know, Jake," I say as I turn on my phone.

They stand from the booth, towering over me. Jake squeezes my shoulder, trying to bring me comfort, but all his touch does is make me flinch away as if he burned me. His touch is wrong.

"Apologies." He raises his hand in surrender. "I know you're spooked. This will be over soon. I'll make sure of it. I know it isn't easy, but try to remain calm, stay busy if that's what helps. I can have an officer outside your house for a twenty-four-hour watch."

"Do you really think that's necessary?" I rub my hands down my face, arms falling limp on the table as the last of my energy fades.

"I do, Demi. I think you should have police protection at all times. Even at the diner."

"People will think I'm the suspect, Jake. What's that going to do to my business?"

"People won't think that. This town loves you. You know that and no one else can make a cup of coffee like you. Can I take this mug? I happen to like it."

A tired smile manages to form on my lips. "Absolutely, Jake. I appreciate your help."

"It's what I'm here for. Have a good day, Demi. Don't try to think too much about what has happened."

I stare at the empty space across from me where Creed usually sits. I have six more hours before he usually comes in.

He's all I can think about. I don't care about the murders like I should. So far, the first two men were threats to me, so my doctor had to be too in some way.

I'll have to trust the person stalking me, killing for me, because he's doing it for a reason.

Somehow, I've never felt safer.

CHAPTER TWELVE

CREED

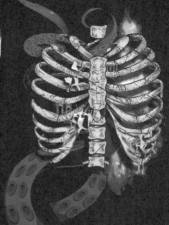

I watch the diner from the tree line, my hands dripping with fresh cold creek water. The doctor bled out fast when I ripped his heart out, soaking my hands until they were seas of crimson. It was beautiful yet the only blood I wanted was the type to flow through Demi's veins. Everyone else smells like they are decomposing from the inside-out.

Before I saw Demi at the diner tonight— because I simply can't stay away from her— I knew I had to wash my hands.

She isn't ready to see the blood I drain. Every drop spilled is in her name, staining every surface it falls on— a brand that will live on forever just for Demi.

This is just the beginning. Anything she wants, anything she desires, anything she fucking craves, I'll get it for her. No matter what.

No matter who.

Wiping my hands on my jeans, I tuck them in my hoodie, and stomp through the long grass of the field by the diner. When I'm halfway there, I lift the hood, once again hiding my appearance so I don't scare her away. She's been afraid enough today.

I find it odd she is comfortable with death but finds my messages alarming. What is the difference?

Opening the door, the damn bell rings, and I flinch at how loud it is. I'm still getting used to my abilities, sometimes, my senses are overstimulated. I keep my eyes cast down, keeping to the side of the diner as I head to my usual booth.

I sit, scraping my nails across the tabletop.

The room is busier than usual. Conversations from other tables are low murmurs blended together.

My hearing focuses on a different table every few seconds.

"—I think we should start trying for a baby. I think it's time."

"—Yeah, we should go camping. That sounds like a great time."

"—She looks fucking great tonight, doesn't she? She always looks good."

I tilt my head, listening to that conversation a little more.

"It's no wonder Daniel was obsessed with her. I think we should give her a go. What do you think? It's probably her fault Daniel is dead."

A growl slips past my curled lip while smoke tangles together as it drifts from my nose. No one faults my mate.

For anything.

She shouldn't have to pay for the bad behavior of a man. The man should take responsibility.

"Tonight. After she closes and walks to her car. We will wait."

"Sounds good to me."

"Me too."

My nails drag across the table, leaving more gashes as I try to control myself. I'm so close to burning the place down, but I can't do that. Demi would never forgive me. This place is important to her. I would never take something away from her that meant something.

"Creed?"

Her voice is soft and welcoming, the sound of home after a long day. It's like water extinguishing the flames building in my soul, wanting nothing more than to release violence and catastrophe. The fury shifts from a boil to a slow simmer.

"I'm so happy to see you." She tries to sit across from me, but I can't have her be so close and yet so far.

Snagging her wrist, I stop her. "Sit next to me."

"O-okay," she stutters a bit, setting down the coffee pot before sliding in next to me.

All my insides settle with her presence. I'm able to breathe. Her leg bumps mine, the small innocent touch makes a purr slip from my lips.

"What happened to the table?"

I show her my nails. "I'm not sure. It was like that when I sat down."

"Weird." She turns to me, filling my coffee cup with a smile on her face. "I'll make sure to get that fixed." I don't think she believes me, but she doesn't seem to mind.

"Don't," I tell her. "Let it be ours." The scratches represent the damage I've done to her but somehow, she remains strong.

"Ours. Is this our booth, Creed?"

"Yes," I say without hesitation, keeping my face turned at an angle so she can't see too much of my face. "This is our spot. Ours. No one else. No one else can sit here again."

"No one? I can't promise that. This is my diner, Creed. People have a right to sit where they want."

I shake my head, doing my best not to get angry. "No one else." I take a breath, moving my leg so it is touching hers again. Touch, as meaningless as it would be to most, means everything to me. "Please." It's as close to begging as I'll ever get.

Her touch is the closest experience I'll have of peace.

"Why won't you look at me?" Her hand reaches for my face, her fingers gliding under my chin to turn my head. "I want to see you."

"I don't want you to see me. The dark is better. It's best if you never have to see what I look like, Demi."

"I can't promise this is our booth then, Creed. Not if you're going to hide from me."

She slides away from me to get away and I clutch her knee with my hand to stop her. I need her next to me. Always. Now that she's mine, being away from her doesn't feel right, especially when she smells of me. It strokes the carnal beasts inside me. I want to show her off. I want to roar and howl, bang on my chest as I show the world Demi is mine.

"I'm not ready to show you. Yet. I will. I don't look like other men, Demi."

She slips her hand in mine, our fingers lacing together, and a sharp breath chokes me. She's choosing to touch me.

Demi wouldn't if she knew the truth. She wouldn't once she saw what I really was.

"Why? Did something happen to you?"

I pick up the coffee mug, taking a large gulp of it, uncaring if it's too hot.

"You don't have to tell me. I'm sorry. I don't want to push you."

"No, it's okay. I want us to get to know one another." I decide to tell the truth the best way I can without scaring her away. "I was kidnapped and tortured. I don't look the same as I used to. I like to be hidden. It comforts me."

"Oh God. Creed, that's terrible. I'm so sorry that happened to you. Did they catch the people who kidnapped you?"

"They are dead."

"Good."

If she could see me, she'd see my brows raise.

"No person deserves to live if that is how they chose to live life. That's just my opinion."

"It's a good opinion."

She leans her head on my shoulder, looping her arm through mine, and the sweet scent of her hair tickles my nose. That memory floats through my mind again, the only good one I have. I squeeze her hand tighter, never wanting to let her go.

Do I have a chance with Demi? Can I be myself around her? Will she forgive me once she finds out I'm the cause of all the havoc in town? Will she forgive me for taking her in her sleep? Which I plan on doing again tonight and every night that follows.

Even right now, not bending her over this table and ripping her uniform to shreds so I can fuck her, is an urge I can barely control when she reeks of my come still.

"Tell me everything about you." It's more of a statement than a question.

She lifts her head from my shoulder, and I don't like it.

Lifting my free hand, I cup the back of her head, forcing her to lean on me again.

She giggles.

Oh, that sound...

It makes my cock strain in my jeans.

"There's nothing much to know," she sighs, her fingers tracing the outline of my claws. I don't know if she is aware that she is doing it, but it feels good.

Everything about being with Demi feels fucking good.

"This diner has been in my family for generations. I always knew this is what I wanted to do. When my mom left to travel, she retired and gave the diner to me. I work all the time. I can't tell you what my hobbies are, but I know I love the rain when the sun is peeking through the clouds. It's serene. A beauty unparalleled to anything on this planet."

"That's not true. You're prettier than that. You're the most gorgeous view I've ever seen. Nothing you say will make me change my mind. It's a fact." My tone is stern, not allowing for argument.

Silence passes between us. I probably ruined any chance I had with her. That's fine.

She's mine anyway.

"You're sweet," she states.

"I am not... sweet. You're sweet."

You taste sweet.

That's what I really want to say, but I know I can't reveal my deep dark secrets just yet.

"We will agree to disagree, how about that?"

I finish off my coffee, pouring myself another cup. "No. I am right. Disagree is clearly the answer. I don't understand your reasoning."

"You come here every night. I don't think it's to have coffee."

I scoff, finding that reason ridiculous. "Why would I come for coffee? You are clearly why I am here."

"I know," she giggles again, leaning into me more. "I like it when you're here."

For now.

Until she sees the beast I am.

"What were your parents like? Do you have any siblings?" she asks.

"I don't remember. When they tortured me, they did something to me. I only have one brief memory of that time. It's a good one. You remind me of it."

She's as close to home as I'll ever get. She's the feeling of walking through the door after a long day, relieved and ready to relax. She's the ease after turmoil.

The rainbow in the sun and rain.

"God, Creed. I can't believe that happened to you. I want to know everything. Maybe we can get together sometime outside the diner? My break is over. Are you going to stay?"

"I always do."

I lift my eyes, her brilliant smile telling me I've made her happy somehow. My beasts like that. They want to always make her happy.

When she leaves, I follow her retreating form, her hips swaying with every step. I remember digging my fingers into those hips last night, driving myself into her body, filling it full of my come to breed her.

A grumble leaves all my beasts, wanting nothing more than to truly bind her to us.

Demi is going to look beautiful pregnant, round with extra weight. Her tits will be bigger, full of milk, and I can't wait to latch myself onto them to taste the sweet nectar that will nourish my children.

The conversation we had seemed to go well but that doesn't mean anything. No woman would truly want to be stuck with me.

It's why I have to give Demi no choice.

Her fate is mine, but I'll let her pretend everything she feels for me is her decision. Every thought she has of me is orchestrated on my end. I'm the conductor of her future, playing her strings until she realizes it's our song sewed in fate.

Pleased with myself, I kill time by using my claw to carve our names into the booth.

Creed + Demi for always.

I carve a heart around it, blowing away the dust I've created by chipping away at the countertop.

A smell I don't recognize grabs my attention, taking it away from my artwork. I lift my head, inhaling deeply only to find my sights landing on Demi's friend, Caden.

He stares at me too but how he squints his eyes with the waves of uncertainty rolling from him, he can't decide what I am.

The feeling is mutual. I don't know what he is either, but he isn't human. I could try to confide in him, but that would be a mistake. He's Demi's best friend and will protect her at all costs.

Demi taps his shoulder, forcing him to look away from me. I curl my lip, staring at where she touched him. I wish I could rip him apart. Limb from limb. She's mine. Every touch. Every breath. Every word.

Everything belongs to me.

Life isn't fair when I can't kill whomever I want.

Luckily, I have a list.

A waitress takes a step to the left, giving me the perfect view of the three men who plan to attack Demi when the diner closes.

I'm going to enjoy ripping them to shreds. Do I burn them? Rip their hearts out? Bleed them dry? Drown them?

Maybe I'll do it all.

I'll take them to my cabin and have some fun.

But then, I won't be able to see Demi tonight, and I must see her. I have to slide between her legs to claim her all over again. They aren't worth losing that time away from her.

Standing, I decide to leave before the group of men do so I can get to them before they can get to her. I make it a point to walk by their table. All three are sitting there as if they don't have a care in the world, watching Demi as if she belongs to them.

"Fucking freak." One of them spits at me while the others laugh.

"Don't call him that!" Demi chastises them, coming to my defense. "He didn't do anything to you. You should show some respect."

"You like that freak show, Demi? Does being scared turn you on?"

I could take the time to spare their lives, pulling them into my vampire trance, but I won't. They don't deserve it.

"You don't have to be an asshole—"

"—It's okay, Demi. I'll be seeing you later, okay?" I give her my back, forcing myself to walk away when every instinct is telling me to stay by her side.

"Wait!" she shouts after me as I push the door open.

That damn bell jingles again.

I swear, I'm going to rip it out. How does she listen to that all day?

"My number." She scribbles it on her order pad, folding it, then handing it to me. "Call me. Sometime. If you want. No pressure."

I tuck it in my pocket, smirking at how cute and innocent she is not knowing I already have her number. I'm the one who scares her when her phone rings.

"Maybe you'll see me before I call." She'll definitely experience me later.

Before I get trapped in her light blue stare, I push the door open and walk out, disappearing into the night.

My boot splashes in a puddle, soaking the ends of my jeans. My dragon pushes to the surface, dying to spread our wings and fly into the night. Looking up, the stars are out by the millions. Black and blues paint the sky. It's a rare sight to see lately from all the rain we've been getting. It's hard to believe I'm going to be killing three men under such a serene view.

Is that how the world works?

Atrocious acts always happen under the guise of beauty.

CHAPTER THIRTEEN

DEMI

"Earth to Demi." Fingers snap in front of my face, yanking me out of my trance from watching Creed leave.

Every time I'm around Creed, we get closer. Emotionally, physically, mentally. It's almost as if I can feel him inside me.

I miss him already. I want him to come back and sit in our booth, watching me, waiting for me, and just being happy that I'm nearby. I've never had that before, someone so eager to be next to me at all times.

I love it.

I'm not sure how the relationship can move forward if he can't show me his face. I don't think any relationship could work like that. I don't care what he looks like. What I like is how I feel around him. I've never felt so safe just by being near someone, but his intensity takes up an entire room, and it's all focused on me.

I bet he wouldn't let anyone touch me.

I want to learn more about what happened to him when he was kidnapped. It must have been terrible for him to endure all that and not remember anything.

"Demi!" Caden raises his voice a little to get my attention again.

"Sorry. I'm a little out of it. What is it?"

"Are you okay? Tell me the truth, Demi. I'm worried about you. It isn't like you to stare off into space. The last of the customers just left and I've been asking you if you want to countdown the drawer or if you want me to."

Embarrassment fills my cheeks, no doubt making them red. "I'll do it. You and everyone else can go home. I'll see you tomorrow."

Caden steps into my personal space, sniffling as if he is coming down with a cold.

"Unless you're sick. Don't come to work if you have the flu. We will manage."

"You're different," he says out of nowhere, which has nothing to do with what I just said.

"Because I'm worried about you? It's important you take care of yourself. You have plenty of sick days, Caden." I'm confused and insulted by his accusation. I've always cared about the well-being of my staff.

The register dings open, tapping my stomach since it's level with me.

"No, I mean, something about you is different. I can't tell. You smell different."

I count the one-dollar bills first. I'm a professional at counting in my head. "Caden, it's the same lotion, shampoo, and perfume I have always used. I'm not sure what you're talking about."

"And you're spending time with that guy that comes and hangs around in here. Something about him isn't right, Demi. What if he is the person going around killing people? I don't want you hanging out with him."

I suck in the side of my cheek, biting it to stop myself from saying something. "You don't control me, Caden. I can make up my own mind and decide what is good for me. Creed makes me feel safe. He isn't a threat."

"Isn't a threat? He has his entire body tattooed gray, wears fake nails, and contacts, but you don't think he's a threat? He screams trouble, Demi. Something about him doesn't sit right with me."

"Well, it sits right with me." I slam the drawer shut when I'm done counting, tucking the money in the envelope. "I'll take this to the bank tonight. Don't worry about it."

"Demi, come on. You know I'm right. Something inside you has to know I'm right." He backs into the door, giving me a sad, forced smile when I don't reply. "Have a good night."

When he leaves, I let out a long breath and drop my head in my hands. Anytime my mind wanders to Caden's words, guilt slams through me like a wrecking ball, smashing against every surface of my bones.

It's painful.

In my hollow bones, somehow, Creed has found a place to live. Denying him would mean agony, a thousand shattered pieces of myself will be all that's left of me.

Caden is wrong.

"Don't listen to him, Demi. You're a big girl. You can handle your own problems. You don't need anyone to warn you away from anything." I give myself a weak pep talk, but I don't really have anyone else to talk to about this.

Caden is my best and only friend. I work too much to have lasting friendships with anyone else. It's a lonely life, but ever since Creed came into it, I don't feel as lonely anymore.

That has to count for something, right?

Giving one last look over to the main room, my eyes land on our booth. The one where he makes me feel like the only woman in the world, that maybe I can have a life outside of this diner.

Wishful thinking always did get me into trouble. I tend to run away with every dream, letting it take over until I know it's too big to hold onto, to want, to need. Only to realize then you have to settle for second best because that's more realistic. That's life. It isn't a fantasy world, no matter how much you want to get lost in one.

Maybe that's what Creed is. He's my fantasy world.

My hopeful heart dims as I flip off the light, the red glow of the milkshake machine the only thing illuminating the darkness. I step out into the cool brisk night, the air nipping at the tip of my nose, promising winter.

The lock audibly slides into place with a 'click' when that sensation takes over me again. It's different this time. Something about the feeling of this person watching me doesn't make me feel the same. My instincts are telling me to run, but my feet are frozen.

I can't move.

Goosebumps travel in warning along my body, my mind unable to send the necessary signals to my legs to get me to move.

"Run, Demi. Run for me. Now. Run, now!"

Creed's voice enters my mind, I don't know how, or if I imagined him talking to me, but I listen.

I don't wait another second.

I push away from the door, not just running, but sprinting to my car.

"You bitch!"

It's all I hear when I'm tackled from the side. My head hits the bumper of the car sending a deep ache through my skull. My body hits the pavement next, my shoulder catching my fall.

I cry out, hearing something pop followed by a burning pain. A hand grips me by the back of my neck, pressing me into the ground hard. I cry out, hoping my neck doesn't break.

"How does it feel to be hopeless, Demi?"

I stop breathing when I hear Daniel's friend's voice. I can't remember his name. I'm drawing a blank.

Another set of hands slide up my legs. "She is fucking beautiful. I can't wait to have a taste."

"No, please," I sob, fighting them with all the strength I have, but it isn't enough. "Stop. Stop! Let me go!" My head is lifted up by my hair. I'm positive my hair is going to rip out of my scalp, when I'm slapped across the face.

"Shut the fuck up, Demi. No one can hear you."

My head swims, blackness tinting the edge of my vision. Cool air hits my legs as my clothes rip, the sound of my dignity being taken from me.

"Daniel always wanted you. I can see why." He grips the meat of my ass while another holds my arms to the ground. His finger dips in my crease, grazing over my pussy.

"Help me! Someone, ple-e-ase," my voice breaks as I cry.

A zipper lowers.

"No, no, no," I squirm to get away, my body heavy from the blow to the head.

His cock slips between my cheeks and begins to rock. "You'll like it, Demi. I'll finally get a taste of what's so special about this cunt and then my boys will have a round. Relax, you'll get wet, and you'll end up liking it." He spanks my exposed cheeks, gripping them so hard, I know I'll have bruises.

"Please," I beg. "Please, stop." My fingers claw at the rough pavement, the pebbles and ridges of the parking lot dig into my fingertips. The skin tears.

My arms are pressed into the ground harder, and a knee is digging into the middle of my back to keep me still.

Three against one. I have no chance of beating them. Thunder rolls in the sky, the promise of rain hangs in the air.

It's always raining lately.

All I can hope is that it washes away this moment forever.

The light drops begin to fall, a sweet caress over my bare skin, but it does nothing to stop the panicked heat and sweat from rising in my body.

The only comfort I have is the relaxing scent of rain, how it is fresh, releasing the aroma of the field nearby. I shouldn't notice something so beautiful when something so ugly is happening.

But that's rain, isn't it? Beautiful and soothing, yet devastating and haunting.

Perhaps I'm being haunted by Daniel's ill intentions.

I sob so hard I gag, my attacker still using the crease of my ass for his pleasure.

"I can't wait to take you, Demi. You know you deserve this. You teased Daniel for so long and he wasn't man enough to take it from you. I'm going to show you what happens to a tease."

An explosive roar echoes through the eerie night. My ears ring from the intensity, but the overwhelming sense of safety returns in my greatest moment of fear.

The man on top of me is ripped from my body, his cock not penetrating me because whoever this savior is, saved me from that horror.

"You dare touch my mate. My beloved. You dare take what isn't yours!" A familiar but primal voice grates the air with its rough tones.

Mate? I must not have heard him right. I've read about mates in the paranormal romance books that I love to read, but that's fiction. It makes me worried if he thinks I'm his mate. He might need mental help if that's what he said.

I roll, turning my head to see who saved me. My vision is blurry, but the orange glow engulfing my attacker is hot, reminding me of fire. I can feel the warmth of it on my skin. Another roar rumbles, making fear slither down my spine. If I could run, I would.

"She's mine. Not yours. You touched her. You die. It's simple."

"No! No, please. I won't touch her again. No!" His screams slowly fade into a gurgle.

"You didn't stop when she said no. Why should I?" A crack of a bone breaking snaps through the night and the chaos ends quicker than it began.

I must have hit my head harder than I thought because he is in one spot one second, and in a blur, a totally different spot the next. My sight sharpens and blurs when I blink to try to clear the fog. That's impossible.

One man tried to run away to save himself, but my savior cackles like a mad man, grabbing my attacker's head, then twists.

Darkness creeps upon the edges of my vision. I close my eyes, thankful I can't see what else is about to happen.

The splat of something falling in front of my face makes me snap my eyes open. It rolls, coming to a complete stop. I smell the strong metallic scent of blood.

It's a heart.

"I'll make them all bleed for you," is snarled before another deafening primal growl threatens.

I wish I could say thank you. I wish I could hold on, but the dark abyss of unconsciousness is too strong.

My mind is drifting again, my eyes drooping from the headwound when I hear a whoosh similar to wings. Giving all the energy I have left, I focus on the blurred man saving me, watching as he vanishes into the night to catch the other man who tried to assault me.

I don't know what happens next. I give into the pain, wondering if the trauma to my head is causing me to hallucinate.

"Demi? My Sweet Honeysuckles."

I try to open my eyes, struggling to even get a peek at the man who saved me. He sounds like Creed, but it can't be. I manage to crack my eyes open for a moment, seeing glowing eyes staring at me.

I'm lifted into the air, which has to be another hallucination.

"I have you." He kisses my forehead, arms wrapping tighter around me, so I'm pressed to his chest.

What did I say about wishful thinking?

And here I am, finding myself in trouble, proving my damn point.

CHAPTER FOURTEEN

CREED

Adrenaline is a villain inside me. It pumps through my veins, taking over every move, every thought, and every ambition. I want to conquer the world—her world and everyone in it.

I cut through the black clouds, the rain pummeling my skin like needles because of the wind. When I get above the storm, while cold, it's peaceful. I glance down, taking in the appearance of my mate.

She has blood dripping down her temple. Her uniform is wet, dirty, and torn. This is my fault for straying so far away while stalking them.

If I hadn't been there, I don't want to think about what could have happened. Killing her attackers doesn't feel like enough. I wanted to do so much more than kill them. I wanted to play with them, torture them— give them hope of survival.

Then take it all away, slaughtering them like the pigs they are after months of begging for their deaths.

Flashes of white boom in the clouds, a symphony of light playing just for us. My wings adjust to a different angle, lowering us gently through the vicious thunder-heads, barely missing the bolts of lightning zipping by us. I don't nosedive, considering I have the most precious object of all my wants and dreams in my arms.

Her house comes to view. The backyard is perfectly fenced in, and I can imagine our children playing, but I'm not sure this house will be big enough for all the babies I want us to have. We will figure it out.

Landing gently in the yard, the grass comes to my mid-boot. She needs me to help her. She shouldn't be taking care of this house by herself. It isn't right. A woman like Demi shouldn't be doing anything alone. She's too special, too beautiful, and too smart. After working all day, she deserves to come home and not do anything.

I want to spoil her. I want to bring her all the gold, jewels, clothes, and anything else she desires. When she's pregnant, I'll massage her entire body every day and feed her by hand, so she doesn't have to lift a finger. She'll be all mine.

Always.

She whimpers in her sleep, her emotions syncing with mine. She's scared and it tastes bitter. The pain she's experiencing reminds me of the knife that slowly cut into my skin at the institute... everlasting, slow, and with sharp stings that come from the very tip of the blade.

Stepping into the house, I close the sliding glass door behind me.

"Damn it, I really need to fix the door." Even if I am the one who broke it, to begin with. I don't want to risk anyone else coming into the house.

Demi winces, wiggling in my arms. Her brows pinch together as high-pitched mewls slip from her lips. She has scratches all over her body and her shoulder seems out of place.

"This is going to hurt but you'll feel better." I press against her shoulder, then give it a good yank, wincing when her shoulder pops into place.

She screams, her eyes opening wide for a split second before they roll to the back of her head, the pain causing her to pass out.

"It's okay." I lie her on the bed, stripping away the rest of her clothes, then tossing them in a pile. "You're okay.

I have you, Honeysuckles." I bend down and press a kiss to her lips. "I saved you from them, but I didn't save you from me because only I can have you, Demi. Don't you understand?"

She's still knocked out, but I don't trust her head wound enough to keep her under.

"I'll be back." I kiss her forehead, inhaling her until my lungs can't expand any more. My cock grows hard smelling my scent mingled with hers. God, I can't believe she's mine.

Pushing from the bed with a growl, I catch my reflection in the mirror.

I'm drenched in blood.

Blood from the men who tried to take what's mine.

My hands are naturally very dark, nearly black, becoming a lighter gray up my arm, but it's all hidden under red.

Keeping my wings tucked so I don't knock anything over, I stop at the doorway to take off my boots and make myself at home.

I groan when my toes are free and I flex them, the claws tapping against the floor as I stroll into the kitchen.

My wing catches on the counter when I turn sideways in the small aisle connecting the dining room and kitchen.

"Mother fucker," I snarl, pinching my nose as annoyance boils in my chest. I take a deep breath, wishing my dragon would get his shit together so they would fade into my back.

But it's always the little things that end up setting me off after a long day. Slipping my wing from the corner, I'm finally free. This kitchen is not big enough for me. Now I feel like I need to stretch my wings and I can't, or I'll break something.

I'm tempted to do it anyway.

A rumble bellows in my chest while I open and close the cabinets looking for her mugs. I think back to the security camera, remembering she opened the cabinet above where she keeps the electric kettle and tea.

Everything is outdated. She needs a new home. Luckily, I can give it to her. Snagging a mug that says, "I want a dragon to tame me," I grin, slightly hopeful she's truly into dragons.

I fill the mug with water, then blow a small flame until the water boils slightly, then prepare the tea steeper. Seeing the thick white powder over the leaves has the trickle of my humanity yelling in the distance in the back of my mind.

With snarls and threats, my beasts silence my soul, possessing me once more. This is who I am now.

Are other monsters like me too or are they more stable? Do they have control of their urges?

Knowing it doesn't make a difference, I toss the steeper in the mug, then give it a good stir with my claw. Gripping the edge of the counter, tonight's events play through my mind. I ripped out three hearts and burned their bodies before getting her out of that parking lot. Luckily, she was knocked out by then from all the trauma and stress, so she didn't have to smell their burning flesh. Demi has had a rough night.

Perhaps it's best I leave.

But then I see their faces, their smiles, the hunger in their eyes as they clawed at Demi's clothes to get access to the beautiful, claimed space between her thighs.

Their hands grabbed and clutched her ass, his small cock rocked between her cheeks, showing her what was to come.

Their touch is all over her. Their scent soaks her.

I have to fix it.

Snagging the tea, the liquid spills from the rim and onto the counter while a primal urge to claim her all over again takes over me.

She's the same as when I left her. Unmoving and so still, if I wasn't able to hear her heartbeat, I would be afraid she was dead.

I climb onto the bed, damning myself to a deeper hell, and slide my hand behind her head to lift her.

"Demi, open your mouth. Let me have you. This is the only way." Her eyes move behind her lids, and they crack open, tiny slits that are glassy. I can barely see she's opened them at all. "Good Girl," I praise her, hoping she can't see too much of me.

She'll forget soon.

She parts her lips, daring me to do more than just serve her tea.

The tea is just the right temperature to slip down her throat. Tilting the mug, the steaming liquid pours down into her mouth. Her throat bobs as she swallows until all that's left is a drop.

I place her head back down, bending to kiss her again when I get a whiff of her attackers. I can't wait for another second. Not with her body on display for me to steal and use any way I want. Their scents are drugging me, replacing any affection I felt for her with something dangerous.

I don't bother unzipping my pants. Instead, I take my claw and tear at the material. My cock bobs free and the tentacles unravel from the shaft, wanting Demi.

I'm brutal. I'm a killer.

But I never want to hurt her.

I dive between her legs to make sure she's wet, humming in approval when I see she's already glistening for me.

"You know I'm with you, don't you? You have to." I flick my forked tongue out to taste her, her sweetness bursting in all the corners of my mouth.

Just like the honeysuckles I remember.

"So fucking good, Demi. I can't wait. I need you. I need to erase their scent from you. You understand." I kiss my way up her body, licking every cut I see on her skin so it heals.

Her nipples react to me, beading into small peaks. I suck one into my mouth, then the other, my cock leaking precome from all my suckers.

"Do you feel how fucking wet you make me?" I take her limp hand, guiding it to my cock. "Do you feel that? So much precome and it's all for you. That's what you do to me."

My spine moves, realigning as the werewolf makes itself more known. The hair on my ears grows longer, my claws thicken, turning into talons, and my jaw widens as my fangs become more pronounced.

I want her to run so I can chase her.

Growling into her neck, I flatten my tongue, her fear subsiding even in this moment.

I taste it.

"You were made for me. You'll see. You'll love me one day, Demi." I inch inside her with a loud groan. "Fuuuck, you're so fucking wet." My voice darkens to such a low gravel, it's hard to understand. "No barrier to keep me from taking you now." I slide right in, pressing to the hilt, and get a glimpse of her licking her lips. "You love that, don't you? You love how I take over every aspect of your body."

She makes a sound of distress, wiggling her cunt on my cock.

"Shhh. Shhh. It's okay. You're..." I almost say she's safe with me, but that wouldn't be the truth would it? "You're very much in danger, Demi." I tease my fangs across her neck while grabbing her tits roughly, wanting to be as close as possible to her. Being inside her isn't enough, feeling her cunt grip me isn't enough. I need more.

My suckers remove themselves from her clit making her moan in disapproval. The other tentacle slips from her ass before I glide from her depths. Knee-walking up her body, I straddle her face.

Her eyes are closed. Blood has dried from where the wound dripped. I bend down, groaning as I lick the gash. Even dry, her blood is delicious. My cock weeps again, my suckers dripping with so much precome, it drops onto her stomach.

"Look at me. I'm in so much need. You're going to take care of me, aren't you?" I continue lapping her temple until all the blood is gone. "You take over me." I sound angry and frustrated with how I growl it out, but I'm far from it. "I just need you so much, my beloved." I press my forehead to hers. "You remind me of a time when happiness and heartache had separate homes in the chambers of my heart."

Her breath feathers across my chin. I straighten, my knees aching from how long I've been straddling her, but my cock is still secreting precome. I thrust my fingers between her lips, her warm wet mouth inviting and soft.

She must think she's having a dirty dream because she begins to suck my fingers, softly, not too hard since she doesn't know everything that's about to happen, is happening in real-time.

Pulling my fingers free, she whines.

Opening her mouth, I thrust my cock inside, my eyes drooping from how good she feels. "Fucking hell, Demi. You're trouble in every hole." I rock, careful not to choke her.

I almost want her to wake up. I want her to see all the ways I'll ruin and make her mine.

Her eyes turn to slits again. The part peeking through nothing but watery pools. Demi's long lashes curl, shadowing over her cheekbones.

"Do you see me, Demi? Do you really? Or are you so fucking high you can't tell who is fucking your mouth?" I ease in and out, staring at her face for any sign of recognition.

I feel her emotions. She might not see me, but she knows it's me.

"That's it. It's okay. Shh, drift back to sleep, mate. I'll take it from here."

Listening like the good girl she is, her eyes close, falling into her drugged stupor.

Increasing my pace, my sack slaps her chin. She chokes, gags, and spit begins to drip.

"You're making a mess," I moan, tilting my head back when her teeth glide along my suckers. My entire body shivers from how good that feels. "Yes, do that again. Do it. Let me feel that fucking mouth." I grab her delicate jaw, keeping her head steady and in place while I quicken my strokes. "Your lips look so good stretched out and wrapped around me. You can hardly take it."

She coughs again, more saliva dribbling down my cock.

"You're going to make me come. You and I both know my come isn't meant to slide down your fucking throat." I slip my cock free, spit clinging to it in strings from her lips. Falling to her side, I turn her, my chest to her back. Lining my cock up to her entrance, I thrust in hard, filling her with every wide, long inch.

"Oh, Creed," she sleepily mutters. "I knew they were wrong about you." My Sweet is talking in her sleep.

"They are absolutely right about me." I slam my hips against her, pressing my hand to her stomach. I feel it bulge with my size, my beasts wanting to breed her. "I'm the terrible man they warned you about. I'm fucking you right now, raw. I'm going to fill you with my knot, locking my come so deep inside you, your womb will have no fucking choice but to carry my child. You're mine. Your body is mine. Your soul. Your mind. Your fucking womb is mine, Demi." I bite into her neck at the same time my knot pops into place, locking inside her just like I promised. I drink long swallows of her blood, the vampire inside me at ease at last tasting my beloved's blood while plunging into her at the same time.

What does that mean? What does this mean?

Retracting my fangs, I continue the rough pace, my knot tugging at her entrance with every stroke. "Oh fuck. Demi." My wings shoot out behind me since I'm unable to spread them. "Fuck. Oh, God. Yes, that's it. Take it, Demi. Take my big cock. Take all my come. Drink it." I wrap my hand around her throat, the tips of my claws threatening to pierce her skin. My knot pulls, trying to pop free but can't. I growl from the sensation. She's so stretched. Another half an inch and she would tear. Her little body wouldn't be able to fit me.

The mattress squeaks, the headboard thumping against the wall with every abusive thrust I give, but she greedily takes.

I groan into her neck, licking the spot I bit, but watching it fade. I hate that. I don't understand why the one on the back of her thigh scarred but this one won't.

Using the frustration to my advantage, I pound harder, grunting as my suckers cause a tugging sensation along my shaft from suctioning to her walls.

Staring down at her, emotions vary on her face as her pussy clamps down on me as she comes. Wave after wave of pleasure hits her, and with every spasm, she soaks my cock.

The extra tentacle from the tip of my cock latches into her womb causing both of us to orgasm. She sucks me in while I overflow her with every drop that escapes me.

"That's it. Just like that. You're doing so good." I push her hair out of the way, nibbling on her ear. "Do you hear me? Can you feel me? If you can, I want you to know something, you are mine, Demi. No one else can have you." I moan again as another small orgasm escapes me, my sack still full with how much come I have to give my mate. "You belong to me. I own you. I've marked my territory. No other can have you. Hear me in your dream, slip my voice past the haze of drugs. Hear. Me. And if you must..." I taste the slender curve of her neck again "Hate me." Her skin gives like butter as my fangs slip into her vein to have one last drink.

Her hate will never overpower my want.

Nothing she can do or say will stop me from fucking her every single night.

No one can save her now.

CHAPTER FIFTEEN

DEMI

DEMI'S DINER

I wake with a start, gasping for breath.

I'm naked again.

There's a slight throb in my head from when—*Right*.

From when Daniel's friends almost raped me. I don't remember much after that. Everything is hazy. I don't know who brought me home or how I got here. The last thing I remember is... flying? I think. That's not possible.

And then Creed's eyes, but again, I had another sex-filled dream about him, so I wouldn't be surprised if I imagined him.

My entire body is heavy. It's as if I had a wild night out on the town and drank too much.

"Ow," I whine, swinging my legs over the edge of the bed.

Placing a hand on my head to try and stop the dizziness, I stand. I sway, the floor waving like the ocean. Nausea rolls through my stomach, and I bolt to the bathroom, barely making it to the toilet before I vomit.

"Gross," I mumble, wiping my mouth with toilet paper before flushing.

I debate on calling into work today. The thought of showing up to the diner after what happened, I'm not sure I can do it. I'm not sure if going to work will ever be the same.

There's so much I need to do. I need to file a report and talk to Jake. He'll view me differently or worse, he won't take me seriously. That doesn't sound like something Jake would do. He is always kind and compassionate, but this is different.

I push up from the toilet, sagging onto the vanity to help me stand up straight.

Flashes from last night surface. I turn around, noticing finger-shaped bruises on my ass just like I remember. They're all over my thighs too.

"What the hell is that?" I lift my butt cheek, turning my head over my shoulder as much as I can to get a better look. "Is that..." I trail off, spreading the skin with my fingers. "A bite mark?" I narrow my eyes, trying to remember if one of my attackers bit me, but I don't remember.

Brushing my fingers over it, I shudder, my skin pebbling from how sensitive it is.

"Oh, wow." I continue to touch it, caressing the scarred indentations. Lust travels to my clit. The more I touch the bite, the more aroused I become. This mark looks old, as if I've always had it. If my attacker bit me, the indentations from the teeth would be red and irritated. "What the hell is happening to me?"

I drop to the heels of my feet, my toes aching from standing on them so long to look in the mirror, noticing the dried blood in my hair.

Right! My head. I hit it on the car. I bend over the sink, part my hair, and carefully search for the wound or knot that should be on my scalp. I press lightly, but the only thing I feel is a dull ache.

Nothing is there.

Am I imagining everything? What if I didn't get attacked? I'm sore between my legs again. There's no other answer. I stare at the shower, debating if I want to rinse away the evidence, but the only evidence is a little blood in my hair and bruises on my ass. I don't even know if I was raped.

I dreamed again, that much I know, and I orgasmed a few times, so I could be sore because of that too.

Rubbing my eyes, I decide to throw on my long silk robe, and call Jake.

The screen lights up on my phone when I pick it up. I hold my breath seeing the unknown number.

Unknown number: "I took care of it, Honeysuckles."

My fingers fly over the touchscreen, the volume not turned down so the clicking from the keyboard is all I hear over my racing heart.

Me: "Took care of what? What happened last night? Who are you? Do I need to call the cops?"

Three dots appear as he types out his reply.

Unknown number: "You can if you want. Whatever makes you feel better. Have you turned on the news, Demi?"

I frown, running to my living room, nearly slipping on the slick hardwood floors.

Unknown number: "You should watch it. I did it for you. You needed me. You do need me."

I fumble with the TV remote as my hand quakes. "Come on!"

Unknown number: "You should calm down, Demi. Don't get angry or afraid when you haven't seen the news yet. Sit down on your couch."

The air is stolen from my lungs. Every muscle in my body freezes. Tears fill my eyes, blurring my vision before falling down my cheeks. Can this person see me?

Unknown number: "Don't cry, Honeysuckles. I'm not there to lick your tears away."

I toss my phone to the other end of the couch.

It vibrates once.

Twice.

Three.

Four.

Five times.

"Stop! Just stop! How are you doing this? Why?" I yell on a sob. Wondering how he can see me. "Where are you watching me from? Huh? How did you get into my house!"

Six.

Seven.

Eight.

My stomach turns again each time the phone rings. I stop when I'm about to toss my books from the shelf onto the floor.

I'm not going to ruin my house because of this person. I'm not going to freak out. That will not solve anything.

Walking around the hand-carved coffee table I got from Caden, I sit in the middle cushion of the sofa, and turn on the TV.

My phone buzzes constantly now while I flip to the news channel.

Channel Five News is the best station to receive the most up-to-date information.

"We are here in front of Demi's Diner, a staple in this small-town community where three murders occurred last night. Three bodies have been found. All of them are burned beyond recognition. Hearts have been ripped out of their chest and the medical examiner says in order to identify them, they will have to check dental records as the fingerprints have been burned off the victims. As far as we know, there are no witnesses to this atrocious act. The people are calling our new serial killer, "The Heart Ripper." Police are saying to be on alert. Stay in your homes. There is now an enforced curfew, and everyone must be in their homes before sunset. My name is Mindy Monroe, coming to you live from Channel Five News, where fast and accurate news comes to you. Back to you, Archie!"

I turn off the TV and Mindy's face disappears. She did a great job looking sad for the people who died, but I know she isn't. She's been cold and ruthless since high school. She would do anything to get the next story. It's all she ever cared about.

It also won't take long to figure out it was Daniel's friends who got killed.

I bite my lip, wondering how to take this information. Reaching for my phone, I have fifteen messages back-to-back.

Unknown number: "*You have to understand, I did it for you. You were in trouble.*"

Unknown number: "*No one is allowed to touch you but me.*"

Unknown number: "*They were attacking you. I couldn't allow that to happen.*"

Unknown number: "*Please, don't be mad at me.*"

Unknown number: "*I couldn't live if you were mad at me.*"

Unknown number: "*Demi?*"

Unknown number: "*Oh, good. You're watching the news.*"

Unknown number: "*I like your robe. It looks soft. You look fucking gorgeous in it. I want to watch you take it off so I can see it slip down to reveal your tits.*"

I gasp, covering my mouth with my hand from his crass words.

Unknown number: "*No one else is allowed to touch you.*"

Unknown number: "*Only I can touch you, Demi.*"

Unknown number: "*And only I can happen to you.*"

Unknown number: "*Only I can happen to you.*"

Unknown number: "*Only I can happen to you.*"

Unknown number: "*Only I can happen to you.*"

Unknown number: "*Only I can happen to you.*"

The repeated message hammers home how serious he is. It doesn't scare me like it should. I mean, I'm scared because this is a lot to handle. So many people have died, but no one has ever done anything so wrong for me.

Me: "*You killed them for me?*"

Unknown number: "*It was the only way.*"

Me: "*Why?*"

Unknown number: "*I don't think you know how serious I am when it comes to you. I'll kill anyone who gets in my way, Demi. I don't think you understand how important this is. If you run, I'll chase you. If you move, I'll follow you. You see, there isn't you without me. Not anymore. I am your shadow."*

The doorbell rings, preventing me from replying to him.

My phone vibrates.

Unknown number: "Answer it. It's Jake. He's come to question you about the bodies."

Me: "At this point, they probably think I'm a person of interest."

Unknown number: "If they dare put handcuffs on you, I'll stuff his badge down his throat. The only restraints you're allowed to wear on your wrists, are my hands."

The scar on the back of my thigh rubs against the couch. That partnered with what he just said makes my clit throb and my pussy begins to ache.

I'm wet.

What the hell is wrong with me?

I stand, keeping my robe pulled tight, and answer the door.

Jake is standing there with his partner Waylon.

"Sorry to bother you, Demi. May we come in?"

"Sure. Yes. Of course, Jake." I swing the door open to give them space, feeling a bit exposed with what I'm wearing. The purple silk robe doesn't leave much to the imagination, but knowing my stalker can see me, I don't want to change into something else.

I want to indulge him. Something about his statement, "Only I can happen to you" sounds so familiar, but with all the events that have occurred, I can't remember where I've heard it.

"Do you want anything? Coffee?" I ask them as they take a seat on the couch.

"No. I'm hoping this will be quick, Demi. You know the diner is closed today because of the bodies found in your parking lot?" Jake whips out his notepad, then clicks his pen to take notes.

His eyes are sad and full of regret. He doesn't want to be here questioning me.

"Yes, I know. Caden did send me a message, I haven't messaged back." I decide to sit in the recliner across from them. My robe parts, exposing my leg all the way up to my mid-thigh.

I don't fix it.

I hope he sees. Assuming, they are a he and not a she.

"He said he hadn't heard from you since last night, and your car is still at the diner," Waylon says, clearly implying I was up to no good. I don't like Waylon's method. He seems to be the kind of cop that believes everyone is guilty until proven innocent.

And while he might be partly correct because I won't be giving them all the information I have; I did not play any part in those three men getting murdered.

I narrow my eyes at Waylon. "I don't think I like how you're talking to me, Waylon. You're in my house, I want you to remember that. I've never done anything to scratch your interest. I don't even have a parking ticket." I slide my eyes to Jake. "I'll tell you everything because I know what you're going to ask. I left the diner and I was attacked by three men. I'm assuming they are Daniel's friends? I recognized their voices. They tackled me and ripped my clothes off. I hit my head on my car pretty hard. I was knocked out. I don't remember what happened after that. I'm sorry, Jake. I don't know how I got home, but whatever happened, someone saved me."

"Did those men rape you, Demi?" Jake's eyes fly from concerned to pissed, warmth blazing like a copper penny shining to a light.

"No." I look down, noticing my broken nails from where I clawed the ground last night. "Whoever saved me stopped them, but anything from that moment to me coming here, it's blank. Everything is a blur. The only marks I have are on my butt. I would prefer not to show that to male police officers," I state.

"Demi, we think this person is killing anyone who is connected to you. You are the center of this. You need to stay at home."

"I can't stay home. I have a business to run."

"And your employees? What will happen to them when they get too close to you?"

"Nothing has happened to Caden. Don't you think he would have been the first one to have been killed? Daniel assaulted me, Keith assaulted me, and his friends assaulted me, but the doctor isn't part of the pattern. I don't know how to explain that."

"We're still working on that too. We might think it's because he examined you. He saw you. You were exposed to him. We aren't definitive."

That makes sense to me. "I see," I say as it dawns on me.

"You are his target. The center of all his desires. Be careful. We have everything we need. We can go. If you have anything else, let me know, Demi."

They get up to leave, the couch groaning from their combined weight. I follow behind them, remembering I was supposed to have an officer outside my house.

"Jake, what happened to the officer I was supposed to have for protection?"

He hangs his head, placing his hat on slowly when he steps outside. "Officer Barnett was the only one who could watch over you. He's missing."

"Missing? Why haven't I heard about this? What happened?"

"We can't file a report for twenty-four hours. We don't know. He and the car just vanished. I'll keep you updated, okay? Just stay safe for me."

"I will. I promise."

They put their black aviators on in unison, giving me a two-finger salute before they climb into their cop car. Slamming my door so hard the entire house shakes, I sprint to my phone to check my messages.

There aren't any.

Suddenly, grumbles louder than I've ever heard before cause the ground under my feet to vibrate.

"What the hell?" I grab onto the counter when the vibrations become so violent, the vase above my sink falls from the edge, shattering at my feet. I jump away to avoid being cut.

The grumbles morph into the sound of a thousand people shrieking all at once.

The containers on the counter begin to tremble, the sides clinking together. The ear-piercing screams blare louder the closer they get. The wails are long and painful, even mournful which tugs at my heart.

And then it's gone.

I rub my temples, exhaustion settling in my bones as the weight of everything falls on my shoulders.

"Demi Hawthorne?"

I scream grabbing the nearest vase and throwing it at my intruder. It shatters.

He doesn't move.

Another person— thing— man— ghost? No, a man, ghosts don't exist. I'm hallucinating. Yes, that's it. From the wounds I sustained from the attack.

This is all a figment of my imagination.

I run into the kitchen to grab a knife from the block, swinging it in front of me. "I've had a hell of a few days and I'm not afraid to start stabbing bitches, I swear to fucking God. Leave me alone!"

Another intruder emerges, then another, until I feel like I'm surrounded.

"She's feisty," one of them announces with a smirk, scratching his chin as he looks me over. "Cute too."

They look human, but not. They are gigantic. I bet if I stabbed them, it would be more like a paper cut.

"Enough, Famine," the big guy in front says. "Demi, we aren't here to hurt you. We are here to help you. We've been alerted of the attacks. We are Hell's Harvesters. I'm Abaddon, the leader of my crew, that's War, Famine, Death, and Conquest." He points to each person.

"Hey."

"Nice knife, but I have a bigger one." The one he calls Death whips out a giant fucking scythe. "I suggest you put yours away before you hurt yourself."

"Fuck you," I sneer.

"Okay, this is getting out of hand."

"Out of hand?" I screech. "You break into my house—"

"—We didn't break anything. We came through the door."

"I locked the door," I mock in a childlike tone to the one called War. I keep the knife in front of me, backing away until I'm at the door. I jiggle the handle. "It's locked. And what are these names? Are you in a motorcycle club? Are those your road names?" I question, sounding more confused.

"Sure, let's call it that. Demi, we were alerted of a paranormal creature here. We know everyone and everything we create, but don't recognize him. Who is he? Where is your mate?"

Confused, a laugh bubbles up my throat until it obnoxiously bursts from me. "I'm sorry, what? Paranormal? Mate? What the hell are you talking about? Are you talking about a book?"

He tilts his head and steps forward, sniffing the air. "You reek of him. You've mated already. You're pregnant with his child. I smell it on you. It's okay to tell us about him. We won't hurt him, but we need to understand why he is killing humans."

My mouth parts in shock. I wave my hand at him. "I don't know what insanity you're spewing, but I'm not buying it. I'm not mated. I'm not pregnant. Fun fact, I'm a virgin. I've never had sex. So I have no idea who you're talking about."

"This is bad," Abaddon says. "The murders, he has done them for you. He thinks he is protecting you, but he's also nearly feral. He won't allow anyone near you. The fact that we are here will be trouble. He'll go off the deep end."

"Listen, I'm sure you're nice guys." My shoulders sag with defeat. "But I'm really tired." My eyes begin to well with tears. "I have had a hell of a night. People are dying around me. I— Can you please go?"

"No. It's time for brutal honesty. You want to know how we got into the house?"

"This will be good," says the man who calls himself Famine, a manic glint in his eyes as he rubs his hands together.

Abaddon's solid body disintegrates into a sheer black fog. He steps through the wall before walking back, taking his main form.

"We are Hell's Harvesters. These men are the four horsemen. Consider us the paranormal police." He steps forward again, getting closer to me and I try to sink into the door. "The sounds you heard as we pulled up? Those are the souls that keep our bikes running. The screams of the ones who have been damned."

"That's what you want to do to... my mate?" Am I really believing this?

"I don't know," he says honestly. "He has killed a lot of humans, which usually we can turn a blind eye to, but he has mated you without your consent. You are pregnant. Paranormal beings can smell that. Right now, you're afraid, confused, yet relieved."

I nod frantically. "A trophy for the demon." I finger-gun him with a cackle before bursting into tears. I'm not sure I can believe this.

"Who do you think your mate is?" he urges, wanting me to speak through my panic.

"I— I don't know. I don't know who you're talking about. It's only been a few days."

"That's all it takes for our kind. A mate isn't like a husband or wife. It's more than that. You're bound together, your souls complete one another. You feel safe around him, loved, you miss him when he isn't around. If he dies, you die. Your beings are intertwined and now you're carrying his child, which isn't a surprise since that's our goal when we finally meet our mates."

"Fuck yeah, I'm never going to stop breeding my mate when I find her or him." Death shrugs, his scythe moving with his shoulder. "I don't care about the label. Just the person."

"That's... good?" I look at Abaddon for help.

He rolls his eyes. "Demi, I need you to think. You know who it is. You've been with them. You feel... like you two are the only ones who exist."

"How did you find me?" I whisper, sitting on my couch in a daze.

"Smelled you at the diner when we checked out the scene. We can't seem to smell him. His scent is everywhere as if he is multiple beasts but that's impossible. We followed your scent trail here."

I place a hand protectively over my stomach, suddenly feeling warmth burst into my heart. "How can I be pregnant and not remember having sex?"

"He must have an ability, but I've never seen a creature mystify their mate," Famine states.

"He could have drugged her if he felt like there was no other way."

"Drugged me?" I echo the question, knowing that has to be the truth because the last few days have been so odd. "I think that's it," I say under my breath.

"We will deal with that later, but Demi," Abaddon stands in front of me, squatting down. "I need to know who it is so we can help him."

"If you do anything to him, I'll die. You can't kill him."

"We were going to until we smelled you and the child. We can't. So all of my fun is taken away," Death gripes, polishing his scythe.

Abaddon reaches out to touch me, and I flinch away, not wanting one of his fingers on me.

"You will find that you won't want the touch of another man except your mate."

I sit there on the couch and think, wondering who could do this unforgivable act to me. To impregnate me without me knowing, to take my virginity without me being coherent for it. I can't stop crying because this situation is crazy. It can't be real, but what other option is there?

Am I really going to play into this fantasy?

"He's watching," I admit in a barely audible whisper. "He's been texting me from an unknown number. There are cameras in the house. He told me today." Well, he didn't outright tell me. It wasn't hard to put two and two together. "Is that normal for a... mate to do?" I'm unsure of the word mate, but even my soul knows it is right.

"No, which is why we need to find him before any more people have to die."

"Some of those people deserved it," I grumble, gasping in horror from my admission. "I'm going to hell, aren't I?"

"Nah, you're fine. Plus, it isn't as bad as people think." Conquest, I think his name is, sits next to me. "Demi, we can't waste any more time. Who is he?"

The only man who comes to mind has suns for eyes and the skin of a storm cloud. Everything from the last few nights flies through my mind. All the dreams I thought I had were him whispering to me.

Only I can happen to you.

He protected me from everyone but himself.

"His name is Creed. That's all I know. I feel..." I exhale. It's long and heavy as I try to find the words to explain it.

"Fated," Abaddon completes my sentence for me.

"Yeah, exactly. Like I'm meant to be with him. When I'm not, I miss him so much I feel like I'm going to die. It's dramatic but true."

"That's what a fated mate means." Abaddon flashes a sharp, toothy smile that leaves me uneasy.

"What do we do now?" I ask.

"We find him."

"He might come here. We just have to wait."

"It's why we are going to leave and go to the diner. We cleared everyone out. We won't be bothered."

"Did you kill them?" My voice is unsteady as I stare at the men.

"Fuck no. We made them think nothing happened. To forget and go home." Famine picks me up, flashing me his fangs. "Time to go to the diner, Cutie."

I'm out of my house in the next blink, in nothing but my robe, with the screams of their bikes ringing in my ears. The souls are wailing to get free, and it almost breaks my heart until I think about the horrible things they had to have done to become screaming fuel for demons.

If I reject Creed, what will happen to his soul?

Would he scream for freedom? Would he scream for me?

CHAPTER SIXTEEN

CREED

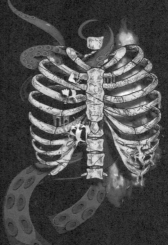

Who the fuck are the men at her house? Who the hell do they think they are interrogating my mate, entering my den, and spreading their scents through my home?

The familiar warmth spreads through my chest, rage adding fuel to the fire boiling inside me. My mouth opens on a roar, the flames engulfing the TV. The screen begins to melt and the only way I have to see her when I'm not there fades away from me as the picture finally fades.

I grab the TV, my claws sinking into the melted frame of the television and with a carnal roar releasing deep within my chest, I rip the TV from the wall and throw it out the window.

Glass shards clink across the floor, the cool breeze whistling as it enters the cabin. My chest rises and falls with frantic pulses. My fists clench at my sides, wondering where they are taking Demi.

They are kidnapping her.

"She's mine!" I snarl, another stream of fire billowing from my mouth which sets the curtains on fire.

I watch in fascination, the bright orange fire flickering happily as it eats the walls. The end table by the recliner catches fire next, crackling as it feeds. I stand to watch the destruction caused by me, letting the only home I've known since becoming this beast fall to ash.

This cabin is no longer needed because Demi is my home. I can live in the sky or the woods, watching her from afar to protect her, loving her at night the only way I know how.

The fire grows, spreading across my arms, trying to possess me too. The wicked heat does nothing since my dragon protects me from the catastrophe fire brings.

Growling as I roll my neck to prepare for war, I walk out of the house in preparation to find Demi.

Just as I step outside, the left beam supporting the roof and porch groans before falling over. The roof caves in, crashing through the half-ablaze porch. It collapses just as my feet hit solid ground.

I turn, watching the cabin become ash, the tips of the flames reaching for the sky. The small house was never permanent. It was always supposed to be temporary. I was never going to stay here forever. I was going to use this town to feed the monster I am, but Demi surprised me.

Temporary turned to always.

And no one will take that away from me.

Demi is the only person in existence I live for. If it weren't for her presence, I would have killed myself already for what I've become. I don't know what I am, and I don't know the correct way to be.

Demi makes that feeling easier to handle.

Getting out my phone from my pocket, I text her, wanting to avoid calling so she doesn't hear my voice.

Me: "Who took you? Who did this to you? Are you hurt?"

The dots appear as she types out her response and even seeing them on the screen has my wings bursting out of my back, preparing for flight.

Her: "No more than you have hurt her. We're at the diner if you ever want to see her again."

I reread the message over and over again, snarling at the man who dared put his hands on my mate. His scent will be all over her. I squeeze the phone in my palm, crushing it until the screen breaks. The phone is in pieces by the time I release the grip on it.

Dropping the dust of the only way I had to communicate with Demi, I crouch, a menacing grumble building in my throat. I leap into the air, uncaring if anyone can see me. My main focus is Demi.

Maybe whoever took her will see me and run away if they care about their life. Then, I'll just have to convince Demi she didn't truly see me for what I am. It was her head trauma from the other night playing tricks on her.

I'll be able to fix this.

I can repair what's been broken.

My wings cut through the clouds, flapping harder and faster than they ever have to get to the diner. There's a lump in my throat thinking about something happening to Demi. I reach for our bond, searching for her emotions.

There are so many, they cause my wings to falter from how strong her feelings sink into me. She's scared, confused, and hurt, but not physically. I lose control of my flight, tumbling through the sky. I try to regain my position, but my wings can't seem to work in tandem while I pull on the thread binding me to my mate.

My Beloved.

My everything.

The ground is coming fast. My wings twist around my body, the talons along the edges hooking together from the havoc. Reaching for them, I grip the sharp hooks that protrude from the leathery flesh, twisting and tugging in hopes they will free themselves.

The ground is closer. The grass in the field between the woods and Demi's Diner won't be enough to cushion my fall. The velocity is too much. When I hit the ground, it will probably kill me.

Maybe that's what is best.

If I die, Demi can be free.

I shut my eyes, thinking about her scent, and I'm taken back to running in a field, the sun warming my skin, a moment in time when I was truly human. Honeysuckles are everywhere. Happiness blooms from the brief memory, but then I open my eyes to see the ground about to take my life.

I'll never experience honeysuckles again if I leave Demi.

She's the bloom in the darkest part of my life and I'm the cold, creeping in to wither what's good in her.

But I bet what's left would still be so satisfying.

I spread my wings with so much force, the talons that were stuck together rip from the bone. The pain is nothing compared to a life without Demi.

Inches from the ground, I soar, my wings finally catching traction. Slowly, I lower myself into the tall, swaying grass. I force my dragon to tuck my wings away, my back rippling as they sink and mend into my flesh. Then, start the journey of trudging through the field. The grass tickles the tips of my fingers, the blades slick from an early morning rain.

I stop just before I set foot in the parking lot, the pavement is pitch black, a pool of ink as a pathway to hell. There's still yellow tape surrounding the diner, abandoned by the police. I pluck it with my claw, tearing it in half. The useless ribbons float to the ground to allow me in.

Do cops really believe that a little tape will keep people out?

I step forward, my boot slowly hitting the pavement from heel to toe. My beasts are on alert, perking up inside me and snarling. To the right, there are five motorcycles parked, carved from bone with skulls all over.

A wicked air haunts me. The threat of power is overwhelming. All of my senses are on overdrive. The people who own these bikes aren't human. I can smell it. Humans have a different aroma, plain and light. All but Demi. Demi's blood is sweet, decadent, with a hint of florals, rain, and sunshine.

These people are dark. Smoke, heat, ash, and violence fill my senses. Bitter and cold.

I open the door to the diner, that damn bell jingling above me.

"So good of you to join us, Creed. You've been leaving a mess for us to clean up."

I step further into the dining room, following the sound of the sardonic voice. "Where is Demi? I want her. I want my mate!" I push the podium over, the wood splintering once it hits the ground.

"She's safe."

Smoke becomes a fog in the room, pouring from my nostrils and mouth with the threat of fire. I can't do that. This diner means too much to Demi. Burning it down would be unforgivable.

"Interesting. You don't smell like any creature I've come across." The voice comes from all directions. I can't tell where he is.

I study the main dining room floor, looking for a figure, but all the booths are empty.

"Give me my fucking mate!" I roar, slamming my fist on a table, breaking it clean in half, and instantly regretting it.

"Tsk. Tsk. Demi won't appreciate you destroying her diner." The voice becomes closer, but the shadows give away no answers to where he is.

"Give me my beloved and I'll think about not killing you."

"Beloved? Interesting. You aren't a vampire. I know one of the most powerful vampires in existence and you do not smell like his kind."

I swipe my hand in the air as I spin around, hoping my talons would gauge him. My growl is menacing, fire licking my lips from the lack of control I have.

A chain of some sort wraps around my neck as he pulls, my back hitting his chest. My skin begins to burn. A howl filled with pain sends me to my knees. This is unlike anything I've ever felt. I claw at the chains, but my fingertips begin to blacken. Pieces of skin drift through the air, turning into ash.

"You act like a vampire, burn like a vampire, but you're so much more than that, aren't you?" He tugs the chain harder. "Silver is a bitch, isn't it?"

The stench of my own flesh burning weakens me and I fall to my knees.

"No! No, you said you wouldn't hurt him. You promised!" Demi's voice comes from the back of the room, and I try to get free of the chain around my neck, but all I do is fall to my burnt hands.

"Demi," I rasp, trying to crawl to her, doing everything in my willpower to be near her, to be engulfed in her presence.

That will give me strength.

"Oh my God!" She slides to her knees in front of me, the silk robe parting at the leg to show her smooth flesh.

I snarl, lunging forward. The chain digs into my neck, then he wraps it around like a collar, keeping me still.

I'm close enough to cover her exposed leg, situating the robe so her body is hidden. "Mine." My voice is hoarse from the agony the silver is causing. My skin sizzles and smoke rises from the wound as I'm cooked.

Demi's finger slides under my chin and forces me to lift my head. I try to fight her. I don't want her to see me. I've done a good job so far at staying hidden. She has only seen parts of me, parts that are questionable, but I'd rather have her question what she sees than finally have answers.

"Look at her," the creature behind me orders, yanking my head. "Look at your mate and tell her all of the horrible things you have done. She deserves to know."

"Look at me, Creed," Demi begs, her soft voice breaking with emotion. "Please. I need to understand. I've dreamed about seeing you."

I keep my head down, staring at the black and white checkered floor. There's a lump in my throat. Sweat beads from my forehead, stinging my eyes, and the only sound is the hissing from the silver kissing my body.

"Take the silver chain off him! You said you wouldn't hurt him. Why is it doing this?" Demi tugs on the chain, but it only tightens, constricting my airflow.

I gasp.

"Oh God, I'm sorry. I'm sorry. I'm only trying to help."

"He isn't human, Demi," the creature behind me explains. "That's why silver is doing this to him. Vampires are allergic to silver. But he is more than that. Never in my eternal years have I ever scented anything like him."

"What are you talking about?" Demi cries, still trying to get the chains off me. "You've made a mistake. Please let him go!"

"You only feel like this because he is your mate. Seeing him in danger and in pain hurts you."

"I don't understand," she sobs. "I don't understand what is going on. I don't care. Please, please, let go of the chains. You're going to kill him!" The scream is rough with her tears, the soul-wrenching kind that digs its claws into your soul, reminding you of your humanity.

My eyes begin to burn with tears, realizing this is where I end. I'll finally get to die, but it will be without the love of my mate. That kind of agony would make the coldest, most heartless beast mourn what they will never have.

The bell above the door jingles.

"What the fuck is going on?"

Caden.

"You didn't lock the fucking door?" the creature controlling me snarls at his men.

"I thought it was," one of his men replies in a shameful grumble.

"Demi, what the hell? Get away from him!" He sprints to Demi, grabbing her by the arm, and all I see is red.

Nothing else matters.

Only Demi.

No one is to touch her.

I lurch forward, talons out, fangs bared, and a vicious growl that would send a regular man to his knees to plead for his life.

"Woah. Holy shit, he is strong." I don't know who these beasts are, but the one controlling me is much stronger than I am. I can't get free.

But I can make it hell on him.

My wings burst free to try and fly to get to Demi instead, but the chains wrap around the high arches of them to subdue me. I'm forced to my knees and the silver eats away at the leather-like hide.

Demi wails, her terror sending her tumbling backward when she sees me, my face, what I am, for the first time.

Caden's arms tighten around her, holding her steady.

It should be me.

I should be the one holding her.

Like a beast trapped in a cage, I roar, shaking the windows from the force. I fight with all I have, pulling on the chain, letting it dig deeper into my neck to get to her.

It can decapitate me for all I care. As long as I get to her first. I'll give my life if it means happiness one last time.

And I smell it.

The putrid scent of her fear. For the first time since meeting her, I've only ever scented kindness, curiosity, and a hint of lust when she was around me. When I'd sneak into her house at night, fuck and knot her, breeding her for my own, claiming her to be mine for all eternity, desire and love poured from her in waves so strong, I drowned myself inside her until we couldn't breathe.

The urge to get to her fades, the rage leaving my body. My face contorts from fury to sadness. My breathing is loud with every exhale, a roughness attached to it.

Again, I collapse to my knees. "Do what you want to me," I say, turning my head away so no one can see the emotions swimming into my eyes.

"Let go of me, Caden. I'm fine. Let me go!" Demi yanks herself from his hold, her cheeks wet with tears spilling from her eyes like waterfalls. "Why? Why didn't you just tell me the truth?"

"Look at me," I whisper, locking gazes with my mate, her blue eyes reminding me of heaven all over again. "I can't even look at myself in the mirror," I spit, trying to prove how much I hate myself. "I'm a monster. Truly. The human side of me barely exists and when it does, my beasts silence it."

"Beasts?" she questions, confused. "More than one?"

"More than one," I echo her words.

Blood begins to drip down my neck and arms, creating a small pool below my fingertips. It's warm, silky, and the liquid smells of her from how much I've fed.

"Where are you from?"

I yank on the chain in retaliation. "I'm not telling you shit until you tell me who you are."

He hums. "I'm Abaddon. The rest are War, Famine, Conquest, and Death. The Four Horsemen. Together we are Hell's Harvesters. Think of us as paranormal law enforcement. You've left a trail of dead bodies, Creed."

"I couldn't control myself," I explain. "I am new to this. All I knew was anyone who got in my way of Demi, hurt her, touched her, disrespected her, I wanted to kill. So I did," I sneer. "And I'm not fucking sorry for getting rid of those worthless men. They didn't deserve to be in her presence."

"New to this?" Abaddon gives control of the chains to one of his men. "Explain yourself." He stands in front of me so I can't see Demi, blocking the only view I have of her.

I take a deep breath, but it sounds more like a wheeze with how deep the chains are. "I was kidnapped a few months ago. I was human. I was walking home from a bar one night and taken to some institute."

"Shallow Cove Institute is nearby," Caden adds more context.

I give a slow, exhausted nod. "Yes. I don't know what the fuck they were trying to do there, but they succeeded

with me. I'm this because of them!" I yell, tugging on
the chains again. "I'm a dragon, werewolf, snake, kraken,
and vampire. I've transformed into this physical shape
permanently. There's nothing I can do about it. I was
tested on, abused, beaten, and starved to give them their
results. I lived." I lift my head and stare Abaddon right in
the eyes. "I survived!" I shout, my wings trying to stretch
out again.

"How many of you are there? Are there more like you?"
he asks in a hurry, placing one knee on the ground. Even
then, the man is massive.

"Yes, but I don't know how many. I killed all the scientists when I broke free. I released all the people trapped
to save them. In my file, before I destroyed it, I read
they injected me with different types of DNA. When they
tortured me, they wanted to know how I'd respond. In
the end, any trauma caused the animal inside me to come
forward."

Sobs sound from behind Abaddon.

I know it isn't Caden crying for me.

"That explains why you can't control yourself. You have
no knowledge of what it means to be us." He steps to the
side and points to Demi. "Who is she to you?"

"My Beloved. My mate. My reason to live." I chance a
look at her, and Demi quickly looks away.

"Why?"

"I don't know," I say with frustration. "If I knew, I
wouldn't be kneeling in the fucking diner with a silver
chain slowly killing me!"

"Because she's the other half of your soul. You're bound.
And from what I can tell, already mated, which raises
a few concerns." He sighs, knowing my time with Demi
is over. "Also," he scratches his chin. "Beloveds are what
vampires call their fated mates. The one person in the
world you're meant to be with. It's one of the reasons
why you thought of the word 'beloved.' Fierce loyalty and
possession come with all mates. You didn't know that,

and you acted on instinct because no one taught you otherwise. It doesn't make what you did okay."

"Why Daniel?" Demi asks.

"Demi, I don't think that's a good idea," Caden speaks his opinion.

I snarl. "What you think doesn't matter. You're a liar too. I might not be able to figure out what you are, but you aren't fully human either. Don't be self-righteous when in some way, you're just as bad as I am." I smirk, spitting blood onto the ground as it works its way up my throat from the injuries I'm sustaining.

"What?" Demi hisses, pushing Caden away.

"I'm not him," he points to me. "I'm not a psycho going around killing people for you. Paranormals don't tell the truth about what we are to humans. It's the number one rule. It's not just to protect me, but every other paranormal."

"What are you?" Demi asks. "Because I don't care what you are. I care about the truth."

I wonder if that statement applies to me.

"I'm a storm kitsune. I can manipulate water and other liquids. It's why it's been raining so much lately. It's how my creature feeds. I need the power to remain alive."

"Wow," Abaddon exclaims. "A kitsune? Those are rare."

"My kind are doing fine. We stay quiet and our numbers have been building up again."

Demi takes a step away from him, a distraught expression on her face as tears fall, then turns to me. "Why did you kill all those people?" she asks me, sitting on her knees again in front of me.

I can see in some way I've broken something inside her, something I might not be able to fix.

"I killed Keith for putting his hands on you and telling you to bend over for him."

"I killed Daniel because he touched you. He assaulted you."

"Good riddance," Caden grumbles under his breath. "I hated him."

"I killed his friends because they were going to rape you. They attacked you. I won't apologize for that."

"What!" Caden yells, stepping forward to go to Demi, and a growl leaves me before I can stop myself.

Demi inhales on a sharp breath from the sound.

"When were you going to tell me this? What the fuck happened?"

"Not now, Caden." She holds up her hand to stop him, then gives her attention back to me. "The police officer that was supposed to be protecting me?"

I lift a shoulder, uncaring. "I killed him and dumped his body in the nearest river. He was masturbating in his car to a picture of you in the paper."

"And my doctor?"

My lip curls to my fangs. "He was taking you from me. He put you on pills so you wouldn't have my children. He had to be stopped."

Before I can say another word, a slap sounds. My cheek burns.

Demi hit me.

"How dare you," she seethes. "How dare you take that option away from me. That wasn't your decision to make. And how? How am I pregnant with your baby?"

"You're pregnant? How do you know? Really?" I'm so happy, a tear drips down my cheek. I try to knee-walk to her, but the chains hold me back.

"They can smell the pregnancy on me," she explains, but it isn't happiness reflecting in her eyes.

It's betrayal.

And it smells even worse than her fear.

"How?" she asks, folding her hands over her stomach. "How am I pregnant? I had never had sex before, Creed."

I inhale, finally scenting the pregnancy since it has been pointed out. No wonder her blood tasted sweet the last time I had it.

"You didn't have the right to take that away from me. My first time should be remembered. Not... a blur. It shouldn't feel like a dream. What did you do?"

I wince from how sharp her words are as they are spoken to me through her clenched jaw.

"I installed cameras in your house so I could learn your routine. I wanted to keep an eye on you. I wanted to protect you from everyone, but I knew I wouldn't be able to protect you from me. My want, my need for you, was stronger than anything I've ever felt in my life. I didn't know how to tame it. I still don't." The last sentence comes out as a growl as my beasts begin to surface. "Even now, smelling the pregnancy on you, I can hardly contain myself. I wouldn't if it wasn't for this silver." I tug my neck to the side, the silver embedding itself deeper.

My vampire and werewolf aren't happy.

"I saw you drank tea," I start. "Every night. So I laced it with Ambien because I knew it was the only way I'd have you. That you'd never love someone like me. So I'd break into your house, crawl into bed with you, and fuck you, claiming you as my mate. And you came all over my cock. You loved it. You got so wet for me. You'd moan my name. You knew," I drawl, clicking my tongue before chuckling. "You knew what was happening subconsciously. You can't deny it. All those dreams you thought you had? They were real. Not once did you tell me to stop. I think you liked it. Being taken like that. I think you're more okay with it than you realize and that's what scares you." Somehow, I end up inches away from her face as I lean in. My skin hisses the more I press against the chains. "And when I found those pills stopping me from breeding you?" I roll my head over my shoulders. "I fucking lost my mind and hunted down your doctor to make sure he'd never be a problem for me again."

A tear drips down her cheek, but I won't let her lie to me. I smell her lust too. She's conflicted.

I'm close enough to flick my forked tongue out, licking the teardrop from her angelic face. The saltiness tastes nearly as good as her blood and I shut my eyes to relish the taste.

"You even taste delicious when you hate me."

"You sick fuck," Caden shouts, rearing his arm back and punching me in the face. "You deserve whatever punishment the Hell's Harvesters give you. I hope you rot in hell, mother fucker."

"What we do depends on Demi," Abaddon explains. "If they weren't mated, then it wouldn't be in question."

"Let go of the chain, please," Demi says, her voice so quiet, I hardly hear it.

"What? Demi, no. Did you just hear everything he did to you? Don't forget about Keith, your neighbor."

I roll my eyes, blowing smoke out of my nose. "He deserved it. I'm not sorry about that."

"Just drop the fucking chain! Stop hurting him! God-damn it, just stop!" She yells with so much force, her arm drapes across her stomach, and her words break into a sob. "Just fucking stop. He's still my mate. He's the other half of my soul. You don't think it tears me apart inside seeing him like this regardless of what he has done? Do you think that is easy for me?" Demi continues, barely able to breathe while emotion chokes her. She pounds her chest with her hand. "Do you think any of this is easy for me?" Demi's eyes narrow at me, turning to evil slits. "Do you promise not to cause any issues if they let you go? You'll stay where you are. You won't come near me either."

Hearing how she doesn't want me near her kills me, but whatever my mate wants. Even if it means I stay away from her.

"I swear. On my life."

"You can't trust him, Demi. He's raped you. He's drugged you."

I snarl at the word rape. I don't consider it that severe. She loved it. She moaned and came. She whispered my name.

"You don't know what it was like. You don't understand. I remember some of it. I remember the blurs and I re-member how he felt inside me. I remember how I felt. It's confusing enough. I don't need you whispering in my ear!" she yells at her best friend. "This is for me to figure out. Not you."

"Let him go," Abaddon orders, giving a nod to his men. "Let's trust fate."

The chains vanish in the next instant and I'm able to suck in a much needed gulp of air. My skin stitches itself back together, the wound closing almost instantly, but I still feel weak, like I've been worked over with a bag of rocks.

The heavy rise and fall of my shoulders are in sync with my heavy gasps. I don't move just like I promised. I stay where I am, but the effort has me trembling, keeping all my beasts in check.

All I want to do is whisk her away, fly high in the sky, and claim her all over again. Her pregnancy is all I smell now, and even under the circumstances, my cock rises for her.

"Really? Still?" Abaddon smirks.

"I can't help it. It's my reaction to my mate." I grip my cock, squeezing it for Demi so she can see what she does to me. "No one else makes me feel this way. No one has even come close."

She sits down in front of me, her eyes swollen and red from crying. "Remember, don't touch me." Her sky-blue eyes are brighter because of it, nearly glowing.

"Do you know what love is?" she asks me. "Can you feel it or is this possession as simple as that?"

I dig my talons into my thighs to stop myself from reaching out. "I love you. I've loved you from the moment I laid eyes on you. I knew I'd do anything to have you."

"How can you tell it's love you feel, Creed?" Her fingertips reach for my face, tracing my hairy jaw, then up to my pointed ears, brushing the hair on the tips. She explores my face. "Do you know for a fact that you're capable of love? Here?" Her hand presses over my heart. "On the inside."

That question makes me explode. Angry, yes, but I'm hurt. This is what heartbreak feels like.

She thinks I'm just a monster.

I cry. My tears break me, and I yell, pressing her hand harder against my beating heart. "I love you with all my insides. All of them! Do you know how much that is? Five beasts and a human. Your love possesses me. I'm the only one possessed." I let out a breath, "With all my fucking insides," I growl before letting her go. "All of them," the statement a defeated hush.

"I need time. Can you give me that? I'm angry at you." She holds a hand over her mouth to hold in another cry. "I'm angry, but I don't want to be. There are too many things that you did that are not okay. But I still can't write you off. I can't let the Hell's Harvesters take you away. You're still my mate and I'm pregnant with your child, but I need time. I need you to give me some normalcy."

"I can do that," I say without hesitation, a sliver of hope wiggling its way into my heart.

"We will teach him everything he needs to know about his beasts," Abaddon explains, placing a hand on my shoulder. "He'll need it. Especially if there are others like him. We'll have to find, teach, and save them if they ever want a future with their mates."

"How long?" Demi questions, stroking her finger down my nose, then across my cheek.

I lean into her simple touch; another drop slowly escapes my left eye until it hits her finger.

I don't want to go.

"A few weeks, maybe."

"Then I'll see you in a few weeks, Creed."

She kisses my cheek. The softness of her lips brushing my skin makes me close my eyes, doing my best to remember this moment to add to the few memories I have of happiness.

And then she's gone.

The bell jingles causing me to snap my eyes open to see the door close.

I try to run after her, but Abaddon snags me, and the echoes of screams follow into the darkness he leads me to.

CHAPTER SEVENTEEN

CREED

Being away from Demi is torture. It's been two days, and all I want to do is go back to her, watch her sleep, touch her skin, mark her, bite her, and consume her. It wasn't supposed to be like this. I wasn't supposed to get caught and left wanting her.

"This isn't how it's supposed to be!" I roar, slamming my entire body against Famine while he tries to teach me about fucking control.

Fuck control.

Famine flies through the air, landing a few yards away on his feet, crouched.

Showing his true form.

A winged demon beast. It's the only way I know how to explain him. A third of his face is stitched together as if some part of him tried to be human.

He snarls at me, flashing his fangs. "You have no control. You need it. You need to be able to control yourself with Demi. What you did to her is not okay. You drugged her. You raped her. You forced her to get pregnant. That isn't okay."

"I didn't rape her. She felt me there. She knew I was there. She knew it was me taking her." My wings spread from my body as I lose patience with Famine. "You don't understand."

"I understand plenty. You have no self-control."
Famine's wings are massive, bigger, and wider than my
own.

"Enough, Famine," Abaddon bellows, his voice echoing
in the empty space of purgatory. "You're goading him on
purpose. He has five beasts to wrestle. All dominant. All
alpha. You can't measure his self-control to yours. That
isn't fair. He is mostly made up of primal instincts. We are
only here to help him understand them, not belittle him.
Do I make myself clear?"

Famine straightens, tucking his wings away. "I was only
testing him. His control has gotten better. Yesterday, he
tried to burn me alive. This time, no fire escaped him. A
little smoke, but hey, what else is there to expect from a
dragon." Famine shrugs, shooting me a wink.

I snarl, not liking his carefree attitude. "Asshole."

"Demon." He lifts his arms in another shrug to correct
me. "How could you expect anything less?"

"Okay." Abaddon sighs, pinching the bridge of his nose.
"Enough with that. He needs to learn about each of his
beasts. Training him in control will mean nothing if he
doesn't understand what's inside him. Today, we will start
with your werewolf. Can you shift into more or is this
your form?" he asks.

I glance around, hating the view I have. Everything is
dead and grey, random creatures flutter around us, and
I'm getting tired of it. I want Demi. I want to stare at her
beautiful face, not be stuck in purgatory.

I remain quiet. Not wanting to answer him.

"If you ever want to go home to Demi again instead
of being locked in purgatory for the crimes you've com-
mitted, I suggest you start getting with the program!" he
yells, his voice booming with his demonic nature.

The ground shakes under my feet, cracks vein across
the ground, and lightning strikes right at my feet.

I think of Demi, the way my fingers miss grabbing hold
of her body. I won't ever have that again if I don't coop-
erate.

"Sometimes I get bigger, but I don't become a full beast. I'm this for the most part." I wave my hand up and down. "Satisfied," I glower, wanting nothing more to do with this.

"I can't imagine how hard this is for you. Dragons and Werewolves are dominant alone but together? You must feel them battling inside you."

I shake my head. "No. It isn't like that." My fists clench with annoyance. "I'm the alpha. The beasts are mine. I only feel... constant primal urges."

He nods, leaning against a tree and crossing his arms. "Werewolves are violent when it comes to mating. Very violent. They can actually end up killing their mate if they aren't careful. They hunt their mates under the full moon and knot them—"

"—I know all about knotting." I flash my fangs in a wicked smile. "I've knotted Demi."

"Obviously, she's pregnant."

I grumble in delight, my cock thickening at the thought. "She is. She's mine."

"What if I said she was mine?" Abaddon dares to suggest.

I blur until I stand in front of him, releasing my fire to burn him where he stands.

His hand wraps around my throat so tight, he cuts off the wild blaze spewing from my throat. His skin turns from smoldering coals to his regular stitched flesh again.

"I am a demon of hell. Do you really think your fire could hurt me? You can't hurt me, but I can hurt you. I will separate the monsters inside you and kill you." He shoves me away. "There is always someone out there stronger than you, Creed. You better keep that in mind."

I rub my throat. I don't say yes or no, but I'm starting to realize how serious this situation is.

"Your instincts are unlike anything I've ever seen. Fated mates kill for one another, it's normal. Possessive qualities are normal but because you have so many beasts inside you, it is multiplied."

"What else do I need to know about my werewolf?"

"You love to rip out hearts," War informs. "Werewolves do this if they have a sickness that only affects them. They kill all in their way and usually, when they get to their mate, it's too late. They will kill him or her too, then rip out their own hearts."

"I'd never do that to Demi."

"We know, but I think you might have a little of the sickness that War is talking about. The unhinged madness only affects werewolves. It clouds any reasoning and rationale which is one of the reasons why you are so intense all the time."

"What a nice word. I was going to say a fucking lunatic, but tomato, tomahto," Famine gests, stretching his arm out for a bat to land on him. "Isn't he cute?" He pets the bat under its chin.

Abaddon holds up his finger, turning his head as if he is listening to something. "I'll be back. You—" He points to me and snaps his fingers.

A forcefield traps me inside. I ram my shoulders against it on every side but it doesn't move. I try to breathe fire, but the flames recoil. Smoke billows, filling the space, and my anger wraps around me, causing my shoulders to rise and fall in quick beats.

"—You stay put."

I hiss, my tongue shifting and flicking out in warning.

"Interesting. I think the majority of you is ruled by the dragon and werewolf DNA. You don't have any other snake aspects besides your tongue. And we all know where the kraken takes over." Abaddon coughs in discomfort.

I rake my claws down the invisible barrier. "Let me the fuck out of here, Abaddon. Let me out!"

"I can't do that. I have a special guest arriving and you have to be contained. I'll be back." He snaps his fingers again and disappears, leaving me stranded in the middle of fucking nowhere with War, Famine, and Conquest.

Rage is boiling. My dragon really hates being contained. My wings are too big to spread out in this space.

"Hey, man. Calm down. You're going to hurt yourself. You're okay. You're safe."

"You think I care about being safe?" I shout, fire consuming my entire body. "Let me the fuck out!" I roar, losing complete control of every beast swirling inside me. Black ink begins to seep from my skin, a new development that I've never experienced before.

I slam my body against the barrier again.

And again.

"You aren't in danger. There's no reason to... to... ink." Famine chuckles at War.

"Oh, grow up. He's losing it."

"He isn't inking because he is in danger. He's inking because he's pissed. Tomorrow should really be the lesson on the kraken. They are giant, quiet, but wrathful creatures. Especially when it comes to protection."

I engulf the entire space in flames, the heat licking every inch of my flesh and burning away my clothes. My eyes close and I get lost in the warmth. I think of control, trying to bring myself at ease, but the more I try, the angrier I become. The more I want to kill. The more I want to tear something apart.

"That explains a lot," Famine says out of nowhere.

"Creed."

I must be dying because I hear Demi. Maybe if I burn long enough, I'll die. Then, I'll stop being everyone's problem. I'll stop being her problem, her haunt, her fear, and she can live in peace, away from this thing I am.

"Creed!" she shouts, pounding on the barrier.

I snap my eyes open, seeing her tear-stained face. The flames diminish and the ink absorbs into my skin.

"You were losing control because you felt your mate nearby," Abaddon explains. "You were about to go nuclear. Your flames turned blue, and I honestly have never seen you so calm. That was... unpleasant. I have no idea what you're capable of, but your mate called for me. She wanted to see you."

"Let me out," I demand, needing to touch my mate.

"No. It isn't safe for her or you. You need to know that you can't have your mate whenever you want."

"She's my mate!" This time, it's my beast who controls my voice, shaking the barrier and trapping me. "I can have her whenever I fucking want."

"No, you can't. She's her own person. She isn't your property," Abaddon argues. "You need to learn that. She is a person. She can be hurt. She can die. If you aren't careful, you could do those things. Do you want to be responsible for your mate's death?"

My eyes widen and I shake my head, unable to pull my eyes away from the tears dripping down her cheeks.

I don't want her to fear me.

I only want her to want me.

"What are you doing here?" I ask her, taking a step closer until we are so close, we could kiss if it weren't for the barrier. "You need to go, Demi. I'm unable to contain the worst of me on a good day. When you're here, I can't contain it at all."

"You're wrong. I just saw you. You were on fire and now you aren't. That's something."

"I still feel it inside me. I always do," I explain, sliding my gaze to Abaddon. "Why can't I control myself around her? But here, she's what I needed to remain calm? It doesn't make sense." I slam my fist against the barrier, needing to be free, needing Demi. She's so close. It isn't fair for her to be so close when I'm not able to touch her.

"Because when you're around her, your control has a different definition. You can't control your... urges with her. When you're away from her, your abilities seem unpredictable, but with her near, she helps you steady them. She's your bomb but she's able to defuse you too. That's not different from other paranormals. You just...." He thinks about what to say. "You have more urges, and they are stronger, more difficult to resist, and I'll be honest, I don't know if you can. I think the urges are in your DNA now. It isn't as easy as turning them off and on."

My shoulders sag, helpless, hopeless, that I'm forever this way. My brows furrow and I hang my head, unable to look at Demi. "You should go. You're the one who said you needed time." I turn around, giving her my back. "So take your time."

"I came here, wherever here is—"

"Purgatory," Famine answers. "You're where all the naughty creatures go when they have been bad."

War slaps Famine on the back of the head. "Shut up."

"Creed, Creed, look at me. Please. I've been begging Abaddon to let me see you. It's been two days and I feel... I feel like my heart is being ripped into two pieces. I had to see you. Please, let's talk."

"After this meeting, I won't allow anymore Creed. This is your chance to say what you need to say. We will leave you two alone."

"Can you please get him out of... whatever you have him trapped in?" Demi asks.

"No. If I release him, he'll rip your clothes off and fuck you in the middle of purgatory."

I grumble in delight at the thought.

Yes, I most definitely would do that. Abaddon knows me well.

My wings mesh into my back and Demi gasps, probably disgusted as she watches them become one with my body.

"Wow," she whispers.

I turn around and a pathetic whine escapes me. I think... I'm sad we can't be closer. I fall to my knees and Demi does the same, scooting closer until her legs touch the barrier.

"Your wings are so interesting. They are beautiful in tattoo form too."

"Demi, I know you aren't thrilled to have me as a mate. You don't need to lie."

"I'm not lying. Creed, please look at me. Please," she begs.

I look up, locking eyes with hers. She's still crying, and I hate that I'm the cause, but I love that I'm the cause as well. As long as she's crying over me, she feels something for us. Whether it's good or bad.

"I'm confused. I won't lie to you about that. I feel so much for you, and I don't understand why. I mean... I do. I do understand. I've read my paranormal books. I know what a mate bond is, but I had no idea it felt like this. I don't know where I am right now. Purgatory sounds like a dreadful place and I'm a little scared to be here."

I try to wrap her in my arms, but the fucking barrier gets in the way, and I roar, wishing I wasn't such a liability. "I won't let anything happen to you. Demi, I'll kill whoever and whatever bothers you. You will have no threats because I will eliminate them."

"You mean that don't you? You really don't mind killing if it's for me."

"I'll always kill for you."

"That should scare me, but—" She licks her lips. "It doesn't. I feel... relieved. Just like how I felt when I saw Daniel dead. What's that say about me?"

"It says you're mine."

I watch as she wipes her cheeks, then looks around, swallowing. Fear rolls off her in waves. I can smell it.

"Nothing will happen to you."

"You aren't able to save me if something happens right now. You're in there. This place is scary and dark."

"I will free myself from whatever holds me back to save you. Not even the power of Abaddon will keep me from you. I'm the only one you need to fear. I'm the dark you are lost in now."

"That doesn't scare me," she replies. "It should but it doesn't. I feel better now that I'm here."

We fall into silence, not knowing what to say.

"You came here, why?" I ask her. "Is the baby okay? Are you okay?" I rush, panicked that something is wrong.

She places her hand on her stomach. "We're fine. I think that's part of the reason why I wanted to see you. We... we missed you. A lot. I feel empty without you. I miss seeing you in the diner. In our booth. Just being broody and grumpy. I need to know you, Creed. I miss your presence, your nearness, but who are you? What is this world I'm a part of now?"

"I don't know who I am. Whatever you want to know, I'm sure I do too. I can't remember anything personal. My memory was fucked when they tortured me."

"I'm so sorry that happened to you." She presses her hand against the barrier, flattening it.

I lift mine, aligning our palms together, wishing they could touch, but I feel her warmth, the goodness of her soul, and it puts me at ease. "It brought me to you. I'm not sorry. You can ask me anything and I'll do my best to answer."

"What's your favorite color?"

I grin. "Your eyes."

She rolls them. "But really."

My smile dims. "Really. My dragon loves the sky, and your eyes are the color of a cloudless day."

"What's your favorite food?"

"Such a cliché question, no?" I chuckle.

"Well, I never see you eat when you're at the diner."

"Because my favorite food is you. I eat you, Demi. I drink you until I'm full."

Her cheeks become red and her mouth parts in shock. "Oh."

"My likes, my wants, everything about me is tied to you. Whatever you want to know about me, we will learn together in time because I'm learning too, but right now, you're the center of my universe."

She grins, trying to hide her smile as she bites her lip. "Don't you want to know me more? Find out who you're bonded to for eternity?"

"I have eternity to know that, but I know you. I know you're kind, thoughtful, and take way too much cream and sugar in your coffee. You love tea at night but hate tea during the day. You love being warm and cozy. You prefer blankets over hoodies. You're smart and successful. You're independent. The owner of a successful diner. You're beautiful. There might not be much to me, but I'm yours, Demi."

"How can you say that?" She curls her fingers against the barrier as if she's trying to hold my hand. "There's so much to you and I can't wait to learn your different sides. All of you. You'll learn to accept yourself, Creed. I know you will."

"It's time for you to go, Demi," Abaddon comes back. "The longer you're here, the more you mess with the balance. Humans aren't allowed here."

"But— I—"

She stares at me with those big blue eyes, more tears filling them.

"I'll be what you need," I rush to say. "I swear to you. I vow to you. With all my insides, Demi."

"I think you already are," she says. "Kiss me, Creed."

"I can't." I try to break down the barrier again. "I can't!" My control starts to snap, and the smoke and flames begin to fill the area around me.

"Whatever questions we have, we will face them together. This new world, I'm nervous but excited to learn it with you. Paranormal books were my favorite and now I can live it."

"That explains why she's so accepting," Famine says.

"Shut up. God. You ruin every moment," Death sniffles. "I love a good love story."

"Where's your scythe? You're being emotional. Do you cry when you slay souls too?"

"That's different."

I tune out their ridiculous argument when Demi kisses the wall keeping us apart.

I do the same, as stupid as it looks, I don't care.

"You're mine," I growl when our lips part. "And I'll always remind you of that."

"I'll be looking forward to it," she says before Abaddon snaps his fingers.

And just like that she's gone.

The barrier is lifted, and I stay on my knees, missing the one part of me that actually makes me better.

"It's time to get to work," Abaddon exclaims. "What happens when your dragon fire is captured, Creed?"

"I don't know."

"What happens when you cry your vampire tears?"

"I don't know!" I roar just as a tear breaks free.

Abaddon swipes it, showing me how it glitters in different colors. "That's what we are going to teach you so you can protect yourself because there are good humans and bad, but there are creatures in our world that would do anything for this tear, do you understand?"

"Why?"

"Because it heals, saves lives, gives the person in need a longer life. It could change the world, but the world isn't ready. You protect your tears and your flames."

And Demi.

Always. Demi.

CHAPTER EIGHTEEN

DEMI

I didn't think getting out of bed a week later would be so hard. I'm depressed without Creed. All day for twenty-four hours, he is all I think about. Life only became harder when Abaddon brought me back. The small glimpse of my mate wanting to learn, to be better, to try to understand himself was all I needed to see.

He's brutal and intense, but his brutality is all for me.

I must be sick in the head for wanting him still, but I can't imagine my life without him. Whether it's because he took matters into his hands or did what he thought was right, I know in my heart and soul, I would have chosen to be with him anyway. With or without all the horrible things he has done.

I felt it when he came into the diner. I knew his presence meant my life would forever have a new meaning.

I've had enough time away from him now. I miss him. I need him. Ever since I went to see him in Purgatory I've known, I want us to start again. I regret saying I needed time.

I think.

Maybe.

I had to ask for time. There was so much happening. I needed to think.

But then why didn't I sweep my house for the cameras? Why didn't I throw away the tea? I haven't drank it since, but I want to when he is home. I want him to fuck me like he did before.

I want everything he has to offer and more. I want brutal, unhinged, pure, untainted lust from him. I want him to take me when I least expect it and I want him to hold me.

"Demi?"

Caden's voice penetrates my thoughts as he takes a seat on the edge of my bed.

"Demi, you have to get up."

"Leave me alone, Caden." I turn to my side, rolling away from him, and tucking the pillow under my head.

With my free hand, I cup my stomach, pressing my face into the pillow when another wave of emotions hit me. Creed should be here for this. I look four months pregnant already. I'm growing fast, too fast for a human pregnancy. I don't know when I'm due. Abaddon came to visit me yesterday saying he can't help me either.

Since Creed is so many different beasts, it's hard to say when I'll be due, or if the baby will be one creature or many like Creed.

I also can't see the baby in an ultrasound. Abaddon brought a machine hoping it would make me feel better, but it only made me feel worse. I can hear the heartbeat, but I can't see the picture.

"Here." He hands me my perfume. "You need this. You don't realize it, but I think you're slowly dying without him. You need him back."

"Why did you give me this?" I hold up the bottle. "Hugging this isn't going to make me feel better."

"I know why it smells different now. My sense of smell isn't great because I scent more in the water, but when I opened the bottle, I could separate the components." He takes it from me again and sprays the pillow I'm lying on.

Creed's essence sinks into me. I groan, slipping my arms around the material, then breathing him in.

Pathetically, I cry, letting out my pain as my heart breaks. My lust for him amps up to a dangerous level.

My entire body is on fire. I groan, snatching the perfume from Caden.

"What is this?"

"He peed in it. He marked the entire territory too." He crinkles his nose in disapproval.

That's sick.

I *love* it.

I spray more, basically dousing myself in it until my body becomes so hot, I sweat. "Get out, Caden! Get out!" I scream at him and at the same time, flames leave my mouth.

I don't care about that new ability. All I want is Creed.

He backs away, holding up his hands to show he doesn't mean any harm. "This is me leaving. Don't burn down your own house."

I don't watch him leave, but I do hear the front door slam shut just as lightning cracks across the sky. It's been raining nonstop every single day since Creed left. I think Caden is upset for me and hasn't been able to control his power.

Fire dances over my skin, small flames flickering, but it doesn't hurt. It feels good. Too good.

"Oh God. Creed! Creed, I need you. Please." I rip my shirt off, then my panties, my entire body begins to sweat. I reach for the drawer to my nightstand and bring out my toy. "God. This isn't enough!" The tears only get worse when I see how small the toy is. It's skinny and short.

I want Creed. He's big and thick, that much I remember.

I toss the toy across the room, and it slams against the mirror. It's too light to even crack the damn thing.

Shoving four fingers inside me to relieve the ache, I groan, the fire becoming brighter but the need for his knot becoming more intense. I want his fangs in my throat. I want all of him.

Everything that makes him.

All of his insides.

"It's worse than I thought."

I'm covered with a blanket in the next moment, Abaddon turning his head away to refrain from seeing my naked body.

A loud growl that has liquid heat dripping between my lips sounds from somewhere in the house.

"Creed!" I call for him, the blanket turning to ash from the flames. "Creed! Please! I need you. I need you so much. God. I feel like I'm going to die."

"You will if you don't mate him in return. I didn't think about that because he's so different, but his beasts are strong. You need to be prepared if I allow him in here. I won't be able to get him to leave."

"I don't care," I sob, rolling my face into the pillow again to smell my perfume.

"This is where I leave you then. Just call for me if you need me." Abaddon is gone or maybe he was never there at all.

I'm in such a fevered state, I feel drugged all over again.

Another roar sounds, this one closer, more menacing, and my body arches in response.

"Demi."

My hazy sights land on him in the doorway. He has his shirt off. His muscles ripple with every harsh, fast breath he takes. Sweat glistens on his chest.

"I felt you. You need me," he states through tight fangs. He isn't hiding himself at all now.

"Yes. Yes, please. Creed. I've been needing you all along."

"I know, I felt it in the bond." He slams his hands against the doorframe, his claws digging into the wood, then drags them down. His biceps flex, showing the defined muscle. "I stayed away for as long as I could, but I couldn't deny your call for me. If I do this, there's no turning back. You're mine. I won't be leaving. I'll tie you to the fucking bed and force you to love me if that is what I have to do, but I won't be leaving. Ever again." He drags his nails up the frame again, then down, carving everlasting grooves in the wood for us to always remember.

His wings spread out behind him, curling up to shadow his entire body.

"Please, please, Creed. I don't know what's wrong with me. I need you so bad."

He grips the doorframe, growling. "You need to understand this. I've been away with the Harvesters. I've been practicing my control. But if I take one more step, I'll lose it. If you say no, if you tell me to stop, if you hit me, kick me, bite me—" two trails of smoke billow from his nose. Sparks crackle across his lips. His eyes turn from amber gems to the color of molten lava. "—I will like it. I won't care. I won't stop. I've been away from you for too long. From you, from your scent, from your voice, from your body." He groans, readjusting his hard cock. "This will be it. There will be no going back. There will be no hope for you or me."

"Yes," I say, the flames becoming higher as they flicker upon my skin. The tears dripping from my eyes dry as soon as they hit my blazing cheek.

The wall begins to crack from the strength of his hold, pieces of it crumbling onto the floor. "Demi," he growls in warning, the same fire heating me engulfs his body, burning away his pants until he is standing naked in the doorway.

I sit up, sliding a hand over my stomach to settle between my legs, coating my fingers in my slick when I see his cock for the first time. "Oh," I moan in excitement, watching as the tentacles unravel themselves. The suckers along his cock begin to move and clear liquid begins to drip from them.

I know he said he was multiple beasts, but when he said kraken, I wasn't sure what he meant.

Now, I do.

He wraps a hand around his cock, stroking it slowly, and his hand becomes shiny from the precome leaking from him in copious amounts.

Before I can ask him again, before I beg him again, he's a blur, standing in front of me in all his glory. His wings wrap around me, cocooning us in darkness, and our flames become one until the orange tendrils fade. Just the feel of his skin on mine brings me relief.

I groan, tilting my head back until I'm leaning against one of his wings.

Unexpectedly, he sinks his fangs into my neck, savage rumbles leaving his chest, as he feeds. One hand comes up, applying pressure to the side of my head, keeping it bent. He snarls into my neck, forcefully feeding and taking, something he has become a master at.

Warm blood trickles down my neck and more scorching heat spreads between my legs. I moan with every swallow he takes, my orgasm building to a crescendo, and with the next lick of his tongue, I come.

"Creed! Yes, don't stop. More. Oh God." I rock my pussy over his leg, needing friction, needing more from him.

Why won't he give me more?

He groans next and hot splashes of his come hit my stomach. He rips his mouth away from my throat and stares at me with his wicked, animalistic eyes. His mouth and chin are covered in red. His fangs are long, pointed, and crimson stains his teeth. He slides his tongue over to suck the blood from across them.

His hand snakes out, wrapping around my throat until I'm gasping for breath. Creed's wings create a breeze as they lift and tuck behind his back. Without saying a word, he controls me by my throat, pushing me down until I'm at eye level with his cock.

The tentacles stroke my cheek and before I can open my mouth, Creed is forcing his cock between my lips in one hard stroke. The tip hits the back of my throat.

And he stays there.

"You loved it when I did this to you in your sleep."

I can't breathe enough to gasp, but my watery gaze lifts to his as I choke on his massive cock. The suckers rub against all sides of my mouth, his precome slipping down my throat in waves. I cough, spit dripping down my chin.

"Your mouth feels so fucking good," he moans, sliding back until the head is all that's left between my lips. "But you know what?" He glides it back in, then out, the suckers tickling the top of my tongue. Gripping me by the back of the hair, he sneers. "I liked it more in your sleep." He yanks out of me completely, grabs me around the waist, and tosses me onto my back.

"Yes," I moan, his hands going straight to my belly as he spreads my legs with his knee.

In one hard, abusive stroke, his cock fills me.

"Creed! Oh God, oh God," I chant, the pain of how big he is, stretching me to the brink mixed with pleasure is overwhelming. Snippets of what happened in my sleep, come back to me. I remember how good he felt and how I hated when the dream was over, I was left wanting more.

"Not God, Demi." He bends down, his forked tongue grazing across the shell of my ear. "Your devil."

The headboard slams into the wall and I lift my hands to grab the edge, to try to silence it so my neighbors don't hear. Creed growls and pins my wrists above my head.

"Let them hear. I want everyone to hear how I'm claiming you. How I'm fucking you. How I'm going to make you scream. How I'll make you beg." He lowers his voice, licking the fresh bite on my neck. "How I'll take you so hard, so rough, you'll beg me to stop." He slams into me just as his tentacle suctions to my clit while the other slips into my ass.

My thighs begin to shake from the stimulation. The way he fucks me in tandem with his tentacle, in and out at the same time. I look down, needing to see him inside me. His cock is purple with red suckers, and goddamn, those are everything a girl could dream about.

"I'm going to come. I'm going to come, Creed. Don't stop. Please, don't stop. You feel so good. I've ached for you." I lift my head, stealing his lips for a kiss.

Our first kiss.

He cups the back of my head, pushing our mouths together. He turns his head, his lip fitting between the top and bottom, proving he is made for me. His unique tongue wraps around mine, pulsing for a moment before slithering free.

We moan in unison, our bodies slicking against one another from the sweat and heat being shared. His body flexes, his hips curl, his cock finds and pleasures every part of me on the inside, and everything about him is otherworldly, every inch of him. He's perfect. He is a dream right out of one of my books.

His gray skin glistens from the sweat and while he is taking what he owns, I take the time to admire his differences. My fingers caress his arms, the dark hair tickling the pads of them. The purple and black scales are softer than I thought they would be, nearly holographic as the light from the sun peeks through the windows to shine on him.

He is far from a devil when he is in the spotlight, but if this is hell, I never want to leave.

My fingers trace his sharp jaw. I can tell when he was human, he was still handsome, that part of him lingers, but the primal beasts have shaped him to look vicious with his jaw wide and sharp enough to make anyone hold their breath if they stared at him long enough.

"What are you doing?" He fumbles in his thrusts, confused, his eyes watching my fingers move up his cheeks. He almost seems panicked.

"Admiring you," I reply, brushing the high bones before moving to his ears. They are pointed but the tips are covered in fur.

His eyes close as I stroke him there. His entire body trembles and he purrs, stopping all movements so he is still.

"You like that?"

He nods slowly, his chest expanding as he inhales a deep breath. "I love your hands on me. It feels... like a dream. A good dream. One I thought I'd never have." He cups my stomach again and opens his eyes. "All mine." The growl he announces into the room can be felt in my chest. His eyes morph from kind and soft, an expression I've never seen, to hot coals. "Fucking. Mine."

I yelp when he flips me to my hands and knees, man-handling me— or monster-handling me— into position causing him to slip out. His tentacles are still attached and the one tugs on my clit while the other manages to slide into my ass deeper.

I whimper and mewl, making sounds I've never made before. I press my face into the bed so I'm not too loud. His claws bite into each ass cheek, gripping them until it's painful, and then thrusts in.

"I remember when I fucked you for the first time. I was so pleased to feel you were only meant to be mine. Now, there's nothing stopping me from getting as deep as possible. I did that. I owned it. I claimed it." His fingers dig into my hair, fisting it, forcing my head to turn. "So I better hear what I've claimed. I want you to scream." He licks up my spine as he curls into me.

Another orgasm builds, and the suckers attached to my clit begin to move, a waving movement that rolls my clit.

"Harder. More. Creed. Give me more. I need— I need—" I stumble over my words as I come, explosions burst, my vision darkens, and I drench his cock with slick.

And I scream just like he wants. "Creed! Oh my God," I groan, clawing at the bed, trying to get away from him because it's all too much.

"I don't know where you think you're going." He grips my hips and tugs me back, slamming me down on his cock. He applies so much pressure with his hold, my bones begin to ache.

I mumble in pain, and he grumbles in delight, the wet sounds of us colliding together as he jackhammers into me causing another spasm to roll through me. "You're going to have my marks all over you by the time we're done," he says, lifting me onto my knees with a violent tug on my hair so my back is pressed to his chest.

"On the full moon, you're going to run from me, and I'm going to hunt you." He drags his lips up my throat, palming one of my breasts while he fucks me relentlessly. "And I don't care if you cry, you'll take my cock, won't you?"

"Yes, yes, yes." I press towards him, meeting him stroke for stroke. "You can have me whenever you want."

"In your sleep?"

I reach my arm up, wrapping it around his neck to bring myself closer to him somehow. "You can drug me too. Use me for anything. Everything. I want whatever you want."

He growls again, his arm disappearing behind my head, and I hear his bite, but it isn't my skin he bites into. His blood drips onto my shoulder.

"Drink." He tries to press his wrist to my mouth, but I turn away when his cock begins to grow.

"What is that? Oh my God, it hurts, Creed. It feels—" it feels fucking good.

"It's my knot. It's my werewolf breeding you even though you're already bred. I can't help it. I'm going to lock it inside you, fill you with my come, and complete this mating."

"We are. I don't need your blood." I wince when the knot threatens to lock inside me. It isn't big enough yet, but I feel it stretching it.

Creed's snarl is vicious and sends a sliver of fear through me. "I learned you have to drink my blood since I'm a vampire too. Fucking drink it, Demi."

I like seeing him lose his patience.

"No." I fight him, moving my head left and right.

Blood begins to drip all over me, down my chest, breasts, and dripping onto my bed.

He flips me back over onto my back, lifts my leg onto his shoulder, and slams into me again.

"I said, yes." He shoves his wrist into my mouth, the smoky flavor of his blood blooming across my taste buds. It's better than I thought it would be.

He actually tastes delicious.

I moan, grabbing his arm to press it harder into my mouth. He shouts, his knot locking inside me, tugging on my hole.

Creed comes, his warmth filling me, claiming my insides all over again.

"Yeah, that's it, Demi. Take me into your body. Accept me." He leans down, groaning as more come fills me, and then his fangs slice into my skin, feeding from me at the same time I'm drinking from him.

Every pull at my neck, every suck on his wrist, I get closer to coming.

And then his memories bind with mine. How he feels about me becomes bigger than I have ever felt before. His pleasure, knowing how good I'm making him feel has another orgasm rolling through me. He tweaks my nipple while he drags blood from my vein, snarling and sneers fill the room.

But there is one memory that collides with mine. They mend together, becoming one.

A shared memory.

I'm playing in a field of honeysuckles with my friends next to the playground, and a boy I don't know with shaggy hair is sitting by himself.

"Do you want to play tag with us?" I ask him, the other five kids waiting to run into the field.

His eyes are big and brown, warm and kind. Then he smiles. "Yes! That would be great."

I giggle, tapping him on the shoulder. "Tag! You're it." I sprint away, my friends giggling along with me while we run through the field.

It's sweet.

He catches me first, but we trip over one another. We're both trying to catch our breaths when he plucks a honeysuckle. He hands it to me.

"Do you know how to drink the nectar from this?" he asks.

I shake my head.

He plucks one too, ignoring the shouts of the other kids asking where we are.

"Tug the stem free. Then suck the bottom. It's sweet." He sticks the bottom of the flower into his mouth.

I do as he says, sucking the bottom of the flower into my mouth when sweetness bursts across my tongue. I grin. "It's so good! It tastes like honey."

He tucks the flower over my ear, then taps my shoulder. "You're it."

He removes his fangs at the same time I stop drinking from his wrist. He straightens his arms so he can look at me, his knot tugging at my entrance again.

Tears glisten on his cheeks and he smiles, flashing his red tinted teeth while his eyes dart all over my face. "It's you. You've always been my happiness. You've always been the one thing I will never forget, what I'll always remember. I couldn't remember anything from my past, but I remembered that field. I remembered the sweet smell of happiness." He inhales, another tear breaking free. "You were always meant to be mine."

I run my fingers through his hair, down his cheek, just as my emotions get the best of me, and I nod. Sharing that memory with him was the best emotional burst I've ever experienced. It surpassed the connection we have naturally. It molded it and created something that went higher than the average love.

We're fated.

It's sealed.

I can't live without my stalker.

My mate.

"Out of all the darkness that has made my life hell in the last few months, the one good thing I held onto was the snippet I had of that moment with you in the field." He kisses my forehead, easing us into another position so I'm more comfortable. He's on his back and I'm lying on his chest, his cock still locked inside me even though I'm already pregnant.

I won't complain.

I brush my cheek against his chest, smiling. His wings take me by surprise, expanding fast and I startle, which only causes me to tug on his cock harder.

His knot brushes a spot inside me that makes me see stars and I come again, squeezing his shaft as my body spasms.

"Fuck, I love when I make you orgasm," Creed groans, teasing my back with his talons. His wings wrap around us again. It's safe. I love being hidden in the haven of his body.

The tendons in his neck protrude as another jet of heat spreads inside me.

"How long will this go on for?" I say with an exhausted, yet satisfied sigh. I want it to end, but I never want it to end.

"I don't know, but let's stay still." He gently grabs my hips, his talons biting into my skin ever so slightly, maneuvering us until we are on our sides. "I can sense you're tired, Demi."

One arm tucks under my pillow while he palms my stomach. "You should be. You're growing my child." He kisses my shoulder, a sweet gesture so unlike how he has acted before.

I love both sides of him.

"I'll protect you both with my life."

I place my hand on top of his and sigh, trying not to be worried. "I can't see the baby on the ultrasound, Creed. I don't know if everything is okay. I'm already showing."

"You'll give birth quicker. You won't be pregnant as long as a human. Abaddon thinks the reason why you can't see the baby is because he or she is in an egg."

"An egg?" Trying not to sound horrified, but I'm only human-ish.

"Dragons lay them. So that's why."

I hate how embarrassed he sounds.

"I'm sorry I don't know more. I was turned into this. I don't have many answers."

"Hey." I squeeze his hand in reassurance. "We will find the answers together. We will learn as we go. We're all safe. We're all loved. That's all that matters to me."

"Fuck," he grumbles, pushing his knot further into me. "You love me?"

It's soon, so soon, but I don't care. I feel it in my soul how much this man means to me. "I do," I reply. "When you were gone, I felt like a part of my soul was missing."

"That's how I felt too. They had to keep me chained with silver to stop me from coming back to you."

I lean my head against his chest, my mouth parting as he continues his thrusts.

"Knowing you love me is awakening all my beasts again."

I giggle, turning my head for a kiss, and damn, does he give me his all. He kisses me as if his life depends on it, slow and deep.

"I love you with all my insides."

I know for him, that's more than anyone could ever feel for another person. I'm lucky.

"You'll still stalk me, right?"

He drives in a little harder, causing me to whimper. "Nothing could ever stop me from keeping my eyes on you at all times. Nothing."

I get lost in the pleasure he gives, hoping he never conforms to what is considered normal because his feral sides are everything I need.

CHAPTER NINETEEN

CREED

"The Heart Ripper has gone quiet in our small town. It's been a month since the last body was found. Police have no answers or suspects. It seems we can all give our hearts, a little rest."

I snort when I overhear the news reporter on TV while I sit in my designated booth, tracing the heart I carved on the top.

As long as no one else fucks with my mate, no one will have to die. It's simple and logical. If people would think before they speak or do, maybe I wouldn't have to kill them.

"You're supposed to be taking orders," Caden stops at the booth and fills my mug. "Remember? You work here now."

Caden has grown on me.
More like a wart. On my ass. I tolerate him because he's Demi's best friend.

Plus, he seems to understand my nature, but he keeps a wary eye on me.

I do my best to stay hidden from the majority of people. I'd hate for Demi to get grief from the people of this town because she's mated to me, a monster, someone so different than who they are used to seeing.

Demi has told me a hundred times she wants people to see me, that she's proud to be with me, but I'm not proud of how I look yet.

"I remember." I take the cup in hand, lifting it to my lips, then feel the moment Demi is out the door of the kitchen. Her belly is bigger than she is which makes me puff out my chest in pride.

I did that.

That's my baby. She's carrying *my* child.

"God, seeing you watch her is disturbing."

"Then don't watch me watch her," I grunt, staring at her just like I promised I would. "Because I'm never going to stop."

"You haven't thanked me, you know."

I still stare at Demi, long and hard. "What for?"

"What for? What for! How about for finding a witch to cast that spell on the rain. You know, the storm I created, so everyone thought Demi had already been pregnant so she could still come to work."

"Right. That." He created a storm so that when it rained and people stepped outside, one drop of rain made them believe Demi had been pregnant for months.

"Right. That," he mocks me.

"Thanks." I didn't care about that. I wanted to keep her locked away for my own selfish benefit, but working makes Demi happy, and that's all that matters to me.

He sighs. "It's better than nothing. I'll take it." He hands me a pad and pen. "Get to work."

"You really want me to work? I'll scare away your customers."

"Demi wants you to."

I snatch the pen and pad from him, standing quickly. "Whatever Demi wants, she gets."

Even if I just want to go home to the amazing nest we have built together. The bed is surrounded by gold. Anything and everything gold I could find, I brought it to her.

Now our bed nest is on the floor, filled with pillows, blankets, and my tattered shirts because Demi loves the smell of them.

"You need to stop growling," Caden advises, slapping me on the shoulder. "And reel in the lust. You're stinking up the room."

"Never."

Demi must feel my gaze because she turns her head, her eyes lifting from the customers she's waiting on. She grins, those blue irises causing my shoulders to twitch when my wings try to burst out, but I manage to rein them in. Those eyes make me want to fly.

She presses her hand to her stomach and blushes, probably remembering how we got into this situation.

The fucking bell jingles, ruining the damn moment. Her attention leaves me to pay attention to the new customer.

And I don't like it. I want to kill the person who stole her from me, even if it was only for a second.

When I see who walks through the door, thunder vibrates in my chest.

Jake fucking Holland.

I hate him, and what's worse, I can't kill him either.

He's a cop, Demi's friend, and isn't a threat.

That doesn't mean I can't think about tearing him to shreds though. My beasts love that idea.

"Demi, looking great," he says to her, kissing her on the cheek before rubbing her belly. "Any day now, right?"

"Don't." Caden grips my bicep to stop me from ripping his head from his shoulders for touching my mate and child.

Smoke swirls from my mouth and Caden waves it away.

"You have to stop that. Get it together. She picked you. She's having your kid. She somehow loves you."

It isn't enough. I want more.

Jake takes a seat at the counter instead of taking a booth, so I head that way, keeping my hood up and covering my mouth with a mask to hide most of my face. I stand behind him, wanting to rip his stupid hat off, but I remember what Caden said.

Clicking the pen, I put on my best customer service voice like Demi taught me. "What the fuck do you want?"

He chuckles.

"Ah, Creed. It's good to see you too. A pleasure as always."

"It isn't a pleasure. What do you want?" I can't stand how nice this guy is, which is why it didn't bother me when I might have used my vampire ability to trance them, thinking I've been here in this town the entire time. No one knows except Demi that I did that.

I got away with murder. And I'll keep getting away with it if it means protecting my family.

"I'm starting to think you don't like me, Creed."

"I don't," I answer, obviously. "I don't like anyone besides Demi. She's everything. I don't have all damn day. What do you want?" I try not to snarl with impatience. I don't think customer service is for me. Maybe I'll work in the office, away from people.

I hate people.

He sighs, finally taking off his hat. "I'll take a double cheeseburger with everything on it, fries, and a chocolate milkshake."

I won't admit it to him, but that sounds delicious.

"Was that so hard?" I click my pen, then slip it into my pocket.

"You won't be making my food, right?"

"No. I'm not allowed near sharp objects."

"There's hope yet."

I sneer, spinning on my heel and nearly running into Demi. I drop the pad, wrapping my arms around her to steady her. My heart beats so hard and fast, I hear the blood rushing in my ears.

"Are you okay?"

She cups my jaw, toying with the mask hiding my face. "I'd be better if you showed your face. I miss seeing you."

I lean into her touch, pressing my hand over hers. Already, the anger, the urge to kill, the hate, it fades when she touches me. I almost feel... human.

"You know I can't show my face here."

"Why not? It looks more human than you think, but okay." She relents because she knows how I feel about this conversation.

I flatten my hand on her belly, sensing a readiness in the baby. "How are you feeling?"

"Not too bad. I—" Water splashing onto the floor stops her from saying anything else. "My back was hurting, but I thought it was just from carrying around this baby."

Instinct takes over. "We have to go. Now." Before she can argue with me, I sweep her into my arms, stepping into the puddle on the floor from her water breaking. "Caden! You're on your own. We have to go."

"Keep me updated! Tell me if you need anything!"

"I can take you to the hospital in the police car. I'll hit the sirens," Jake offers, putting on his hat as if I've already said yes.

He doesn't understand. I can't say yes. In order for my mate to have this baby, we have to fly, I have to knot her and stretch her so she can easily pass the egg without pain. That's what the crash course in dragons taught me with Abaddon.

A hospital can't help us.

"No offense, but stay the fuck away from us right now," I growl, unable to stop the beasts from sounding.

He stops dead in his tracks, eyes wide, confusion and shock pouring from him in waves.

But not fear.

Interesting.

I push out the door, the stupid bell ringing, and I can't take it anymore. "Goddamn it, this stupid fucking— god— damn— thing." I reach up and snatch it from its place, tossing it on the floor. "No more bells either!"

Demi giggles, wrapping her arms around my neck. "You're cute when you're panicked."

"I'm not panicked." I blur behind the diner, spread my wings, and launch into the air. "I'm in need and you will be too once I get high enough."

"That's insane, I'm having a baby. I don't want to— oh— oh!" she clutches her stomach as a contraction hits, but the strong scent of lust follows. "What the hell?"

With long, quick cuts through the air, my wings work overtime as I take us higher and higher until we can no longer see the ground.

It's just us.

Lost in the sky, getting closer to space, and if I could, I'd take her to the stars.

"Why is this happening?" she yells as another contraction hits, then paws at my pants. "I don't like that I'm in pain and need your cock. It doesn't make sense. It will hurt." A gut-wrenching scream leaves her as she clutches her stomach. "Oh my God! Give me your fucking cock before I kill you, Creed, I swear to God!" she threatens, unbuttoning my pants before ripping the zipper down. "This makes no sense."

With my claws, I reach between her legs, thankful she's wearing a dress today, and rip her panties from her body. She's fucking drenched. From lust, from her water breaking, from needing me... I can't wait to give her what she wants.

"Because you need my knot in order to successfully have the egg." The air is cooler the higher we get and to keep her warm and safe, flames emerge all over my body while I pull her closer to me. Fire engulfs us and I immediately feel a change in her. She wraps her legs around my waist. I lift her enough to guide my cock to her soaking wet hole, then push in, keeping my arms tight around her body so she doesn't fall.

She's trusting me completely. It's up to me to keep her safe in the air. She has no wings, no ability to protect herself, and no way to save herself if something goes wrong. I love having her trust. I'll die before anything happens to her.

"Fuck, Demi," I growl when she begins to rock her hips, my cock easily sliding in and out of her from how drenched she is for me.

"You feel so good. This feels better than it ever has. Oh God, Creed. I'm going to come already. Yes!" She curls her hips, grinding her clit against me. "Yes." She tightens her arms around my neck, her lips parting as her orgasm gets closer. "Oh, yes, there, right there, fuck, Creed."

"You look so fucking beautiful when you're fucking me. Come for me, Demi. Let me ease your pain." She starts to rock harder and faster, my wings working overtime as they cut through the sky to get to our home, our nest, as soon as possible.

My tentacle locks onto her clit, suctioning the small bundle of explosive nerves while I slip the other between her cheeks, toying with her puckered star.

Her lips press against mine as she shouts down my throat, her walls contracting around my cock, massaging my shaft, causing the knot to already begin to form at the base. Our tongues collide, but then she latches onto it, sucking and stroking it.

I groan, my eyes rolling to the back of my head.

Curling my hands around her shoulders, I drive into her as best as I can mid-flight. "You were created to take every inch of this new body of mine. You were sculpted by hands knowing you were mine. Your cunt was imagined with me in mind." I thrust, driving in as far as I can, forcing her to take every thick inch of me.

There are large amounts of slick from her orgasm and her body preparing for the egg. Her thighs shine from it, my pants are drenched from the sweet nectar.

"I have to let you go," I whisper into her ear on a whine, squeezing my eyes shut from how fucking amazing she feels. "Demi, you're so hot and tight, you're fucking addicting. God," I snarl, clawing my nails down her back, tearing her dress.

"Let me go?" She shakes her head, pressing her forehead to mine. "You can't. I'll die."

"I'll catch you, but I have to let you go. My dragon is pushing for it. Letting you go must be part of the process." I don't want to leave her. Pulling out of her will be one of the hardest things I have to do. "I'll catch you, I promise, then I'll knot you. You want that, don't you? You're craving my knot."

"Yes, but I'm scared." Her fingers grip the hair at the base of my neck.

"That's the point, Demi." I lift her from my cock, the tentacle slips from her ass while the suckers refuse to let go of her clit. The force causes her to orgasm again and more come cascades from her.

My tentacle finally removes itself. "Remember, you're mine. I won't let anything happen to you."

I release her.

She drops fast, falling helplessly through the sky. Demi holds on to her stomach, her eyes squeezed shut as her body flips, so she's faced down, watching the ground become closer.

I shred the rest of my clothes and spew fire into the air, and dive for her.

My wings are aerodynamically flattened to my back, slicing through the clouds to increase my speed.

Even from above, I can smell her fear, yet there is still so much lust. Her dress is blown into pieces, shredding from her body since my claws have already torn the material. Her body is on display for all to see, which has me pulling my wings above my head, pushing them closer to my body to produce more speed.

When I'm inches away from her, my wings circle her, bring her into my embrace, and her ass settles against my pelvis, my cock easily sliding into her cunt again.

"Oh, fuck, Demi," I growl, biting into her shoulder to try and contain the feral, violent rush of desire pumping in my veins.

We're still falling, fucking, and her cries of fear only make me want to pound my hips into her harder.

"That's it, take my fucking cock. You're so scared, aren't you? You have no idea what will happen, and it feels so damn good." I slide out, the tip of my cock the only part of me left inside her before I drive in again.

Her flesh gives under me as I sink my claws into her cheeks, clutching her ass with most of my strength to use her body as support while I hammer into her.

My wings suddenly spread out, the ground coming at us so fast, I can see the different shades of the green blades of grass just before we hit the ground. In the nick of time, we soar into the sky again, my knot swelling and locking inside my mate.

She orgasms again, spasms vibrating my shaft, and come begins to burst from me, stream after stream, flooding her womb.

"When you're healed, this body is in so much trouble," I warn through clenched teeth. Wrapping my hand around the back of her neck, I jerk her head back, aligning her body with mine as I land. "And you'll fucking deal with how I want to take you and how much. Won't you?"

"Yes," she hisses, trying to lift herself up, then back down to fuck me, but the knot stretches her, causing her to stop.

"What the fuck is happening? What the hell are you doing to her?" Mr. Pete gripes from the other side of the fence.

"You don't see anything, Mr. Pete," I state, cutting him a hard glare, but I know the moment I step inside, he'll forget all about me from when I tranced him.

"Please, get me to our nest. I need to push soon. Please, Creed. Please," she begs, her body becoming feverish with sweat.

I kiss her temple, tasting the sweat beading across her flesh, exhaustion mixed with anticipation, desire, worry, and happiness burst through me. Each of her emotions tastes different.

But it's the worry that concerns me.

"What's wrong, Honeysuckles? Why are you worried," I say into her mind, able to telepathically communicate because of our bond.

Sharp pain cuts through our connection next, nearly causing me to trip, but I hold on tight.

"I'm afraid."

I look down, noticing tears pouring down her cheeks while she pinches her eyes shut.

"There is nothing to be afraid of. I won't let anything happen to you or our child. You're safe with me."

"I'm afraid something will be wrong. I love you, but you don't know either, and don't for a second think it will be your fault if something is. We don't know what will happen. I'm scared of heartbreak. I'm scared to lose him or her."

A lump in my throat forms at the thought of something being wrong with our child. The thought hadn't occurred to me. I know it won't be my fault, but as a father, it feels like it would be.

"Everything will be okay, Demi. I promise."

"You can't know that."

"I do. Because I've lived through nightmares and I've created darkness for you, this is our happy ending. This is our field of happiness."

I lie her down in the middle of the nest, the bed pushed all the way to the side. I can't help but moan when she tugs on my knot again while we settle onto our sides.

"I feel better in the nest," she whispers, finally at ease. "A lot better." She places my hand on her stomach, and I feel the contraction hit. The egg moves into position, but my knot hasn't deflated yet. I'm still stretching her, filling her with my come so when she pushes, she'll be slick, and the egg will pass easier.

"Good." I kiss her shoulder, pressing my cheek against her back, and settling into our blankets.

My knot finally deflates and as I slip out, she shouts as another contraction hits. I move between her legs, trying to stay calm, but all my beasts are nervous.

Everything has to be okay.

I spread her legs, placing my hands on her knees, and getting the most perfect view of her cunt. She's dilated. I can already see the top of the egg. The blankets beneath her are already messy from our orgasms.

"You can do it, Demi. You're phenomenal. You're strong. You're beautiful. I'm the luckiest monster alive to have you. You forgave me, you accepted me, you somehow manage to love me, and I know I could never live this new life without you. Push, Demi. Push for me."

She screams at the top of her lungs, raking her nails down my arms so hard she draws blood.

"I can't. I can't do it," Demi sobs, clasping my arm. "I can't. It hurts so much."

I lean down and dab the sweat from her forehead with one of the blankets. "I know. I know it does, but you're so close. I know you can do this."

She cries out again, tears dripping from the corners of her eyes, and I think none of this would be happening if I didn't force her to get pregnant without her knowledge.

Watching her give birth, solidifying my place in the world, I have no regrets.

The egg finally comes out and Demi groans in relief, lying back on an exhausted huff while she gasps for air.

"Oh my God." My voice quivers as I reach for the egg, carefully placing it in her arms. "You did it, Demi. You did it. I knew you could." Tears spring to my eyes as I sit beside her, cradling our child in her arms.

"The shell is gray with purple scales. Like you. Just like you," she says with excitement, finding the energy to laugh. "When will they hatch? Do you know?"

"Another three months is what Abaddon said."

She sniffles, kissing the top of the egg. "I can't wait."

I run my claws through her hair, melding my body to hers so I can be as close as possible to my new family.

A family I don't deserve, but a family I'll always cherish and protect.

I'll kill and slaughter entire towns for them if that's what it takes.

"You were right, you know," Demi whispers.

Tearing my attention away from the egg is one of the most difficult things I've had to do, but I do it to meet her eyes. "About?" I ask.

"You are the only one that can happen to me— to us. You've opened up a beautiful world to me that I didn't know existed. You're unconventional, but you're unconventionally mine."

I grin, crushing her lips with mine.

My only happy memory has become a future of honeysuckle fields.

EPILOGUE

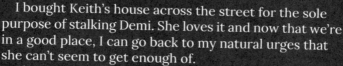

CREED

Two months later

I bought Keith's house across the street for the sole purpose of stalking Demi. She loves it and now that we're in a good place, I can go back to my natural urges that she can't seem to get enough of.

Blood is still on the floor where I killed Keith and I'm going to leave it there as a trophy. It shows I'll do anything for my family. I'll go to any extent. Right now, I'm waiting for Demi to pull up to the house after a shift at the diner, wanting her to see what I've done to the yard.

I didn't tell her about it, so I can't wait to see her face.

The screen on my eighty-inch flat-screen TV allows me to see everything that goes on at the diner and the house. I have access to Demi twenty-four hours a day. No matter where she's at or who she's with.

She's mine.

The car pulls into the driveway. I don't take my eyes off the screen as she climbs out, staring at her new yard.

Honeysuckle bushes are everywhere, even the mailbox is covered, and only the lid can be seen.

I snag my burner phone from the counter and text her from an unknown number.

Unknown number: "Do you like your new yard? I did it for you. I wanted to show you just how much you mean to me."

I press send, waiting a moment before she checks her phone.

Demi: "Who are you? What do you want?"

I love the games we play.

Unknown number: "You."

She looks around, acting as if she has no idea who is messaging her.

The screen flickers again, showing the bedroom where our egg is safe. I always breathe easier when I can see it. I've been keeping it warm with my fire every night. Another instinct I followed.

I check the time, rolling my head over my shoulders and then cracking my neck. The moon is almost full.

And I'm ready to hunt.

There are woods behind her house that will give us some privacy. We tried to plan for the woods by the diner, but we weren't comfortable enough to leave the egg.

So we settled.

Demi: "My mate will be home soon. You need to stop messaging me. Stay away from me."

She tucks her phone in her purse and takes one last peek over her shoulder before disappearing into the house.

"Oh, I'll never stay away," I growl. "You can count on that."

The first thing she does when she enters the house is check on our egg. A big smile stretches across her face. She tucks the blankets around it, then kisses the top like she does every time she comes home from work.

It was decided while we waited for the egg to hatch, I'd stay home and watch it. I'm not good with people so the decision was easy. I'd protect our child. Luckily, I haven't had to kill anyone yet.

Demi begins to undress, making my cock tent my jeans. I stand from my chair, stepping closer to the screen while

I watch my mate. My tongue flicks out, my werewolf clawing inside me to go to her.

I need to be closer.

Taking one last look at the monitors, I slip out the door and run across the street.

"What are you doing?"

I pause sneaking into the gate that leads into the backyard. I won't enter through the sliding glass door, but I'll go through the guest bedroom window I cracked earlier this morning for our special occasion.

"Mr. Pete. You ruin everything. What I do in my house is none of your fucking business. Now shut up, I have to go fuck my mate."

"Your crass tone is unpleasant. Demi wouldn't appreciate how you talk about her."

I smirk, opening the gate. "She loves it when I talk about her, Mr. Pete, especially when I'm fucking her, degrading her, ruining her for everyone." I lean in close, locking eyes with him again to pull him into my trance. "You'll stop asking me what I'm doing every fucking time you see me, or I'll kill you and bury you under my new garden. I tolerate you for Demi."

"Okay," he nods.

"Good. Now mind your own business." I finally pass Mr. Pete, locking the gate behind me, and press my back to the side of the house.

My shirt snags on the brick. When I get to the corner, the moon fills me with raw feral power. It's as if electricity is dancing over my skin. My cock surges to life, heavy and weighted, pressing against the zipper. I fall to my hands and knees, growling and becoming more animal as the moon rises.

I peer into the glass, my vision sharpening on Demi in the kitchen. She's having her tea, wearing nothing but one of my shirts.

My spine cracks as my body begins to grow, my legs splitting my jeans open as they thicken. My fangs become thicker, longer, and I tilt my head back, howling into the night.

Demi screams from inside the house. I lower my head to see her again and the mug drops from her hands, shattering on the floor when she sees me.

Her heart beats faster, thrumming beautifully with adrenaline and fear. While this is planned, her reaction is genuine. She never expects me to appear more monstrous. With my claw, I scratch down the glass, then give it a soft tap.

The entire sheet breaks. Pieces clatter to the ground, but they aren't sharp enough to pierce my skin as I walk over them, cocking my head and licking my lips while I stare her down.

She steps over the broken mug, careful of her feet. "Creed, just wait a minute, okay?"

I growl, fire licking my lips.

I won't wait.

The glass breaks under my weight as I ease into the room.

She bumps into the couch as she backs away from me. A wave of lust hits me, something sweeter, something... potent.

My gaze falls between her legs, watching a thick trail of her nectar drip.

It smells more intense than before. Abaddon warned me about her experiencing a heat, but given what I am, he didn't know if, how, or when it would happen.

I lick my lips, taking another step, and she jumps when glass breaks under her feet. I smell blood next, the vampire in me dying to lick it from the floor.

Demi makes a break for it, dashing out the broken door and across the lawn.

I lick her nectar from the floor, then her blood, not wanting to leave a drop of it behind. When I stand in the doorway, she's climbing over the fence. Her eyes lock onto mine, the moon at its highest, and with a snarl, I run.

She drops from the fence and runs, doing her best to outpace me.

Like that could ever happen.

I leap into the air, my claws hooking into the wooden fence. My wings refuse to work, not helping me at all because this isn't for my dragon, but for my wolf.

Jumping over the fence, I land on all fours. Scenting the air, I try to find which direction she ran in. Smart girl. She rubbed her scent all over different trees. I taste the rough bark, wishing it was her cunt.

I'll have her. Soon.

Catching the strongest of her scent, I run in that direction, leaping over fallen logs, and crushing fallen leaves in my haste. I snarl, howling once more to tell the world of my hunt.

She finally comes to view. Her shirt is torn, and her hair is a mess with twigs. Demi looks over her shoulder to see me, and she cries, pumping her arms to run faster.

But the drug kicks in from her tea.

She slows.

Demi stumbles, losing her footing, then runs into a tree. Her shoulder catches the most of force.

She groans, catching herself on her hands as she falls. Her shirt rides up, giving me a view of her ass and my mating mark.

I launch through the air, pinning her on the ground. She fights me a little, wiggling her body against me to try to get free, but the drug works faster the more she tries to escape me.

Like that could ever happen.

I never told her when I spiked the new batch of tea, so she didn't know if she'd be drugged or not.

My tongue licks across her neck and my fangs tease her ear. "Did you really think you could get away from me? Did you really think I'd fucking allow you to run from me for too long?" I reach between us, shredding the last of my pants as they fall free. My cock slaps her ass and I grip it, guiding it to her entrance, then with a rough thrust, stretch her gorgeous cunt.

She groans the best she can as the drug begins to take over. Demi is stronger now though since we're mated, so she fights the lullaby of the drug longer than she did before.

"Fuck, Demi. You're going to take my knot, like a good fucking girl, aren't you? You probably won't even know. You'll be asleep, coming on my cock, blissfully thinking you're in a dream."

She whimpers, fisting dirt into her hands, slurring my name when I drive in again. I can't control myself. I take her roughly. Fucking her with long, rough, deep strokes. We slide across the leaves, her pussy mine for the taking as the fight leaves her body.

I bite into her neck, latching onto her shoulder while I ride. Small, clipped sounds fall from her lips with every stroke I fill her with. My tentacle slips into her ass like it always does, but the other has to push through the ground to find her clit.

So messy. So fucking dirty.

I pull in long gulps of her blood. The taste is an elixir, deliciously designed for only me. Honeysuckles and rain.

"I should string you up and tie your wrists together, so you can't touch me. I'm going to fuck this body until you're so sore, you beg me to stop." I suck her earlobe into my mouth and chuckle. "But I won't. I won't ever stop, Demi. I own you," I sneer, pushing into her harder. "You're mine. I've claimed you. No other will ever have you like this. No other will get to feast on your body. And if they try—" I slam into her harder than I ever have, using my enhanced abilities for a split second. "I'll fucking kill them and then bathe in their blood to show you what happens when someone tries to take you from me."

My jaw drops as my orgasm warms the base of my cock. My knot begins to swell. I flip her over onto her back, ripping the shirt away from her body so I can have a view of her tits. They are bigger, swollen with milk for my child, and I purr in satisfaction.

Her eyes are hooded, glassy slits watching me from the corners of her dreams.

I bend down, sucking her nipple into my mouth, moaning when milk bursts across my tongue. I drink as I fuck her, squeezing her other breast. Milk drips over my hand, leaking down her body, giving me more to clean up.

"Mmm," she groans.

"You love being used and I fucking love using you, Honeysuckles." My claws dig into her shoulders, the skin breaks, and blood beads. "God, even your milk is fucking sweet." I wrap a hand around her throat while I hammer into her, looking down to see her belly swell from the size of my cock. "I can't wait to fill you again. You're going to be pregnant by the end of the night, Demi. You'll always be pregnant."

"Mine." I thrust. "Mine." Digging my talons in the dirt, I use it to pull myself further into her cunt. "Mine!" I force my knot inside her, locking us together, and roar, a primal howl telling all I've hunted and claimed my mate.

"Creed," she slurs from her unconscious, clamping around me, my orgasm setting off her own, and with every spasm and contraction, my come seeps further into her womb.

Her belly swells as I release, pouring so much, there's no doubt, she'll be pregnant again.

With her asleep, I bend down and lick the milk from her body before wrapping my arms around her, holding her close, and walking back to the house. Her cheek rests on my shoulder and with every step, another stream fills her from tugging at her hole.

While the leaves crunch under my feet, I welcome myself to her neck again, drinking her blood since I crave it so deeply.

When we get to the fence, I scale it easily, landing on the other side, then head to the broken door.

Whoops.

I'll have to clean this up later.

Without cleaning us, I take us to the nest and lie down so we can be with our egg. Settling in beside her, I hold her stomach while I continue to pulse my come in her depths.

It was obsession at first sight when I saw her.

And it will be obsession at last.

For always.

EPILOGUE TWO

DEMI

DEMI'S DINER

A month later

I wake up when I hear a cracking noise.

Rubbing my eyes of sleep, I watch the egg, hoping what I heard wasn't a dream. The gray and purple coloring of the shell has gotten so much deeper in color. The egg has easily tripled in size and I'm curious to know how our baby will appear.

Human? A dragon? A kraken? I don't know, but whatever they are, I love them.

A crack forms along the side, then again.
I squeal with excitement, slapping Creed on his chest to wake him up. "Creed! Creed! It's happening. It's happening. Wake up."

He doesn't just wake up. His wings spread and he flips into the air, crouching next to the egg, wide awake.

I wish I could wake up like that.
"Tuck in your wings, Creed. You're scratching the walls" I point to the damage, teasing him.

"Sorry, Honeysuckles. I'm excited." He grins, showing his sharp fangs.

"Me too." I take his hand and we surround the egg, just watching and waiting.

The cracks begin to be too much and pieces begin to fall onto the nest.

"You can do it," I urge, wanting to help, but Creed told me we couldn't interfere. The baby had to work its way out of the shell. "Come on, sweetheart. I believe in you." My eyes burn with tears, my chest filling with impatience and happiness.

The top of the egg bursts free but sticks to our baby's head as he or she wails into the air. Arms are next, then legs.

And then, the rest of the egg falls away.

"You're beautiful." I cry, picking the last of the eggshell from his head. "A boy. Look at him, Creed. Look." I press my cheek against our son's, staring at my mate.

Big tears fall down his sharp, monstrous face. "A boy. A son. I have a son," he chokes, sliding his claw down the chubby cheek. "You're okay with how he looks?"

"He's perfect. I wouldn't have him any other way." He has gray skin like his father and the same purple scales, but they cover his body and stop at his face. He is hairy like a werewolf, his ears pointed with the same hair as Creed. He even has the same tentacles between his legs.

But the one thing he has from me?

He has my blue eyes.

They are round and big with long gray lashes women everywhere will be envious of. He has a powerhouse set of lungs as he wails.

"You want to hold him?"

Creed nods, holding out his arms.

"There we go," I whisper. "That's your daddy."

When they lock eyes, our son stops crying, and Creed lifts him to his face. Fire leaves his lips, the same with my son, and their flames dance together, becoming one.

"What was that?"

"I don't know. I just knew I had to do it," Creed explains. "If his fire ever dies, I can give him mine." He hands our son back to me when he begins to cry. "I think he is hungry."

"I think so too." I pull up my shirt and settle him at my breast. He latches on easily, feeding like the beast he is.

Just like his daddy.

"What are we going to name him?" I ask. We never talked about names. We wanted to figure it out together when the baby was born.

"Well," Creed begins, clearing his throat. He's shy.

"What is it?" I urge him, wanting to know.

"What about Storm Blackstone? Because I found you in the rain and thunder."

I smile, looking down at our son. "That's perfect. He's perfect. Hi, Storm. Hi," I croon at him, crying because I'm so happy. Creed lies down beside me, combing his fingers through my hair while keeping his other hand on Storm's back. His palm engulfs Storm.

"My own field of happiness," Creed whispers, watching us intently. "My Honeysuckles."

I press my cheek against his head, my heart filling with more love than I ever thought possible.

"I love you with all my insides," I whisper to Storm.

To know my fate was bound all those years ago as a child and I didn't even know it.

All thanks to a game of tag and a field of sweet flowers.

The End.

Maybe you kind of like me? Join my readers group where I post updates, art, and nonsense.

Facebook group: January's Raynestormers

ABOUT THE AUTHOR

I'm January Rayne. Thank you so much for reading Honeysuckles, my first dark romance. I hope it didn't disappoint. I love writing, reading, and learning as much as I can along the way of this journey. I want to thank everyone who supported me when it came to getting this book done. I had so many doubts and I debated on releasing Creed's story at all. Thank you to my team, Carolina, Tiff, my husband, my alpha readers, my arc readers, my friends, and my family. I couldn't do this without you. My motivation is dedicated to you all.

Always be kind. Always love. And as Creed would say, "I love you with all my insides."

SCAN HERE FOR EASY ACCESS TO FOLLOW ME ON SOCIAL MEDIA:

Made in United States
Troutdale, OR
10/19/2023

13839782R00159